THE NECESSARY DEATH OF LEWIS WINTER

Malcolm Mackay

WINDSOR
PARAGON

First published 2013
by Mantle
This Large Print edition published 2013
by AudioGO Ltd
by arrangement with
Pan Macmillan

Hardcover   ISBN: 978 1 4713 2838 1
Softcover   ISBN: 978 1 4713 2839 8

British Library Cataloguing in Publication Data available

Printed and bound in Great Britain by
TJ International Limited

THE NECESSARY DEATH OF
LEWIS WINTER

To Sam & Alex

CHARACTERS

Calum MacLean—A twenty-nine-year-old gunman, living in Glasgow. Freelance; life is better alone. How long can that last when you have his talent?

Peter Jamieson—He's worked hard and smart to build his little empire. Still growing fast, and he needs the best people to do his dirty work if that's to continue.

John Young—Jamieson's right-hand man. Sharp as a tack. Loyal, conscientious; twenty years side by side will do that.

Lewis Winter—Twenty-five years of criminal activity, and still near the bottom. One good deal can change all that. Change everything.

Frank MacLeod—Gunman for Peter Jamieson. The best, frankly. But you can't fight age. You pass sixty, and things need replacing, like a hip.

DI Michael Fisher—It takes dedication to fight organized crime. You pursue the bad guys, whoever the hell they are.

Hugh 'Shug' Francis—Ambition means wanting more, even when you have enough. A car ring is enough, the drug trade is so much more.

Zara Cope—It's not the life she'd have chosen, an older man wanting her to settle down. But Winter's a good man, learning to fight for more, and she likes that.

Nate Colgan—You do what Nate tells you, when he tells you. Even his employers know that. Only his daughter, and maybe her mother, Zara, think differently.

George Daly—Unconventional muscle. Be a good friend and keep your head down. Pray for no promotion. Responsibility is deadly.

Martin 'Marty' Jones—Loan shark, pimp, pain in the arse, profitable. That last one is why people suffer him.

Kenny McBride—Being a driver for Peter Jamieson isn't hard. All you have to do is know the way and not screw up.

William MacLean—Thirty-one and he runs his own garage. Not a bad achievement. If only he didn't have to worry about his little brother Calum.

PC Joseph Higgins—Not an obvious young cop, with his rough family background. But he works hard, and works quietly.

Stewart Macintosh—You're in your early twenties, you're free and single. Of course you're going to go out and have a good time.

David 'Fizzy' Waters—He's been working on cars with Shug since they were in school. Always backing him up, no matter what.

Glen Davidson—A freelance gunman, looking for something more profitable. Not subtle, but very, very confident.

PC Paul Greig—A lot of people don't trust Paul. Probably why he's still a PC at thirty-eight. But there are few who know the streets better.

Tom Shields—Another young guy, just looking to have a good time, much like his flatmate Stewart.

Neil Fraser—Typical muscle. Big and angry. Blunt of fist and blunt of mind. A useful employee for

Jamieson.

PC Marcus Matheson—A young cop, so bright and determined. A lot will depend on who he learns from.

Adam Jones—Manager of Heavenly nightclub. It hasn't earned its name, but like his brother Marty, he's profitable.

Norman Barnes—A lawyer. He takes what cases he's given, and they're rarely anything pleasant.

DC Ian Davies—Retirement isn't too far away if he can keep his head down. The joy of working under Fisher is that Fisher doesn't trust others to do much of the work.

1

It starts with a telephone call. Casual, chatty, friendly, no business. You arrange to meet, neutral venue, preferably public. You have to be careful, regardless of the caller, regardless of the meeting place. Every eventuality planned for, nothing taken for granted. Tempting to begin to trust; tempting, but wrong. A person could be your friend and confidant for twenty years and then turn away from you in an instant. It happens. Anyone with sense remembers that bitter reality; those without sense will learn it.

Saturday afternoon, football on the radio in the background, sitting on the couch with a book. *The Painted Veil* by William Somerset Maugham, if you must know, and he's fascinated by it. It has lured his attention away from the radio; he doesn't know what the score is any more. The older he gets, the less important that seems. The telephone rings—landline, not mobile—taking his attention away from everything. A marker placed across the line he's on (never fold the page to mark your place), and he's getting up.

'Hello.'

'Calum, how are you, pal? John Young here.'

'John. I'm well. You?'

'You know, same old. Been a while since we saw you down the club. Thought I'd call you up, see how you were. You keeping busy?'

'Busy enough. Comes and goes, you know how it is.'

'I do that. You hear about old Frank MacLeod—

1

in having his hip done? Yep, out of the world for a few months at least. Hell of a thing, for a guy so active.'

'I heard. Shame for him.'

'Sure is. Can't picture him with his feet up. Be good to see you again, Cal, been too long. You should come down the club tomorrow, after lunch. We'll shoot a few frames of snooker, have a few drinks. Be fun.'

'Sounds like a plan. I'll drop by about two-ish.'

'Good stuff, see you tomorrow.'

The clues are all there if you care to look for them. Perhaps you don't care to; most people don't. A casual conversation: two people who know each other on a first-name basis, without being too close. Friends who see each other on a weekly rather than daily basis. Friends who don't care. Phone calls like that are made so often, so why care? It's a job offer. A very definite offer of something long-term and lucrative. Does he want long-term and lucrative?

Small flat, small car, small savings, but always enough. He works for need, not luxury. Long-term means risk, and risk is to be avoided. There are gamblers in the business, but they all lose eventually, and the cost is final. So don't gamble. You don't need to. There are two reasons why people do: one acceptable, and one not. The unacceptable reason is greed, the prospect of more money, which they don't actually need. The other reason is the thrill, and that's different.

He hasn't been in the club since he heard about Frank's operation. Old man goes into hospital to have hip replaced. It's no news to most. Those who know Frank—what he does—know different. He's

2

old, but he's still great, still important. Like a boxer who loses speed but learns tactics, he's as dangerous as he has ever been. He's from a generation ago, the golden-olden times before the intrusion of modern technology, modern policing and modern sensitivities. So many were left behind. Time marched, but Frank had always moved a step faster. The work he had done in the past was still needed, just the process was different. Now he was gone, for a few months at least, and would have to be replaced. He would be replaced by a younger man. A short-term replacement, for now.

Now Calum can focus on nothing. Another job is another job—nothing more. That doesn't concern him. Being enveloped in the suffocating bosom of the Jamieson organization concerns him. For the likes of Frank MacLeod, it was comforting, a guarantee of work and security. For Calum MacLean, it's a threat of enforced regular work, a loss of freedom. What is worth that?

2

The club is in the city centre, a small entrance leading into a large building. Nobody on the door on a Sunday afternoon. Usually a handful of people in at the bar, upstairs at the eight snooker tables. Not today. Today on the door a sign: *Closed for cleaning*. A tatty sign, trotted out every time privacy is required. Suspicious, obvious, but people didn't ask questions. Calum ignores the sign, opens the door and walks in.

It always seems dim inside, even with every light on. On his right he can see the large, scuffed dance floor, and on the far side the DJ's booth. There's a bar running the length of the side wall, gaudy lighting, bottles of every variety—none that he likes. He doesn't drink alcohol, although he's never understood in his own mind why. Self-control, most probably. It's not a moral thing. He loathes the club too, loathes that lifestyle, the sweaty cattle market, the pointless racket. It always came back to him that he hated it because the point was to attract women, and he isn't deemed attractive to women, no matter how dark it is.

A wide carpeted staircase in front of him, short steps that are easily misjudged. A lot of people have tripped going up them, overreaching. Calum is always careful, fearful not of being hurt, but of looking stupid. At the top of the stairs is a pair of wooden double doors with rectangular windows. He pushes one open and steps into the snooker hall. Eight green tables, two rows of four, plenty of room between each. Scoreboards on the walls, little machines beside each one. Pay a pound, get thirty minutes of light on your table. They make little money, not enough to justify the space they require, but they're one of Peter Jamieson's bewildering array of improbable passions. There's a bar against one wall, small, old-fashioned. No flavoured vodka here, just beer and whiskey. It's closed today. Cleaning, apparently.

John Young is standing at a table in the middle of the room, chalking his cue. The balls are scattered about the table, none yet potted. He may just have started, he may have been hopeless. Calum has never seen him play before, doesn't

4

know. He knows Jamieson is good. Everyone knows Jamieson is good. Everyone knows Jamieson has had lessons from professionals. Young must have learned something from his boss.

'Calum, how are you?'

'Fine.' He's walking across to the cue rack and picking one out. He's wearing jeans and a T-shirt; he can only play well in a T-shirt. Sleeves get in the way.

Young shoves all the reds back into the centre of the table and racks them in the triangle. He carefully places the balls on their spots. Everything precise, placed by a man who plays often, and plays with a serious partner. 'Good weather out,' he finally says.

'It is. You break.'

Young bends, lines up the shot and hits it. Only one red runs loose, the white coming right back up the table. Safe—a break to make the next shot difficult. No letting you win.

It stays serious until it becomes obvious that Young is going to win, and easily. Calum has effort, Young has skill, and it takes ten minutes for those two to be widely separated. Then talk.

'You been working for anyone lately?' Young asks. This is the first real mention of business, the first open acceptance that this is what the meeting is really about.

The question is misleading. Calum works, he has to. What Young wants to know is if he's been working repeatedly for the same person, or just drifting around. He probably knows the answer already; he wants to see if Calum can surprise him. He can't.

'No. Bits and bobs. Freelance. As ever.'

Nothing for another minute or two. More shots carefully picked out, even when the frame is won, even when the maths prove it. When it's over, and the balls are being laid out again—best of three—Young speaks again.

'We're without anyone now. Shame to lose Frank for a few months.'

'Didn't see it coming?'

Young laughs. A short laugh, not a happy one. 'Frank's one of those guys that can't admit when there's something wrong with him. Not until it's too late. He should have warned us. He knew for ages and said nothing.' He shrugs, a what-can-you-do shrug.

Calum's turn to break. It's messy: reds everywhere, white in the middle of the table. Trying too hard. Young feels confident enough to talk early.

'How old you now, Calum?'

'Twenty-nine.'

'Gettin' old.' Young laughs, self-deprecatingly; he's a podgy but youthful forty-three. His eyes twinkle when he laughs, like he means it; his forehead crinkles and his tousled dark hair seems to fall forward. He looks jolly, but you never forget who he is. 'You thinking about settling down?'

It's a professional question, not personal. 'I haven't thought about it at all. Time might come. I don't feel like I need it. I like my freedom, but I'll see how the wind blows.'

Young nods. It's a demand. He's saying that if he settles with Jamieson, then he doesn't want to be overworked. It's a demand that Young can live with, one that fits with other wishes.

Talk quiets. The frame is getting more serious.

6

Young was too casual, too confident. He's missed three shots that he should have made, and Calum is ahead. Calum misses a shot he would usually miss. Young concentrates. He starts knocking in shots, making a break that requires skill. He needs to get as far as the blue to guarantee the win, and he gets there at the first attempt. They shake hands. Young thanks him for coming.

3

When he knows the boy has gone, he puts his cue back on the rack and crosses the room to the back corridor. At the far end is Jamieson's office. Two knocks and Young enters without waiting for a reply. They've been friends since they were in their late teens, since they were both starting out in the trade. Thrown together by circumstances—a chance meeting on a shared job—they recognized immediately how much each could do for the other. Jamieson was in charge, that was clear; Young the right-hand man. No other right-hand man earns so much or is given so much control. He's trusted.

'You are the brains,' Jamieson would tell him when drunk, 'I am the balls. It works.'

It wasn't that Young lacked courage, or that Jamieson wasn't smart. Young could get his hands dirty, but Jamieson's instinct for the nasty work was unrivalled, and evident from a young age. Jamieson was intelligent, but Young was tactical, and that was an important difference. Separately they were talented; together they were lucrative.

Jamieson has to be in charge. He has to be seen to be in charge. It doesn't matter what either of them thinks; their employees and their rivals have to believe that the man they fear most is the man in charge. Perception. PR. You would be amazed how important that is in a trade like this. Being in charge comes with a downside, though. You're at the top of the tree, where everyone can see you, where so many others want to be. Jamieson can handle that, no problem. Besides, their operation isn't yet quite big enough to spook the top dogs into action. Yet.

Jamieson is sitting where he always sits, on the swivel chair behind his desk, facing away from the door. The desk faces the door, the chair rarely does. There are two televisions on a long stand behind the desk, both showing horse racing, another passion. He gambles, not because he needs to, not because it's a thrill, but because he has a need to beat other people. In this case, the bookies. He isn't trying to be rude when he sits with his back to you; he's just the sort of person who can be consumed by the things that interest him.

Horses don't interest Young in the least. Miniature Irishmen torturing dumb beasts in the name of a sport funded by the gullible and controlled by the idle rich. His seat in the office is on a small leather couch at the right side of the well-lit room, just beside the large window. There are newspapers on the table, mostly local, some national, scanned for any references to their work. These days you need to spend more time checking websites to make sure people don't make unfortunate references to you. Young sits and waits.

'I spoke to the boy MacLean,' he tells Jamieson when he's sure both races have finished.

'Boy? How old is he anyway?'

'Twenty-nine.'

'That all? Feels like he's been around for ages. What did he say?'

'I think he'll do it, if he's one of two or three. Doesn't want the full workload.' Jamieson is concentrating now, sitting forward, hands gently tapping on the table. This is his tool to focus on what matters, the constant patter of hands on desk. 'He ain't exactly a bag of laughs,' Jamieson smiles. 'But I like him. He's good. Smart. Quiet. Frank says he's the best of the new breed. I agree. We'll make him an offer.'

4

Young waits three days before he calls Calum again. The current job can afford to wait three days. It's also like dating—you mustn't seem too desperate. If you give the impression of hurry, then people will demand more in return. With Calum, it could scare him off. The boy is clearly wary of commitment. That's naive; Young's experience tells him that. In a few years he will be craving it. The regularity, the comfort, the safety net. Doing a job in this business is like being fired from a cannon: doing it freelance is being fired without a net to land in. The big organization, it protects you, it has ways of keeping you safe. Eventually the pressure of the job will wear Calum down and make that safety attractive. But not yet.

Calum is back on his couch, playing video games. *God of War III*, if you're interested. He finds it frustrating. The phone rings—mobile this time. He pauses, picks up the phone, looks at the screen. Young.

'Hello.'

'Calum, it's John Young. How are you, busy?'

'No, not busy at all.'

'Good, come down the club. Me and Peter want to speak to you, okay?'

'Right away?'

'Right away.'

A job offer, obviously. Important? Maybe, but he's waited three days, and that suggests not urgent. Perhaps that's what it's supposed to suggest. It'll be temporary, but it could be designed to draw him into something longer. Frank MacLeod isn't going to last forever. Nobody in this business does. Calum switches everything off, leaving nothing on standby. He gets a coat; it's a colder day. Blustery outside. He picks his car keys from the top of the fridge in the kitchen, and leaves the flat.

There's nothing in the flat that can tell you what he does for a living. There's certainly no gun. No one who works with a gun and has any sense keeps a gun in their home. There's no documentation. Keep no reminder. Some people keep souvenirs. Those people are stupid. Dangerously stupid. Maybe a bit sick. They will be caught. A police raid will tell nothing about Calum. No emails. No tweets. No text messages. Tracking phone calls would tell that he was in touch with people like Young, but you can't go to jail for the friends

10

you keep. Calum has never been arrested, no convictions, never seen the inside of a jail cell. He's been in the business for ten years. He won't gloat about avoiding arrest until he's retired.

Avoiding arrest is not the same as avoiding suspicion. Not sure how he's doing on that front. Do the police know that he exists? Surely. They must know about Jamieson; everyone else does. Jamieson is the up-and-coming figure. Calum has done work for Jamieson before. He's done work for one or two more established figures as well. He's not tied to any of them, though—that's important. He's a moving target. A chance that the police don't know him. A chance they don't know what he does. That's what he wants for himself, and what Jamieson wants from an employee as well. Starting with a clean slate.

He goes into the club by the front door as he always does. No point sneaking in. If people are watching the club, then they're watching the back as well as the front. Sneaking in the back only makes you look more suspicious. Up the stairs, through the door. The snooker hall is open to the public, the bar open. Six people using three different tables, another four people at the bar. One of the men at the tables is Kenny McBride, Jamieson's driver. Driver is a broad description. Jamieson can drive himself most of the time. Kenny's a taxi for the boss. He's a driver on important jobs. He delivers things. He picks things up. Anything that needs a car. Calum nods hello, walks past.

Along the corridor, all the way to the end. Nobody outside the office door, no obvious security. Never is. No paranoia yet, although that

11

will probably come. It does with most. Jamieson is mid-forties. Not old. More youthful than most people his age. Not big enough yet to be plotted against. So most people think. A hands-off approach to security. Ruthless, yes, but casual too. Calum knocks on the door three times and waits to be shouted in. He doesn't have the sort of relationship that allows him to enter uninvited. Somebody calls for him to come in. He opens the door, steps inside and closes it behind him.

It's just Jamieson and Young. The TVs are off, which means business. Jamieson is behind his desk. Is he trying to look like a businessman, trying to look respectable? Unlikely. He has bucketfuls of self-awareness, he doesn't feel a need to try and look like the good guy. The desk isn't to make him look respectable; it's to let you know he's in charge. Young's sitting to the side on the couch, as always. Neither one of them is intimidating. But then neither one of them is trying to be. Young isn't capable—too podgy and relaxed. Jamieson can do it. He can scare, when he wants to. His eyes, that's what does it. It's almost always about the eyes. If your eyes can't do scary, then you can't do scary. Jamieson could give a look when he chose.

'Good to see you, Calum, been a while,' Jamieson says, nodding for him to sit on the chair in front of the desk. 'Take your coat off.'

Calum does as he's told, because you do what you're told. He places the coat over the back of the chair and sits in it. Now he's facing Jamieson, and Young is only just out of view. That's disconcerting, deliberately. You don't know what Young is doing. You don't know if he's mouthing something to Jamieson. You don't know if he's

12

made a gesture or not. You can't see his reaction. You don't even know if he's paying attention. That's the point. You will leave that office not knowing what at least one of them is thinking.

'Let's get down to business,' Jamieson says, with that cold face that tells you to pay attention. 'Have you been doing much work lately?'

He wants to know if Calum has killed many people lately. Kill too many in a short space of time and you will inevitably draw attention to yourself. Jamieson's clever about that, good instinct. Don't hire someone who's been too busy. Don't hire someone who hasn't been working at all. Not too hot, not too cold, but just right. A Goldilocks employee. You answer because you have to, but it's awkward. Nothing wrong with Calum's answer, but you have to trust Jamieson with the answer. You have to trust that the only people who hear it are the people in the room. No bugs. They're rare, but not impossible.

'I've been keeping to a regular schedule,' Calum answers. 'I don't like to overstretch.'

It's the right answer. It means little, but it's right enough for now. Jamieson knows Calum is smart. Calum knows what answer Jamieson wants to hear. In this case it's true, and Jamieson believes him, but takes everything with a pinch of salt.

'I might have a job for you, if you're interested. You know we're short.'

'I heard. I might be interested. Depends, though.'

'On?' Jamieson's frowning now. He doesn't like conditions. He particularly doesn't like guys who haven't even hit thirty making demands, when people like Frank MacLeod rarely do.

13

'The schedule I work is good for me. I don't want to break that.'

Jamieson nods. Not unreasonable. Also fits with his own plan. No more relying on one man to do such important work. Frank was great, but now he's broken and there's nobody to step in. They have to recruit from outside. From now on, they always have at least two.

5

'You know Lewis Winter?'

Now it's real business. It's considered that the job has been accepted. Calum hasn't said he'll do it, but he's laid down a single condition and, by moving on to the job, Jamieson has accepted the condition. You don't talk money. They both know what the ballpark figure is. Now it's specifics for this job. Calum is on board. Jamieson and Young have both accepted it. Now they will treat him as though he's one of their people, in the organization. Maybe just for this one job. It's been like that before, when they had a big job and Frank chose him to ride shotgun. You're in the family for one job. Then you're on the outside, with them keeping an eye on you, making sure you don't say anything you shouldn't. Also making sure you stay useful to them, for moments like this.

'I know of Lewis Winter. Met him once, briefly. Wouldn't say I know him.'

But Calum knows enough. He knows who Lewis Winter is, and he knows what Lewis Winter does. That's enough. Lessons from Frank MacLeod, lessons from others with experience. Don't learn from the ones who have been caught and tell their stories to all and sundry. Don't learn from those who know how to do it; learn from those who know how to do it well. They tell you to learn everything. Not a glib comment. Learn who everyone in the business is and what they do, because you don't know when you'll run into them. So you learn who people like Lewis Winter are, even though they're not important people. You learn every nook and cranny of the city, because you don't know when you'll be there. Calum has done it. He's kept himself up to date. He drove around the city, exploring areas he didn't know. He made sure he knew the industry better than it knew him. He made sure he knew Glasgow better than it could ever know him. If he needed to move quickly, he would know the route. He might only need the knowledge once in his life, but that once could decide the length of that life.

He had met Lewis Winter through a mutual friend. They were at a party where Winter didn't belong. He was there with his much younger girlfriend. It was only three or four months ago, and someone had introduced them for reasons inexplicable to Calum. Perhaps because they were the only two criminals the mutual friend knew, and he thought they would get along. Winter is into his mid-forties. He has grey hair around the temples; he's struggling to keep his weight down. He looked as though he had just lost. He isn't a man for a party. He isn't a man blessed with great success. If he's the subject of this conversation, then things aren't liable to get any better for him.

'Winter's become a problem. The job would be

for you to deal with him.'

Calum nods. Nothing out of the ordinary there. Surprising that Winter should have become a problem to a man like Jamieson. Winter is small-time, always has been. He is a man cursed. Every success was swiftly followed by a crushing failure. Twenty-five years of it, no sign of a change.

'Sounds simple. Anything I should know?'

Jamieson shakes his head briefly, a slight shrug of the shoulders. 'Anything you think you should know?'

A key distinction to make. What you should know is what you need to know, not what you want to know. You want to know why Jamieson plans to murder this man. You don't need to know that. Lewis Winter is a long-term, small-time drug dealer. Jamieson is involved in many facets of criminal life, drug dealing included. Lewis Winter steps on Peter Jamieson's toes. If Jamieson's not seen to take action, then he could look weak. Perception is vital. The things you need to know relate only to your ability to do the job well, and to the consequences. You need to know if there's anything hidden that could catch you out; if your target has friends or contacts who might catch you up. Only what will help you do the job. Only what will help you live with the consequences.

'Does he have any sort of security that I should know about?'

Not a question he would usually ask about Lewis Winter. Winter is small-time, he has no security. At least none to speak of. He has no bodyguards. He has no hangers-on who would be capable of causing trouble.

'He might own a dog, that would be about it,'

Jamieson shrugs.

'He doesn't,' Young chips in from the side, his first contribution.

'There you go,' Jamieson smiles. 'He's living with his girlfriend now, that wee trollop.'

'Zara Cope,' Young says. 'A slut, but a smart one.'

'A smart slut,' Jamieson is saying with a smile and a shake of the head, 'those are the ones. Man, those are the ones. You know she had a kid with Nate Colgan six or seven years ago,' he's saying to Calum.

'Does the kid live with them?' Calum's asking, always worried about that scenario.

'Nah, with the grandparents.'

Nate Colgan. It's a name that conjures images that are better left unseen. A hardman. Not a caricature of a hardman. Not someone who walks around flexing muscles, covered in tattoos, playing the role of the angry man. A real hardman. A man that people like Jamieson use, but treat with care. A man you would all do very well to avoid upsetting. A man Calum is worried about upsetting. He met him once. Colgan seemed surly. When he spoke, he was surprisingly intelligent. Not unpredictable. Not an explosion of anger for no good reason. That's not hard. That's crazy. Hard is people knowing what you're going to do to them and being unable to stop you. Calum didn't know what the relationship between Colgan and Cope was these days. Better to avoid her, if possible.

A thought occurs.

'Is Winter still working alone these days?' Calum asks.

17

This matters. Winter alone means killing Winter. Winter in an organization means killing Winter and paying for it later. People can't be seen to be weak.

Jamieson is glancing across at Young. Calum can't see the response.

'As far as we know,' Jamieson begins, 'he's still working alone. He's been making moves in my areas, though, and not being subtle about it. Like he's trying to piss me off. Like he knows he has backup. I don't think he does. Yet. I think he will. I want to get him before he gets backup.'

That's as much as Calum should know. No more detail. No word on who the backup is, how close it might be. It hints at something bigger, though. An ugly hint.

A nod of the head accepts the job. No shake of the hand, not necessary. This isn't a gentleman's club, after all. This isn't a gentleman's agreement. This is business. Calum has agreed to it. If he fails, then he will probably be punished. Not killed. If you kill a man for failure, who else will want to work for you? You ostracize him, though. You make life tough. Calum knows this. He's seen it happen to others. It's happened to talented people. Mostly it happens to the loudmouths, to the idiots who think they can do the job, but can't. It's easy to kill a man. It's hard to kill a man well. People who do it well know this. People who do it badly find out the hard way. The hard way has consequences. Even the talented must be wary of that fact.

6

Jamieson is sitting in the chair, watching the door close behind Calum. Young is still sitting on the couch to his right, sitting in silence. Jamieson is a man of definite action. He makes the call to have a man killed, and he turns back to his horses, or his golf, or whatever hobby is occupying his attention today. Only, today, he doesn't. Today he sits tapping the table, still looking at the closed door.

'He's got a lot of talent, that boy,' he says softly. 'Something about him I'm not sure of.'

'He's just socially awkward,' Young shrugs, 'that's his way. Smarter than your average bear.'

'Aye,' Jamieson nods, 'that's a fact. Frank told me that, first day he met him. Said the boy was smart, said he had the guts for it too.'

Courage and intelligence are worth little alone. It's why Jamieson and Young work together, and always will. It's why so many people are almost good at what they do. They have one or the other. A stupid person can have enough courage to make them useful in this industry. A smart person can do a lot. To be great, you must have both. You have to know when to rely on your brain and when to rely on your guts. Some people have enough of both to keep themselves free and working for decades. Sometimes even people with an abundance of both make a mistake. One mistake. One simple, sloppy mistake. Twenty years in jail. Unemployable thereafter. The smartest of all know not to take their brains for granted.

'You worried about the job?' Young's asking

19

him. It's rare to see Jamieson being uncertain about a job.

Jamieson shrugs. 'I don't care how good the boy is—this is the sort of job that can trip him up. Trust me. I ain't saying he can't do it. I ain't saying he'll botch it, not at all. He's the best we can get for the job. But these are the ones. Look at it. We don't know what we're sending him into. We don't know what Winter's got.'

He says it reluctantly, because he knows that it's an implied insult towards his friend. It's always Young's role to plan the job. It's Young's role to know what they are likely to be up against. They think they know, but they can't be certain.

Young sighs impatiently. They've been over this before. Lewis Winter is now working with others. He's moving into new territory because he believes he can get away with it. He's making himself more high-profile because he needs to, if he's going to attract the new business he wants. They know that he's becoming a danger to them. They know that he has bigger people behind him. Or that he will have. They aren't there yet. There's a promise of support. So you get rid of him before the promise is realized. It makes sense. It's logical to Young. He's justified it to himself. It's necessary to kill Lewis Winter. Now Jamieson is questioning.

'He has no support yet. I've been having him watched. The only contact he has is over the phone. There's no extra security. Not yet. We know that. The boy himself will check. He won't just blaze in there. He's smart.'

Jamieson nods his head. All of that is true. 'The boy will follow him. So long as he doesn't follow him so long that the support arrives.'

20

'He won't have to worry about Winter's new friends. We have to worry about them. He doesn't. He has to worry about the girlfriend. Maybe he has to worry about one or two dickhead hangers-on.'

Jamieson smiles and nods. There are always hangers-on, people who want to be a part of it. They find a sop like Winter and attach themselves to him, try to bleed him dry.

'What about that wee gold-digger?'

The gold-digger. There are plenty of them floating around too. Always have been, always will be. No worse than the hangers-on, and in many ways more fun. The same aim: bleed you dry and move on. Most gold-diggers are of no consequence. You enjoy their company, you give them a little something and then you move them quietly along. Some are more dangerous. Some are harder to get rid of. Zara Cope has always been one of those. A smart girl, one who knows how to make it last. One who knows how to get more than money. She knows how to get control. She's been with Winter for a while now, moved in with him. She's always with him, pulling the invisible strings. She has her claws in deep, and she will surely be there when Winter expires.

Young's shrugging. 'He'll judge how to deal with her. He's smart enough to work it out.'

'Hope he doesn't kill her,' Jamieson says quietly, 'I wouldn't want to piss off Colgan.'

'Would it piss him off?'

'He still carries a candle for that bitch,' Jamieson nods solemnly. 'I don't know Colgan well, but I know that much. Obvious.'

'The boy will judge it.'

Jamieson turns and reaches for the remote

21

control, putting on one television. Not a lot of sport on this afternoon. Not a lot of work to do, either. Building up to things. Should be building more quickly, but new things keep getting in the way. New things, like Lewis Winter's new friends.

7

The first thing is easy. You find out where the target lives, and you track him. If you know the target well, then you can skip a lot of this. Many people end up killing those they know well. It's people they worked with, people they've seen around the industry many times. They may have partied with them. They may even be friends. But you do it, because that's the job. The victims know that, as well as the aggressors. If you don't go into the industry with your eyes open, then someone or something will soon open them. You soon learn how it works. You track them to learn their routine. Everyone has some sort of routine. Sometimes messy, sometimes only a sliver of routine in a chaotic life. The routine is when you get them.

Calum doesn't know Winter well enough to skip any of this. The boring necessity. He finds out where he lives—that's easy. No secret. Winter must know he's at risk in this business, but his track record suggests that he doesn't plan well for these eventualities. Every time he takes a step up the ladder, it breaks underneath him and he tumbles back down. He has ambition, and nothing else. He has some brains, but no sense. He has no obvious security at his house when Calum drives by. When he leaves and goes to meet a couple of street dealers who work for him, he goes on his own. He's oblivious to reality. Or maybe he doesn't care. There are people like that. There are always people who take huge risks and don't even try to protect themselves from the consequences. They're either not afraid of death or don't care much for life.

Winter has been knocked down enough times by life not to care much for it. As he talks to these two idiots—young men who sell product to their friends and family in exchange for more for themselves—he doesn't care. He's taking risks that don't matter to him. A lifetime in the industry, and for what? He's little further forward than he was when he started. Younger men than him are running major organizations, buying up legitimate businesses, achieving. He's dealing with two monosyllabic, illiterate junkies. This is what it's all come to. He's earning less than thirty thousand a year on the deals he's doing. He has a house he can only just afford to pay the mortgage on. He has a girlfriend who was the well-known cast-off of many better men than he. She's demanding. She's changing his lifestyle to suit hers. She's heightening his ambitions to match her own. He needs to pay for her love. So he's taking risks.

He had hated school. He'd worked for a haulage company for a couple of years, but he'd hated that too. Then he fell into the business via an old school friend. A little bit of dealing, nothing big, just at parties. Working on the bottom rung of the business, but having fun while you're doing it. An employee for a big organization that got you

23

regular work, that looked after you. Back then he had enjoyed it, but that was such a long time ago. Now a middle-aged man, trying to be a big player. Unable to make money or connections. He had a success in his late twenties, a big deal. He was going to get rich. The police didn't get him, but they got almost everyone else involved in the deal. The one guy who didn't get caught. That made his name poison for a while. Then another potential deal, in his mid-thirties. Working with a partner, Jimmy Morrison—don't call him Jim. But Jimmy screwed him, did a runner, took all the cash. Left Winter penniless and humiliated. A laughing stock again. Still trying to recover.

Then an offer to get involved in something bigger. Out of nowhere. Make some moves, prove you can hack it. Get on Jamieson's patch. He's the first person going to be knocked off his perch. You start the moves. We'll be right behind you. An offer from someone Winter trusts. Someone Winter knows has the ability to back up the offer. So he makes the moves. If it goes wrong? So what. Jamieson will kill him, and that'll be the end of it. What a loss. A life that gives him nothing. Take it. Feel free. Peter Jamieson is welcome to possession of this life. If it goes right, then maybe life becomes something more. Maybe something worth living. Zara stays for good. Children. No more hanging on by his fingertips. A big player. Relax. But he has been here before, and he knows that hope is evil. It sucks you in and spits you back out, laughing at you all the while. No, accept the risk; don't get carried away by the possibilities.

'Why have you still got so much left?' Winter is asking angrily. He doesn't do anger well. He always looks too downbeat to be worked up. Comes across as huffy instead.

'Ah dunno these people. They dunno me. They ain't buyin'.'

'They're buying from him,' Winter tells the man. He used to know their names, but he can't remember now. They won't last anyway. They never do.

'Ah dunno.'

'How much time have you spent trying to shift it then?' Winter asks, knowing the answer will be a lie. They're so bad at lying. Bad at telling the truth. Bad at everything.

'Loads. Loads. People ain't buyin'.'

'I'm running out of patience with you,' Winter tells him, staring into the middle distance. They're in the centre of a quiet street, talking as though they've just bumped into each other. He hates them. Despises them. He needs them. 'Try harder. Make it happen. I want you to have sold the lot by Saturday—you're getting more then. You,' he says to the other one, 'will get more tomorrow. You've done well. I'll see you right.'

The young man smiles and nods enthusiastically. A dog given a pat on the head by a brutal owner. A toothless grin. Pathetic. Scum.

Winter is in his car. He doesn't know he's being followed. When he was young, he would check. He would look around to make sure there was nobody tailing, nobody that might cause him harm. When he was young, nobody ever tailed him. They didn't care. He wasn't important. He's now spent so long not being important to anyone that he doesn't bother to check. If he had, he wouldn't have noticed. There's a lot of traffic, nothing will stand out. He needs to get something to eat. He needs to change the taste he has lingering in his mouth. Those junkies. They represent him. They are what his livelihood depends on. They are the scale of his achievement.

Calum follows behind, intrigued. He doesn't know the two junkies, but he knows what they are. Peddlers. They're the sort of people who sell for a few months until they become so unreliable that they have to be cut loose. They're a real risk to deal with. If you cut them loose and they get talkative, then you could be in trouble. You might have to deal with them. Winter has to take the risk, though. The alternative is to spend every night going round the city trying to sell his own product. It wouldn't be long before people got to know who he was and what he was doing. It wouldn't be long before someone jumped him, or the police arrived. He needs others to take that risk. But they are hopeless to rely on. It's obvious that Winter has come away from the meeting angry. Now he's stopping outside a café.

He eats lunch alone. Back in the car, another meeting, this time at a house on the south side of the city. Calum notes the address. Find out who that was. A quick google on his mobile tells him nothing. Too well maintained a home to be another junkie. Maybe a supplier? Probably not important for the job at hand. Then home. Back to Zara Cope, the love of Winter's life. Ha, the love of his life. Calum sits in the car at the bottom of the street and watches the house. Boring job. Boring, boring, boring. Necessary, though. Has to be done. Will have to be done for at least another couple of days. If no routine shows itself after that time, he might have to keep on watching. Never rush it.

8

Zara is watching TV. She looks bored. That scares him. He stands in the doorway, not sure what to say. She's so pretty. Shoulder-length dark hair, full lips, high cheekbones, large eyes. Striking. A confidence in her look that's complacent and well established. Superior. He's sixteen years older than her, but that's not what stops him talking. That has never been the cause of the barrier between them, the discomfort he feels. The discomfort is the difference in lifestyle, the difference in what they want. Perhaps that all comes from age, he supposes sadly. Can't escape it. The one thing you can't change. She wants parties and fun. He's already done that. He wants something more. He wants marriage, children, and compassion. She looks up at him, standing there watching her.

'What's up?'

He has a tendency to stand and watch her. Watch her get dressed, watch her in the kitchen, watch her watch TV. She doesn't mind—whatever entertains him. She knows she's pretty. Worth watching. She's always been aware of it. When she'd first begun to hang around with these underworld types, they had all been sniffing around her. She was eighteen; the men who mattered were in their thirties and forties. She was well raised, intelligent, well spoken. She was a cut above their usual meat. It had seemed like

27

innocent fun. Nothing serious. They used her, she used them. Not too many; she didn't let herself get a terrible reputation. Not like some. Then she got a little older, and other pretty young things appeared. New experiences. She was still beautiful, she just wasn't the kind of beautiful that important people wanted to play with. Not the shiny new toy any more. When she started, she thought it was fun, something extra in life. Now it was all. She didn't know any other life. It was this or nothing. If Lewis could pull off the new deal, this might be worth sticking around for.

'Nothing,' Winter answers. 'What d'you want for dinner?'

Zara shrugs. 'Whatever's in. Are we going out tonight?'

The question means she's decided that they are going out tonight. It's not that she bullies him. She only has to hint and he accepts. He fears what her reaction will be if he refuses her obvious wish. He's seen her huffy side, the petulance. Nothing to rock the boat. Nothing to let her get upset and be dramatic. He wants this happy family. He has to accept the sacrifices it takes.

'I thought we might,' he lies.

'No need for anything heavy then,' she says with a smile.

She looks happy now. Good actress, he knows that. To see the smile is enough. Might not be real, but it's pretty and it warms him.

It's his turn to cook. They take it in turns, and she does do most of the housework. Hard to think of her as a housewife, but there you go. It's a role she seems increasingly willing to throw herself into. People change. What people want from life

28

changes. He's thinking about that while he's rummaging in the freezer. Not looking forward to another night out. Almost every night now. Only way to keep her entertained. He's always looking for signs that she's growing up. Anything that might suggest that she's turning into the same sort of person he already is. Sometimes he thinks he sees hints of her maturing, then she does something to obliterate that hope.

He's encouraged her to see more of her daughter. The idea of playing the kindly stepfather appeals. She's only visited the girl twice that he knows of since they started dating; he's never met the girl. It seems uncaring to him. Inexplicable. How can you not love a child you've brought into the world? He's not a father. He wishes. It would be what he needs. A life to truly love, and to be loved back. Zara doesn't love him; she tolerates him. She benefits from him, so she stays—he understands that. He accepts it, because it's how it's always been in his life. He expects nothing more, but he longs for a relationship that can be different. He sees other people with it. Why can he not have it himself?

Poor judgement. He knows it. He's always known it. Zara isn't the right person, not for that sort of life. He'll never be able to play happy families with her. They could fake it for a while, but she would get itchy feet. It wouldn't last. There's the fear, though. He thinks about it as he sits opposite her, both eating some chicken-and-pasta dish that he's thrown together. It's flavourless, but she's already talking about where they should go, playfully complaining that his choices are always dull. The fear. If he dumps

29

Zara, and looks for something more meaningful elsewhere, he might not find it and be left with nothing. What they have may not be much, but it's better than nothing. He agrees to her suggestion of a nightclub—one that she always enjoys, he always hates.

Zara can see that he's not happy with the suggestion; he's such a poor liar. He plays along, though, as he always does. Too insecure ever to disagree, ever to fight back. Too weak? In some ways, she thinks, he is. In some ways he's pathetically weak. He's scared of what lies ahead in his life, miserable about what's gone before. He never talks about it, but it's written all over him. In other ways he can be courageous. He tries to make things happen. He has ambition. He's willing to take a risk to try to make life better for both of them. That's impressive. He wants things for both of them that take courage to achieve. His ability to silently go about risking his life for their betterment—that impresses her.

She reaches a hand across the table and places it on the back of his. He stops and stares at her, unsure of the gesture. It's not her way. Is it the prelude to bad news?

'This deal you're doing,' she tells him. 'I want you to know that I'm proud of you. It takes guts. I know you're doing it for us, and it means a lot to me.'

Her eyes twinkle when she smiles for real, and they twinkle this time. It makes him feel soft, it makes the world seem like it's turning back to face him again. It makes him feel the risk is worth it, and that he wants to live through it. That brings another fear. The fear that just as she is changing,

30

just as the relationship is growing, he'll fail again.

Winter smiles and nods. 'Things are gonna get a lot better,' he's telling her, 'for both of us.'

9

A taxi arrives at the house just after half past eight. It idles outside, not blowing its horn. Probably a regular pickup, knows to wait. They emerge. She comes out and walks slowly down the front path, in a coat that covers her to her knees. Winter is still at the door, locking the house. They won't be back for a few hours. When they do get back, neither of them will be in much of a condition to get the key into the lock. Winter's wearing a dark coat and dark trousers; he looks too old for a night out. He turns and walks briskly down the path, catching up with Cope before she reaches the taxi. He opens the back door for her; she drops in and out of view. Winter goes to the other side of the car and drops in, without looking around.

Calum sits in the darkness and watches. How paranoid is Winter? Evidently not as paranoid as he should be. Not looking around, not checking to see if anyone's there. If it's occurred to him that he might be a target, then he's not taking the threat seriously. He's never been a target before, never been worth the effort. He doesn't know how to play the game. Calum starts his car, letting the taxi get far enough ahead before he switches on his lights and pulls away from the kerb. He'll do nothing more than watch tonight, no matter how tempting an opportunity might arise. Sometimes the temptation is strong. You sit back weeks later and realize that the first chance was a better chance than the one you took. So be it. It's never worth rushing.

They're heading into the city centre. There's enough traffic to hide in easily, no trouble tailing them. The taxi stops on a busy street. They get out, the taxi pulls away. Damn it. Nowhere to stop. Calum has to carry on down the street. He watches in his mirror, picking them out. They're going into an upmarket bar—seems more his place than hers. Perhaps just a few sedate drinks. He finds a parking spot on the next street. Now a risk. How close does he get? Would Winter remember him if he saw him? Chances are that he wouldn't. Chances are he could sit right next to Winter and he wouldn't have the slightest idea who he was, but you can't take the risk. Some people remember faces well. If he sees Calum, remembers him and knows what he does for a living, then the job becomes extremely difficult. It's not that he can't still kill Winter; it's that Winter would tell people that Calum was out to kill him. When he turns up dead, everyone will know who did it.

He won't risk getting close. He won't even risk going into the same bar as them, even though Winter probably wouldn't see him and might think it a coincidence if he did. He's walking down the street, looking for a building opposite that has a view of the front of the bar. There's a chip shop, but that's only a temporary solution and his stomach is already angry with him. All he can find is an alleyway to stand in. Dark and dank, and the sort of place other people might use for unattractive purposes. Calum stands and watches,

32

out of view of everyone. He can see the entrance to the bar. He mustn't be seen by others. Mustn't be seen watching the bar where a soon-to-be-dead drug dealer is drinking. Sort of thing that turns up in court. CCTV isn't a worry. It might have picked him up on the street, but it won't see him in the alley. The police won't check it anyway. He won't be hitting Winter for at least another forty-eight hours. He'll be sure to keep a safe distance the day or so beforehand.

His stomach is making noises he doesn't like. The smell in the alley doesn't help. It's nothing specific, just a dirty smell. A mixture of all of life's ugly things, all pushed into the corners. He tries to hold his breath for long spells, but that doesn't help much. Hopefully they'll be having a short night out. He doesn't want to leave his vomit splattered all across the alleyway. It's the peril of watching. When you watch a target all day, you must eat what you can grab. You eat in the car, you drink in the car. Calum draws the line at going to the toilet in the car, but he knows of people who have pissed in bottles while they watched. You eat junk. You sit still for hours on end. A recipe for disaster.

The alley is becoming a bad idea. If someone rolls out of a bar and needs to vomit, they would use the alley. If someone rolls out of a bar and needs a piss. If a couple roll out of a bar and want some time alone. People go past, they don't see him. After forty minutes Winter and Cope emerge from the bar. It's a blessed relief to see them. They walk along the street, not seeming to look for a taxi. Calum waits, watching, and then picks up the tail on foot. They have a few drinks inside them, but they aren't drunk. Not yet. On the way, but not there. They're talking to each other as they walk. She's doing most of the talking, leading the conversation. They seem happy. Content, at least. Calum follows them for two streets, to a nightclub.

This seems much more her place than his. They disappear inside. Calum stands outside and contemplates. A lot of people coming and going. They could be in there for hours. If he goes in, then he will certainly be picked up by the security cameras. He won't take that risk. He could wait outside for hours, but he would have to stand. There's nowhere to park his car nearby, and a man standing outside for hours on end will draw attention. No point in hanging around here. Best bet is to go back to their house.

He sits in his car, parked neatly down the street on the opposite side from Winter's house. It's a nice street, comfortable. Surprising that Winter is earning quite enough with the little set-up he has to afford a nice house in a nice part of town. Maybe he isn't. A lot of people in the business have a habit of living beyond their means. Calum isn't one of them, quite the reverse. He would like to see inside the house. Not to judge Winter's spending, but to see the layout. If you're going to be in the house, then it's good to know your way around. He wouldn't even try to break in. Calum has broken into two or three houses in his life, but only when absolutely necessary. It's not something he considers one of his skills. Never leave more evidence than you need to. Don't take a risk that you can avoid, no matter the possible benefit. The house was the most likely place for the hit. He would learn his way around if he found himself inside. It wasn't so big that it would confuse him.

It's nearly two o'clock when a taxi pulls up outside their house. A man Calum doesn't recognize gets out of the back first. He seems young. Too young to be Winter anyway. Then the front passenger door opens. Winter this time. Two women get out of each side of the back. One is Cope, the other Calum doesn't recognize. She seems to be the partner of the younger man. All four are drunk to the point of imbalance. Cope leans on Winter, who is trying (and failing) to look like he's enjoying himself. The other three are laughing. Someone says something. Three drunken laughs, and a silent Winter. He's fishing in his pocket for the front-door key. He fumbles it into the lock with great effort. It takes more than thirty seconds for him to get the door open, and the four disappear inside.

Calum sits outside, and watches for another hour. The living-room window faces the road. The light goes on and stays on. Half an hour later an upstairs light goes on. The living-room light is still on. Will probably be on all night. Four drunks. Some go upstairs, some stay downstairs. The lights will be on all night. They'll tell him nothing. After an hour of nothing he starts the car and drives home. He's learned a lot about Winter over the course of the night. A midweek drinker, dragged to clubs where he doesn't belong. Drinking more than he can handle. Picking up hangers-on. There are obstacles. There are also huge vulnerabilities.

10

Sitting at home, thinking. A well-earned and much-enjoyed night's sleep, an hour at home before picking up the tail again. Think about what you saw. Consider every aspect of it. The first problem is obvious. Too many people. Last night was the victim plus three. Tonight could be the victim plus umpteen more. If they're in the habit of having people back to the house, then the house becomes a much less enticing location for the hit. But where else? If it's not the house, then it's hard to know where else you can do it with any degree of control. Anywhere out in public and you're not in control of the hit, not ever. You're relying on too many intangibles. You're relying on things leaving you alone.

The house. It has to be. So easy if they go drinking again. If it was just the two of them, easy to control. They come home drunk and it's easy. Drunk people are unpredictable, but they're weak. Judgement impaired. Physical ability destroyed. Very drunk, and they might not know what's happening to them before it's too late. You learn very quickly what a friend alcohol can be. An enemy too. It's responsible for so many good people falling apart. In this industry. In this city. Curse of the gunman, they say. Long periods of inactivity between jobs. What do you do? People get bored. They fall into drink. Not Calum. Not yet. Winter's drinking to keep up with Cope. That's the vulnerability. That's when you get him.

Calum knows the location. He knows—if

nothing dramatic happens that day to change his mind—when he'll carry it out. One more day tailing. One day resting, keeping his distance. Then, following night, the hit. The location, the time. The picture of the event is forming in his mind. It looks convincing, pleasingly simple. But for that one problem. If there are other people in the house, then he has to consider taking someone with him. Doesn't need to be another gunman; he'll still do the job. They only hit Winter. Never hit a target you don't need to hit. Ever. One murder gets the police interested, two gets them excited. Take an extra pair of hands to keep the witnesses out of the way. Has to be someone he trusts. There are a few of them. Only a few. First impressions: easy, apart from that one little problem.

A second day tailing Winter. Much the same as the first. Nothing new to learn. Winter went and met one of the same junkies from the day before. He gave him something, more product to sell, probably. Then on to another meeting, this time with someone who looked a little more presentable. Probably a supplier. Small-time. They weren't taking the precautions a big-time supplier would take. Calum doesn't even know where Winter gets his supplies from. Not important, so long as it's not someone who'll miss him. Sometimes you get blowback you don't expect. You kill someone who turns out to be more important than your employer realizes. They have connections to important people. The important person sees the attack on their man as an attack on them, and feels the need to retaliate. Doesn't happen often. Most people know the connections in this business, but it does happen.

That brings back the memory of the meeting with Jamieson. The suggestion that Winter might have connections with bigger players in the pipeline. Kill him before the connections are finalized, and they probably won't consider him important enough for revenge. Kill him when the connections are established, and they might consider it an attack on them. Whoever they are. Who are they? Who would most likely tie themselves to someone like Winter? Someone who couldn't make connections with a more established and successful dealer. Someone either new to the trade or new to the area. Whichever one, it's a relief to believe that. New to the trade and you'll get little support. New to the area and you'll get none at all.

Winter ate lunch away from home again. He could have gone home, he seemed to have all the time in the world, but he chose not to. Interesting. What does that say about his relationship with Cope? Too much of a good thing, perhaps. After eating at a café, it was on to a pub. Grotty place, real dive. Calum waiting outside. Winter wasn't there to drink. He was there for a deal. Organizing something, cutting some sort of deal. Maybe with the landlord. Use the pub as a place to sell. Make sure he has exclusive use of the place. Maybe just making a deal with someone in the pub. He was in there for the best part of an hour. Hard talking. Trying to persuade someone that he was making a move up the way. That would be his biggest challenge—persuading people that he's worth taking seriously.

Calum reflects, as Winter comes out of the pub,

looking stone-cold sober, that this is happening rather suddenly. Someone turns up and gets Winter to step on Jamieson's toes. Persuades Winter that big things are coming and that he can be a part of it. Persuades Jamieson that big things are coming and that he has to stop it. Why target Jamieson? Not yet one of the top dogs, that's why. Already important and making a lot of money, but not yet so big that he can't be brought down. It's someone credible. Someone credible enough to persuade Peter Jamieson that immediate action must be taken. It's worth the drastic option.

He's run out of things to do with his day, so Winter goes home. He doesn't look like a man excited by his new business opportunity. He looks as though it's all weighing him down, like he isn't convinced by any of it. Maybe he isn't yet convinced of the potential rewards. Maybe he isn't willing to believe that any of it is true, until nothing can possibly go wrong. With his many failures behind him, that seems more likely. Understandably cautious. He goes home and disappears inside. Calum settles down outside, hoping to see the couple leave the house in a couple of hours' time. Please go out. Go get drunk. Make it a nightly occurrence. Be the kind of people who can only find fun in alcohol. That guarantees an easy hit.

They don't let him down. A taxi arrives at the house, later than the evening before. They come out of the house, both looking a little flustered. It looks like they've had a disagreement. It looks as though the night out is a last-minute arrangement. Calum suspects it was Cope's idea. Winter looks miserable. Same routine as the night before. He locks the door, then hotfoots it down the path to open the taxi door for his woman. They both get in, the taxi drives away. Calum waits a few seconds, then follows at a distance. Same as the night before. Into the city centre. The taxi drops them outside a nightclub, a different one from the night before. Not impossible to park nearby, but Calum decides not to bother. He goes back to the house to wait for them.

He's hoping they'll be alone. He taps the top of the steering wheel, thinking. What sort of party did they have at the house the night before with the young couple they brought back. Sexual? Easy to control the situation if they all have their pants down. They were all so drunk the night before it's hard to imagine such a sexual adventure being anything other than a chaotic mess. Possible, though. People try all sorts of stupid things when they're drunk. Drugs? Not likely. Maybe Cope, maybe the young couple, but there's no word of Winter using his own product. He wouldn't have survived so long if he did. Most dealers that have a brain don't touch what they sell. If you fall into the trap you lay for others, then you're going to fail. Alcohol is quite enough anyway.

The taxi pulls up outside the house. Calum glances at the clock on the dashboard: twenty past midnight. Earlier than the night before. The taxi doors open, both Winter and Cope get out. Nobody else. The doors close, the taxi drives away. The couple make their way up the garden path towards the door. She has her coat off. She looks attractive; it's easy to see why her claws always catch someone. There's no laughter this night. Alone, they don't make each other laugh; it takes

40

others to introduce that into their relationship. They're drunk, but not to the extent of the night before. A shorter night, less drinking. Winter's able to get the key out of his pocket easily enough, get it into the lock at the first thrust. They disappear into the house. The downstairs lights are on for about ten minutes. Then an upstairs light. One of them has gone up, the other is still downstairs. The downstairs light goes off ten minutes later, then the upstairs light goes off as well. This is a quiet night for them. Calum goes home.

11

George Daly waits for the man to get back up. Rob something, that's the other man's name. Robert. He can't remember the surname. Doesn't matter.

'You think it's okay just to take money and not pay it back, Robert, is that it?' George asks him. Keep voice calm, slow movements.

When he had started doing this sort of work for Peter Jamieson he had tended to do what all newcomers do. You get excited. You let the adrenalin control you. Sometimes you go too far, or say too much. Often you give the impression of being a maniac. George isn't that. He doesn't enjoy the work he does, but it pays the bills and he knows he's good at it. Smart enough to be good at the muscle work. Smart enough to know he doesn't want to go any further than this. He doesn't want to do the work Calum does for a living. He doesn't want that responsibility.

41

George is twenty-eight, maybe looks a little younger. Curly black hair, which always makes him look rather boyish. He does muscle work. Intimidation work, you might call it. Extortion, perhaps. Beatings. Threats. Whatever you want to call it. He's under six foot, he's not especially muscular. Wiry, but obviously tough. There are some who do muscle work that are large people, but very few are gym monkeys. The kind of men who spend an inordinate amount of time in the gym, building up their muscles, tend not to be the kind of men trusted with these jobs. These jobs can require subtlety, sometimes brains. You must know how far to go, and never cross the line. Meatheads need not apply. They tend to end up being doormen instead.

This Rob fellow, struggling to get to his knees, his hand slipping on the linoleum of his bare kitchen, has borrowed money. Not from a bank. From a lender of less official stature. From a lender who works for Jamieson. Interest rates in the region of five thousand per cent. Not the worst in the city. Such an easy trap. People need money. You lend, no questions asked. They don't understand the rates. They don't understand the consequences. Perhaps you borrow a hundred pounds to provide an enjoyable Christmas for your children, who see little joy through the year. You borrow a hundred; you may end up paying back a few thousand. Of course, most can't, so other methods are used. They end up dealing to pay off the debt. If you're a young woman, there are other ways to pay.

Rob has failed to pay for several months. Five hundred borrowed to pay another debt. He now

42

owes six thousand, and has no ability to pay back. He has nothing else to offer.

'Get up, Robert.'

George is waiting for him to rise. He's punched him only twice, but Robert isn't great on his feet. He's not drunk or high now, but it's a rare lull. That's why George is here. The lender is concerned that Robert won't live long enough to pay back much of the debt. Shouldn't have lent to him in the first place. Wouldn't have, if he'd realized how bad a state his life was in.

'Ah can dae somethin',' Robert mumbles, almost on his feet.

No, he can't. Not reliable enough to deal. Not intelligent enough to work. If he has no money, then he has nothing at all.

All lenders are scum. In this case, the lender is a man called Marty. Not only an exploitative thug, but a boastful irritant as well. Always hanging around Jamieson's club, trying to ingratiate himself. Despite his ability to maintain his temperament, George has often wanted to shut Marty's boastful mouth. He's so used to beating up people that he cares nothing for. He doesn't hate these people, doesn't even dislike them. Mostly he just feels sorry for the people he's sent to deal with. It's the job, though, and he's learned not to care. He would actually enjoy carrying out his work if Marty was the target. No such luck. Maybe one day. People do fall out of favour after all. So far, though, Marty has always been able to make enough money to stay popular.

Not just money. Women too. Marty is a big provider for Jamieson and others of that rank. He finds young women, provides good venues, organizes the best parties. Living to excess, cutting loose because you can afford to. Marty provides. It's how the other half live. The other half from Robert, who is now on his feet. A grim little flat, almost no furniture to speak of. A life not worth living. And now George has turned up on his doorstep to make it even worse.

'Ah can get some money.'

George sighs lightly. They all say that. They say it no matter the circumstances, because they think it's what he wants to hear. It just isn't enough. Marty has already said that this guy has no money, and no prospect of getting it. This will be a final warning.

He waits until Robert has straightened up again. He raises his hand, and he pauses just long enough to allow Robert to duck slightly. He catches him on the ear; Robert falls to the floor again. It isn't a hard hit; George can't be bothered with that. He's made his point.

'You got one week. One week from today, someone's gonna come round and see you. You have the money by then.'

George walks out of the flat and moves quickly down the filthy stairwell to the exit of the building. A typical job. Robert will get some money, by hook or by crook. He'll steal it from somewhere. He'll borrow it from another lender. He won't get everything Marty claims he owes, but he'll get enough to avoid the worst punishment. He'll end up digging an even bigger hole for himself in the process. They just don't live a life at all, George is thinking, as he drops into his car.

He's stopping the car outside his flat. No more work today, as far as he's aware. Finished by lunchtime. If something else comes up, they'll call him. Otherwise, his day is his own. Jamieson doesn't pay him a huge amount, but he makes enough to get by, and he enjoys getting by. A casual life—no responsibility, a lot of fun. He bounds up the stairs, sees a figure sitting on the top step as he comes round the corner. He pauses. You always worry. He might not be a key employee, but you can always be a target. It's people like him, people who are easy to get to, that some will go for first. A revenge attack on Jamieson by attacking someone who doesn't think he needs protection. A little warning for those higher up. Easier to attack than a person who's actually waiting to be attacked.

'What's up, Cal?' he's asking, but he already knows.

They've known each other for eight or nine years. Calum's a year older than George, but he's been in the business a year less. He's risen fast, while George has happily stayed low. They've worked together several times before. When Jamieson's used Calum, and Calum has needed backup, he's always used George. George is the only friend he has who works for Jamieson. He's the only friend he has that he would use on a Jamieson job. Calum isn't the sort of friend who drops round unannounced unless he has a good reason. Too well mannered. Too considerate. He's here because he needs help on a job, and he wants George to be that help. And George can't say no. It's his job. Calum knows it. He thinks George will be happy to help, so he asks. He also knows that George has no choice. George can't call Young or Jamieson and ask if he has to do it. He knows

45

he has to. To wriggle out of it would raise uncomfortable questions.

'Can I come in?' Calum asks, standing on the top step.

'Yeah, course,' George is nodding. He's not going to leave his friend out on the step, no matter what. This is work, not social. This is work he won't want to do. But it's work he will end up doing. He's opening the door, knowing that by letting Calum in he's accepting the job. He holds the door open; Calum walks in. Calum's walking straight through to the kitchen, taking a seat at the kitchen table. It's the strange thing about his flat, the thing George has never been able to understand. People always gravitate towards the kitchen to talk, rather than the living room. He either has a wonderful kitchen or an unwelcoming living room. He's not sure which.

12

George is making a cup of coffee for both of them. Calum never asks for anything, tries never to be an imposition. George is delaying, not wanting to know what the job is until the latest possible moment. It's the part of the job he hates, thinking about it. Thinking about everything that can go wrong. There are plenty of people in the industry who are stupid enough never to think of what might go wrong. There are many who can only summon the intellectual capacity to think of what can go right, what the positive potential is. The outcome. That's what everyone's thinking of. It's what everyone wants to think of. The smart ones realize that when the conclusion arrives, they might not be in a position to enjoy it.

'I got a job on,' Calum's telling him as George sits opposite.

There's a lot of sunlight in the kitchen—that might be why people come here. 'Yeah?'

'Yeah. Might need a wee bit of help. You interested?'

George is shrugging. He can't not be interested. 'I guess. What d'you need?'

'I got a target. He might have people around him when I move, so I'll need someone to keep them out of the way.' Nothing exact. Keep it vague until you have a definite agreement. He trusts George, but that doesn't mean you spill your guts. It's largely because George is a friend that he won't give him the detail until he knows it's safe to do so. Give George deniability.

'What can I do to help?' George is asking, and leaning back in his chair to hear the detail.

'You heard of Lewis Winter?'

'Yeah,' George is nodding, thinking back. 'Dealer. Shitty operation, if ever I saw one. Sure I remember scaring away one of his scabby wee peddlers. He the target?' he's asking with real surprise.

'Yep, he's the one. Been stepping on toes, apparently. They think he's setting something big up, and they want to stop him.'

George is scoffing. 'Winter's never set up anything big in his puff. Doesn't know how.' It's typical to doubt the motives of your employers, to scoff at their reasons. Everyone thinks their boss is paranoid, because in this business every boss has good reason to be. In this case, George means it.

'Seems like he has bigger people backing him up. Or will do. Hopefully not yet.'

'Aye,' George is nodding, 'hopefully.'

Obvious cynicism. It's people like Calum and George who get let down by their bosses, hung out to dry. Send them in to do a job that's so risky you would never do it yourself. That's the way of it. Calum and George are expendable. Winter could have major backup, the kind of people who would make their lives hell. Jamieson wouldn't care, so long as he was off the hook.

'You followed him?'

'Yep. Last couple of days. Usual street work. Meeting people in pubs.'

'Shitty operation.'

'Shitty operation. Place to get him is the house. Him and his bird go out every night drinking. Come home drunk. Sometimes they bring people home with them.'

'Oh, aye.'

'Sometimes they don't. I'm going for him tomorrow night. If they're drunk then it shouldn't be too tough.'

They've both heard that so many times. They'll be pissed, it'll be easy. Sometimes you end up relying on alcohol to do half the job for you, and it has a tendency to let you down. People can sober up awfully fast. They see the danger, something switches in them, and suddenly the alcohol makes no difference. Sometimes they're not as drunk as they look. You get some people who are so used to being very drunk that they can think and act well despite it. Then there's the unpredictability. Some people, when drunk, begin to behave in ways that you would never expect of them. Some gain courage they shouldn't be entitled to. Some become uncharacteristically decisive. They strike back, they do something stupid. They take incredible risks with their safety. Never rely on their drunkenness. Never.

'Winter never used to be much of a boozer,' George is telling Calum. 'Used to be a quiet guy, kept himself to himself. Then he met her.'

'Aye, well, looks to me like it's her who leads the way on the nights out. They go to nightclubs. He ain't a nightclub guy. They roll home pissed. I don't know if they'll have anyone with them. Might. Might not. Best-case scenario, it's just Winter and Cope. Worst case, they might have a bunch of other people with them.'

'So what's the plan? Let them wind down?'

'Nah, I don't want them to be in bed. We let them get into the house. We knock, go in. You get everyone else into one room, I get Winter into another. We make it fast. I want in and out in two minutes. Just hold them there, then we leave. We don't need to do anything clever with this one. No complications.'

George is nodding. No complications is wishful thinking, but it can happen. Sometimes you get hit with all sorts of unforeseen trials. Sometimes everything is exactly as you hope it will be. George hasn't been on too many hits—four in eight years before this one—but he's heard enough. Heard from people like Calum. People who do it for a living. Four or five a year. Every manner of hit. He remembers Calum from way back, when they first met. Back then Calum was a gawky-looking guy. He lacked self-confidence; he was quiet to the point of antisocial. A lot of people thought he was being a jerk. Most of them ran their mouths off, partied it up. People slept around, drugs flowed freely. It was a violent, exciting, thrilling and sometimes short life. The smart ones avoided that.

Calum and George partied their fair share. They slept around a little, they had good times. It wasn't what motivated them, though. A lot of people found their way into the business because they saw the lifestyle and wanted it. People were in clubs and saw young men their own age partying with pretty girls and spending money. The flash kids attracted more new recruits. Yet it wasn't the flash kids who ever ended up being successful. They would make money, sure, if they knew how to stay onside. They would never have true responsibility, though. They would never get a job like Calum's. You don't give a job like that to someone with a big mouth. Show-offs end up being seen by the wrong people. But they attract new recruits. Not Calum and George, though. That wasn't the lifestyle that had attracted them.

For George, it had been the chance to do something irregular. He couldn't settle in a normal workplace. He couldn't settle in a normal life. Some people are just like that. Itchy feet. He did the jobs he was given, he made enough money to live on and he drifted through life. He was content. He didn't need anything more than he had. He didn't dream of riches. He didn't dream of the perfect life. For him, good was enough, and this was good. Calum had similar motivations. He went into the business and did similar work to George. Where George was working for Jamieson, Calum was essentially freelance. He tended to get worse jobs, more dangerous. He had no safety net. He impressed a lot of people. Before long, he carried out his first hit. People gradually became aware of the fact that he was a big talent. He stayed freelance, though. He did as few jobs as he could get away with. Just enough money. Just enough experience. He judged it well.

Calum ends up staying for a couple of hours. Neither has anything else to do today. Calum is making a point of keeping his distance from Winter, letting him live his penultimate day in peace. They talk about everything other than work. The job should be simple, and they've done it enough times to each know what's required of them. Little is required of George, all being well, beyond turning up; everything Calum still has to do is simple. Simple for him. Simple for someone who has done it so often before. They talk as friends, not as colleagues. No business. Make each other laugh. Take some of the tension out of it. Doesn't matter how many times you've done the job, there's still tension to be exorcized.

13

People deal with the immediate build-up differently. Some people will drink heavily. Some will party, get a woman. Those are ways of relieving tension. Others shut themselves off from the world. They need to focus on the job, have no distractions at all. For Calum, the best preparation is to live life as he always does. Don't treat it like it's anything other than a job. Just another job.

Some people get up and go and sit in an office all day. Some people build things. Other people drive around all day. That's their job. They don't think about it, they just do it. For Calum, it's killing people. He will prepare for the job. On the day of the job, he will carry it out. Then, afterwards, he will go through the same process that he always does. Nothing clever, nothing special.

There are still things to do. He needs weapons. Plural. One for him, one for George. George won't use his, if he can possibly avoid it. He still needs a usable piece. You plan for the worst-case scenario. Calum needs something as well. Something very usable. Something reliable. He'll certainly be using his, no matter what. He's committed to the job and that means completing it, no matter how badly it goes along the way. Getting the guns is a nervous matter. Getting them can be as dangerous as using them. There are plenty of places to buy, very few that can be trusted. A lot of people in the business of selling weapons are people on the fringes, people not fully involved in the industry. They have access, and that makes them useful. Doesn't make them popular. Doesn't make them insiders.

Some runners get their guns from legitimate sources. You find people who own them legally, and you buy them. Most do not. For most, the guns are acquired either through theft or from unseemly sources. You find people who own guns legally and you rob them. That happens. You find someone working with guns and you bribe them. That happens more often. Soldiers are a source. Guns go missing from an army barracks. There's a lot of guns there; it's easy for one or two to walk. Handguns always. Only an idiot or a show-off buys

52

something more than that. You can get bigger guns. You can get automatics. But why? You won't need an automatic or a shotgun in a gangland environment, unless you expect a pitched battle. You certainly won't be in a good position to hide the thing, and dispose of it afterwards.

The most common source remains reusage. A runner will buy a gun from someone who's used it on a job. Then they sell it to someone else. Then they buy more guns second-hand, sell them on again. Many guns will go round in endless circles. Many are used on multiple jobs by various people, passing through the hands of several runners in the process. It's a lucrative market, and the one Calum most often uses. He uses the same runner because he's the only one he's thus far learned to trust. Some will use multiple runners to make sure that no one supplier knows how often they work, but you only do that if you trust more than one runner. That takes time. So far, always the same one. Reasonable prices, sell the gun back after use. Essentially rental, although you never know when you might be forced to ditch the weapon mid-job. Usual cost, four or five hundred pounds. That will be more than swallowed up by Jamieson's payment to Calum.

There is another source of weapons. Many guns have come across the water from Northern Ireland to supply people. Many people have come across from Northern Ireland to make use of their criminal skills. Some people like that, welcome them. Others don't. Jamieson doesn't, and Calum certainly doesn't. There are plenty who claim to do his job, although this is a different environment from the kind of killings they're more used to.

53

They're outsiders who think themselves at home. They don't belong, but haven't noticed. Too many friends have welcomed them and allowed them to take root. They have weapons galore to sell, and there are plenty buying. Not Calum. Not ever. Different kind of criminals. Different kind of people.

He visits his runner in the early evening. No warning. Turn up at his house. He keeps them in the loft, only ever two or three in his possession at a time. If they were found, he would look like a dangerous small-time operator. Two or three guns found. How many hundreds have passed through his hands in the three decades that he's been in the business? He's knowingly supplied many killers on many occasions. He's always kept his head down and his mouth shut, and perhaps nothing is more important for a runner. Once you have a name, a public awareness, then you have nothing. Little is said. He knows why Calum is there. He retrieves the weapons, money changes hands and Calum leaves. Two small handguns. No whistles and bells. No silencers, for example. Not needed in a job designed to send a message. Expensive, heavy, unnatural. Very few gunmen like them—gives you a harder shot. Job's hard enough, thank you very much.

Out on the streets with two guns in your pocket. A nervous time. Calum is driving straight home. He'll hide the guns, pushed in through an air vent on a blocked-up chimney in his bedroom. One more thing to do, but that can wait. He has more than twenty-four hours before he does the job. The last thing to do will be done the following morning, and it will involve the help of his elder brother. A precautionary measure, and he takes a few of those. There is an issue with that, though. There's an issue with taking too many precautions. You change everything about yourself and people start to notice. You make radical changes to yourself or your life before every job, and people will notice. Someone will put two and two together. Nothing that draws attention.

The following morning he calls his brother William at the garage that William has a share in. His brother, two years older (certainly not two years wiser), must know what he does. He definitely knows that Calum works in the industry. He must be aware. William has many contacts in the business himself. He played a role in introducing Calum to a lot of people in the business. William now runs a semi-legit garage in the east end. Small place, small-time. Makes reasonable money, topped up by supplying cars to people in the trade. Help out people you trust, make a bit of money. Keeps things ticking over nicely. With Calum, it's a little bit different.

William always helps Calum, every job. Calum goes to him because he's his brother, and he can trust him. William would take any punishment rather than allow his little brother to be found out. He suspects what his brother does, why he needs the cars. Fine: supply him. Don't talk directly about the work. Warn him to be careful. He worries, though. It's an industry where it's hard not to make a little mistake. Little mistake means big punishment. What would it do to their mother, if her younger son were to find himself locked up for life? So he always helps Calum, but there's a growing reluctance. The more jobs his brother does, the more likely he is to be caught. Does William warn him? Does he say something about the business, breaking the unwritten code of silence that exists between them on the issue? Not yet.

Calum arrives in his own car, but he won't leave in it. People take their cars to the garage in all good faith. They hand them over to be fixed or serviced; they're told to come back the following day to collect them. They don't know that the car is going to be used in a criminal job. Once upon a time these defensive efforts weren't necessary. Now, thanks to CCTV, they are. Calum doesn't want his own car being picked up anywhere near Winter's house. So he uses the car of some poor innocent soul, someone the police wouldn't even think of suspecting. Use it, return it. His brother hands it back to the owner the following day— everyone's happy. There's a risk. If the police get a bee in their bonnet about that particular car. They see it on CCTV, decide to dig deeper. Question the owner. Find out it was in the garage at the time. Less of a risk than using his own car.

'How you doin', little bro?' William smiles as Calum walks into the garage. There's another mechanic working on the underside of a car, a customer standing beside the little office at the back. 'Let me deal with this guy, I'll be with you.'

Calum nods and waits. William is talking to the customer, telling him how to avoid repeating the damage he's done to his car. Calum pays little mind, knowing nothing about cars. The man leaves the garage with his car keys in hand, looking haunted by the bill he's been given. William is walking across to his brother, shaking his head.

'Some people shouldn't be on the road. So what's up?' He stays cheerful, but he knows this will be business.

'Can we talk?' Calum's asking, nodding to the office.

They're standing in the little office now, just the two of them. It's cramped. There's a door leading out to the alleyway behind the garage, a desk with a computer and some paperwork, a Pirelli calendar. The windows look out into the garage itself.

'I need a car for the night. I can bring it back middle of the night, or first thing in the morning.'

William is nodding. 'I can get you a motor. Any likely damage?' He asks as a matter of routine. There's almost never a risk. He wants to know if his brother is going to go far in it, maybe use it on country roads. Anything that might make it obvious that it's been out of the garage. He can fix the clock if he needs to.

'Nope. Won't leave the city, all very ordinary.'

'Fair enough,' William says to his little brother. 'I can do you a wee Corsa, not gonna draw much attention. Being picked up tomorrow afternoon, so make sure it's back by then.' He's handing Calum the keys from a little rack.

'You bein' careful?' William asks Calum as the latter is making to leave the office.

'Work, or birds and bees?'

William grins. 'Jesus, if I still need to give you the birds and bees speech . . . I mean work. You bein' careful with work? Careful who you work for, I mean.'

Calum is shrugging. 'I'm always careful what I do, you know that. Why, what's got you spooked?'

William shrugs. 'I dunno. I hear things. Been hearin' people talk a lot these days about changes. Apparently there's new people comin' into the city.'

'Always people coming into the city. I stick to the established.'

'Uh-huh. And the new ones are goin' after the established, so you could be on the wrong side. Just, you know, keep careful. Make sure you don't get caught out by the changes.'

It's strange to hear his brother talk like that. He knows William cares about him, just as he cares about his brother. They hadn't been especially close as children; Calum always had the impression that he annoyed his brother. He wasn't sure why. Then they grew up, and suddenly they found that they had a great deal more in common than they realized. A bond developed. When their father died, the bond became closer. They both felt the responsibility to help their mother, help look after her. She was hardly an invalid, but she was a sixty-year-old woman on her own for the first time in her life, and they each did their share to alleviate that. They were brothers now more than they had ever been. That was what made his brother's words more unsettling.

They don't talk business. Ever. They talk everything else, but there's no need to talk business. Each knows what the other does, what the other's involved in. Calum doesn't need to talk about the minimal involvement William has in the business, because it isn't worth talking about. He knows what his elder brother does to supplement his legit income. He does it well. He doesn't get too involved. And William knows what his little brother does. He doesn't want details. It's usually safer not to know. He doesn't ask. This is the first time he's asked anything at all. He's known what Calum has been doing for almost eight years, and this is the first warning. That spooks Calum a little. What's prompted it? New people in the city? There are always new people in the city, people making moves against the established order. That alone is nothing worthy of comment. William must know something else. He must know something specific that he doesn't want to have to share. They don't talk detail. He knows something specific, something relevant to Calum, something that worries him.

14

A routine meeting. Routine for Young, anyway. Maybe not routine for the cop he's meeting. Hardest thing in the business. Young always said it, and he had heard others say it too. Getting a cop on board. Get someone on the payroll and keep them there. Hardest thing you can do. You have to judge it just right. You have to make sure you approach the right person at the right time. Once you know they're interested, you have to play them just right. You tempt them, you convince them, then you hook them. Once they're in, things change. You have them over a barrel, so they're a little more secure. Still, they have the ability to bring you down if they're feeling self-destructive. They can make life unbearable. They can be much more hassle than they're worth. You have to make them feel happy and secure. Make them feel like they're not doing much wrong. Don't let them know how important they are. If they want to meet you, you meet them. If they want you to keep your distance, you do.

Over the years Young has managed to lure two cops onto the books. He holds them both at arm's length, but they surely know who he is and who he works for. They know they're working for Peter Jamieson, although neither of them has ever met him. Both are male, uniformed officers. One is destined to stay that way. Young picked Paul Greig up years ago, but the man is so utterly corrupt that he's untrustworthy to everyone. Untrustworthy even by criminal standards. He takes money from numerous criminal enterprises in the city, helps them out occasionally. He seems to be riddled with a desire to make life difficult. Young keeps him at a very safe distance indeed. He's one to use only when really needed. A last resort. In case of emergency, call Greig. He had been the first copper that Young had snared; it had seemed like an achievement. Over the years Young had lost trust in him. He was convinced Greig had sold info about the Jamieson organization to other crime figures. That was why he needed a second.

He had heard about Joe Higgins from a number of people in the business. His family had been involved in all manner of unmentionable mishaps. His parents owed money to many different undesirable people. His seventeen-year-old sister had embarked upon a chosen career that she needed to be rescued from immediately. There were questions to be raised about the legality of several things his family had done, and several things he had done himself. A wonderfully calamitous bunch. John Young organized a meeting with the young man. A twenty-three-year-old cop. A lad who made an unlikely recruit for the police force, but seemed to be doing his best. After the meeting Young came away with the impression that Higgins was both an unlikely copper and an unlikely member of his own family. His family were tough, loud and unpleasant. The boy was nervous, polite and eager to please.

Young had laid all the options on the table. He'd been open with the boy, judging that the best approach to take. Don't frighten him; don't try to play at being his best friend. The lad needs help, whether he realizes it or not. Young promised to make all the moneylenders go away. He promised to make his sister unemployable in her chosen field, and instead find her something more dignified to do with her life. He would help the boy, and all PC Higgins had to do for him was provide him with little updates. Nothing too risky, nothing too clever. Just let Young know what was being said, what was happening to other people. Gossip. Police gossip. Nothing that would put his career at risk. The boy agreed. That had been three years ago.

He never asked much of Higgins. If there are risks to be taken, then let others take them. For now, he is cultivating the relationship. He needs the boy to feel comfortable with them. This is a regular meeting—sometimes once a month, sometimes once every six weeks. They're always chatty, relaxed. Young never pushes him on anything. If the boy has something interesting to say, then he has something interesting. If not, no big deal. Next time. No pressure. Never pressure. This time Young is keen to find out certain details, but he can't suddenly push him. He rarely asks for specific detail, and only when he knows it's something Higgins can easily find out. No pressure. This will be a step forward.

They meet in a small flat that belongs to Jamieson, in a quiet part of town. Access is off the road, out of view of the street. It's quiet. Safe. Young always gets there first, lets himself in and waits. He always goes alone. Always. A second person would scare Higgins. He's never introduced the boy to anyone else in the business. If he can avoid it, he never will. Higgins is smart, diligent and well mannered. He's the sort of boy who has the potential for promotion. It's the dream for Young: a detective on his books. Maybe higher even than that. Someone with control over cases. Someone who can direct the flow of the police service away from the Jamieson organization. One day, perhaps. Big ambitions. For now, Higgins is still useful. For now, he can find out little things that Young could use to big effect. Young settles in and waits for Higgins to arrive.

A sitting duck. It occurs to him every time he goes to that flat to meet Higgins. If Higgins knocks on the door and has half a dozen of his colleagues standing beside him, Young would be finished. No way out. That's the risk of getting close to any copper. A knock on the door. Young's getting up, walking across and looking through the peephole. He can only see Higgins. He opens the door, nods hello and holds the door open until the twenty-six-year-old is inside. A quiet boy, but an imposing figure. Youthful face, but tall and broad-shouldered. Now young and athletic; likely to end up fat and with a bad back.

'Want a cup of coffee, anything like that?' Young asks him. They're strolling through to the large, open-plan kitchen and living room.

'Nah, ta, I'm okay.' Higgins is in jeans and a hooded top. Casual. A day off. They never meet when he's on duty. That would be criminally irresponsible.

They sit and Young asks him about his family. He does that every time. Make it seem like he cares. At the same time remind the boy that his parents' financial security and his sister's livelihood all depend on him. She's a beautician now, whatever that is. Young has no idea. It's what she wanted, so it's what she got. She's useless at it, apparently, but Jamieson owns half of the salon, and her brother is useful, so she keeps her job. Higgins has answered politely, as always. He's smart enough not to share any further troubles with Young. Smart enough not to dig a deeper hole. Not yet. The way things are going with his family, though, he may need to soon. Young knows it, but says nothing.

'Heard anything relevant?' Young asks. Standard question. It means have you heard anything that Peter Jamieson and I ought to be concerned about. The answer has always been no, and Young assumes that Higgins is smart enough to alert him immediately if he hears anything urgent.

'Nope, not a lot of interest happening. Most of the focus is still on outsiders.'

Always good to hear. Outsiders are the bogeymen, as much to the police as to the established crime organizations. The police, subconsciously or not, take a better-the-devil-you-know approach. The outsiders become a priority. Takes the eye off the established order. Now and again the police would have a spurt of activity against established people, but they're occasional. One of the points of having a cop on the books was to boost the opportunity of knowing when the police's interest had turned back towards the established. You try to prepare, do all that you can to take yourself off the radar. You have a better chance with advance warning.

Young carries on the conversation, asking numerous questions about things that don't matter much to either of them. Higgins tells him about several crimes of significance that have occurred in the last few weeks. A couple of murders, a drugs bust, a counterfeiting operation. Young has already heard of all of these things, probably knows more about them than the police, but he nods along politely. Don't let the cop know that you have more information than he does. Let him think he's the one with the valuable knowledge. There's no mention of Lewis Winter. Young isn't sure how long Calum will take to carry out that particular hit. He tends to take a little longer than most men in his profession. More careful.

More ponderous. More successful. If it had happened, Higgins would have mentioned it. So he's still waiting.

'What do the police know about Hugh Francis?'

Higgins blinks. 'Shug Francis? A bit. Involved in a lot of car crime. Not so much these days, harder to steal cars than it used to be. A pest, but I don't think he's a priority. Doesn't use violence. Don't think the public are aware of him. Last I heard he'd bought a racing car,' Higgins is saying with a smile.

'Track-day car, yeah,' Young is nodding. He's heard all the charming stories of Shug's geeky adoration of cars. 'You guys haven't looked any deeper into his work?'

Higgins shrugs a little. 'I heard someone say that they had looked into him a couple of years back. Not a lot to find. He's a smart guy, y'know. Hides everything real well. I think they looked at him to see if he had anything else going on, if he was using his car set-up to do other stuff. Don't think he was, or we would have taken measures. Has a good legit business to hide everything behind.'

Young raises an eyebrow. He isn't going to say anything else.

'You think we should be looking at him?'

Young thinks about it for a moment. 'Might be worth it. Could soon be relevant. I can't say more than that.'

He can't say more than that because he can't be entirely sure. It annoys him so much, not to be sure. Someone is making moves against Jamieson and, despite the scepticism of some, Young is sure it's Shug Francis. He has the means. He's smart enough to pick the right targets. Jamieson is the right target. If you want to come into the market, you need to take share from someone. You steal market share from someone worth stealing from. You don't steal share from someone so big they can stamp on you and wipe you out with ease. Jamieson is on the rise, so he isn't liked by the big players. Respected, yes. Feared, absolutely. Liked, no, because they recognize the threat he poses. Someone chipping away at him would not be

65

loathed by the top people in the business. One thing Shug Francis has always been good at is ingratiating himself with people who matter.

They end the chat. Whether Higgins recognized the significance of Young mentioning Francis, Young can't be sure. He seems to treat it as a normal meeting, doesn't give any indication that he understood the difference. Young doesn't bring up specific cases. He doesn't go asking for particular information. This time he has tried, and he isn't sure it even worked. By raising the name of Shug Francis he is making Higgins aware of his interest. He wants Higgins to go away and think about it. He wants Higgins to have a look at what the police already know about Francis, and bring that information back to him. The cop is young. He's inexperienced. He might not realize what he's being asked to do.

The cop leaves first. Young waits for a boring twenty minutes before leaving the building, making sure there's distance between them. He goes to the club, where he knows Jamieson will be. They've discussed the issue so often. Someone is making moves. They need to know exactly who. There would be nothing more damaging and embarrassing than attacking the wrong enemy. They don't yet know exactly who is to blame. Young finds Jamieson playing snooker. He waits patiently for the frame to end, and the pair of them make their way back to Jamieson's office. It's remarkable how relaxed Jamieson is about it. Young agonizes constantly, wondering who their target should be. They know the person is using Winter. Hitting Winter will send a powerful message. He hopes it will also draw the real target out into the open.

'Boy doesn't know anything about Francis,' Young's saying as they take their usual seats.

'Maybe there's nothing to know.' Jamieson knows Francis. Knows he's smart. Knows he isn't a risk-taker.

'I'm convinced. Why is it so hard to find out anything about his operation? Because he's hiding something. He has the whole thing locked down. Didn't used to. I'm telling you, he's making some sort of move. If it ain't against us, then it's against someone else, and I can't find anyone else who's being moved against.'

Jamieson taps the desk. 'So what?'

'So we wait and see what the reaction is to Winter. When he gets hit, something happens. Whoever was working with him will need to approach someone else. They have to come out in the open, just a wee bit. Then we know.'

'He still hasn't hit Winter?'

'Not yet. Soon.'

15

He doesn't like Fridays. Busiest day of the week, workwise. People are buying for the weekend. Hardcore users buy every day. A lot of casual users buy only on a Friday. He has to make sure his people are well stocked for the spike in orders. He spends most of the morning doing that. He meets all six people that he's using to sell his gear. Five of them are users; they're always difficult to track down. Unreliable. All over the place. Chaotic lives.

He stocks four of them, and the one reliable dealer he has. He might make greater use of that non-user in the future. If things are going big-time, then he might make the boy an offer. He's jobless, maybe a little feckless, but he isn't entirely stupid. And he's clean, that's the most important thing. That stupid, using peddler. The one who hadn't been able to sell what he'd been given. He's nowhere to be found. He's gone missing with the gear he had left. Stolen for his own use. That requires punishment. He has to be seen to be tough. He won't attack the man himself, but he will pay someone else to do it. Get back any gear the guy still has, which will probably be none. Then never use him again.

There's another reason why Lewis Winter hates Fridays. Zara wants every Friday to be a party. They have to go out. There is no question, no debate. They are going out. They will drink, they will dance, they will be out until the middle of the night. Twenty years ago he would have enjoyed it. Now, he hates every second. He doesn't like being drunk; it makes him feel more insecure and maudlin. It increases his hatred of the people Zara attracts. They're all terribly young and terribly trendy. Men hover around. He tries to keep pace, but his heart isn't in it. She wants to dance. He knows how absurd he looks. It looks like she's brought her uncle to the club with her. People have different attitudes now. They seem more aggressive in matters of enjoyment. They have no trouble hitting on a man's girlfriend when he's right beside her. The old rules have gone. Sometimes she flirts back.

If she would just stop inviting people back to the

house. They have no business being there. He doesn't want them there; she does. It's his house. It's their house. He's committed to her. Like it or not. He'll have to sit down and talk to her. At some point in the relationship he has to stop feeling like shit. It's making him miserable. It's because she walks all over him. He will say something. Not tonight. She'll already have made plans for tonight. She'll have called some of her friends and they'll all have arranged to go to the same place together. A group night out, to begin with. Some will bring boyfriends, some are single. They're all much younger than he. They'll all enjoy the night out, except him. He's just there to buy drinks. He's there to call the taxi to get them all back home. He's the chaperone.

He gets home after four o'clock. There's nobody downstairs. He can hear loud music from upstairs. He knocks on their bedroom door. Zara calls for him to come in. He opens the door. There's Zara and a friend in the room. Another tanned, blonde, vacant-looking friend. They all look the same to him. The friend is sitting on the bed with a glass in her hand, surrounded by clothing. Zara is in front of the full-length mirror, looking at herself. She has on a party outfit. There's a wine bottle and another half-filled glass on the dresser.

'Hey, sweetie,' she coos at him. She only ever speaks in childish, endearing terms when there are other people around. Keeping up some pretence. 'Nah,' she says decisively, and pulls the short dress up over her head. She throws it onto the pile on the bed. She's now standing in front of the mirror in just her underpants. When she's drinking she likes to be the centre of attention.

She drinks a lot, Winter has realized. He's known it from the moment they met, but it's her chosen lifestyle. She's a party drinker. It livens her up. It was too early in the relationship to say anything about it, back then. As time has gone by, his desire to mention it has dissipated as his desire to hold onto her increases. He doesn't like her when she's drunk. Now he tolerates her.

'Wanna help me pick something sexy to wear?' she asks with a grin.

He can't deny that she is beautiful when she smiles like that. Mischievous. Devilish. 'I think you're a better judge than I am,' he says quietly. He quickly worries that he's set the wrong tone, that she might think him miserable. 'I think you look great as you are.' That's the right tone. She and the friend laugh, and the friend says she bets he does. 'I'm going to grab something to eat,' he's telling them now, recognizing that the time has come for him to make an exit. They want to carry on dressing up. 'You two want anything?' They both say no, they're fine. He knows they don't need anything to eat because they've been drinking for more than an hour already, and plan to keep on drinking.

He makes himself a bacon roll. Nothing much— if they're going to be out all night, then he doesn't want much on his stomach. He sighs more often than is healthy as he makes himself a cup of tea to go with it. He had started the relationship on the wrong foot. Having realized that he was allowing himself to be the junior partner, he should have bailed out early. It was fear and desperation that had allowed things to roll on, and now it feels like it's too late. It would seem as if he was trying to

70

change her. She would argue that she'd given so much of her life to him, and he has no right to try to push her to be someone else. He sees other men making these relationships work. It's a fact of life in the trade that there are women around. He knows men who happily bounce from one woman to another, never losing sleep over losing a woman. He knows others who are married, but know how to have fun. They all seem so much better at it than he is.

He's cleaning up after himself when Zara comes down for another bottle of wine and to tell him that a couple more of her friends are going to come to the house before they head into the city. 'You don't mind, do you?' she asks so sweetly.

'Course not,' he answers quietly.

She has a top on, but is still in just her underpants. She pushes up against him and kisses him passionately. 'It'll be fun,' she smiles, 'I promise.' She takes another bottle of wine and goes back upstairs.

He doesn't doubt that it'll be fun for her. It always is. He tries to remember the last time they did anything that was designed to be fun for him, and he can't.

16

Calum is sitting on his couch, playing video games. *Gran Turismo 5*, if you care. He enjoys it, despite his racing deficiencies. He glances at the clock. It's now ticked past five o'clock. He can feel the nerves starting to tickle at the bottom of his stomach. It doesn't matter how many times you do the job. It certainly doesn't matter how good you are at it. If you're anywhere close to being a normal human being, then you're going to be nervous about it. In a few hours' time he is going to head out into the night and murder a man. It looks like a simple job. He knows he's good at what he does. Doesn't matter. You're taking a man's life, and that's worth being nervous about.

Six o'clock. He switches the machine off. Find things to do. He won't be leaving his own flat until after ten. He and George will head to Winter's house after eleven and check it. If there's no sign of life, they'll leave and come back again after midnight. Calum's confident they won't be home by then. So he and George will sit and wait. There's four hours before he does anything at all. Into the kitchen. Open the fridge. Get something to eat. Not much—the nerves won't allow it to settle. He looks at what's there. Very little. Not much of a foodie. He takes out a packet of bacon, switches on the cooker. There's fresh bread in; he'll have a bacon sandwich and a cup of tea.

Twenty past seven. He's putting the TV on, but there's nothing he can settle down to watch. So hard to settle to anything. He needs to kill time. Another two and a half hours before he leaves the flat. He walks round the flat. There's too much energy in him. You don't want to be bursting with that nervous energy when the time of the job comes; you're much more likely to make a mistake. Some people have ways of expending the energy. Calum knows one gunman who swears by sex before any job. The best sex you'll ever have, apparently. Even if that fellow can't find a young lady to share his exuberance with, he will satisfy himself. Anything to kill the nerves. Calum won't accept that. Worse than energy is the opposite. He knows he makes a lot more mistakes when he's tired and lethargic than he does when he's on the edge.

Pacing the little flat. Starting to feel a little tired in the legs. He knows he has to do something. He's left getting changed until the last minute, making sure he has something to do. A pair of black jeans, a plain black top. Both items bought months— maybe more than a year—ago. Never been worn before, will never be worn again. They'll be carefully placed in someone else's general rubbish bin. Not a recycling one. Then they end up in landfill. There are some who put the clothes into charity shops. Some places have large recycling bins, usually outside supermarkets, where you can drop off old clothes. Some people use those. Calum can't abide the idea of the clothes still being out there, possibly with his DNA on them. Long shot that they would ever be found, but still a risk he won't take.

He has two balaclavas. These are difficult. You don't want to be seen buying balaclavas regularly. It goes without saying that it carries risk. A few years ago he bought a boxful over the Internet. He had them sent to the house of a friend, went and picked them up. It's a risk, always. You buy something that almost only has criminal use. You buy them on a false card. You have them sent to an address where the occupant will happily claim to have ordered no such thing. You then keep the box hidden in the loft of your mother's house, without telling her it's there. It would concern her. She would want to know what you were doing with them. Awkward questions. He had taken three from the box a month or so ago, guessing that he might need one soon. He needed two. George won't have one of his own.

Not every job requires dressing up. Sometimes you're sure there will be no witnesses. Sometimes there's no risk in letting them see your face. Sometimes they need to see your face before you can get close to them. This isn't one of those times. There will be witnesses. Those witnesses will be interviewed by the police. Every precaution must be taken. Calum knows that, and he trusts George to be professional enough to know it as well. No talking inside the house. No sloppy mistakes that could lead to identification.

Calum stuffs the two balaclavas into his pocket. A man dressed all in black, with the ability to hide his face. If he were stopped by the police, in a car that didn't belong to him, he would be caught. Caught with a gun, and he would be looking at a mandatory jail term anyway. The journey to and from work is treacherous for the men in his business. He removes the guns from their hiding place, sliding shut the vent on the chimney. He's always careful not to disturb the little layer of dust on the top of the vent, convinced that it might give the impression that it's never been touched. They would be able to tell, he told himself. If they really looked, they could tell. Don't ever give them a reason to look at you. That's why working for someone like Jamieson is a risk. Being close to an organization that is surely being watched means you will be watched. That flash of doubt runs though his mind again.

74

He's left the living-room light on in the flat, left the television on. Not too loud—just loud enough to be heard if you pressed your ear to the front door. He's getting into the car now. He's still unfamiliar with it, isn't comfortable driving it. It seems to want to lurch forward when you first press the accelerator, and then there's no power to get it up to speed. He's not going to race to the meeting point with George, so speed is no concern. It's the threat of stalling at traffic lights and being asked by a passing cop if you need help. The threat of being involved in some minor accident because you don't have full control of the car. Anything that might draw attention.

Calum's picking George up from a building site. It's a random meeting place where they know there are no security cameras. You don't pick up from home—that's a risk. You pick up somewhere random. You pick up somewhere that you won't be seen. George drops into the passenger seat.

'Nice motor,' he's saying with a smile. It's the sort of small, gutless vehicle that an old lady would drive. Nothing to draw attention.

'Nice enough,' Calum says in response. They pull out onto the street and head towards Winter's house. Calum's glancing at the clock. It's nearly eleven o'clock; it'll be a little after by the time they get there. He's expecting the house to be in darkness. He's hoping it will be. No surprises. Please, no surprises.

17

He needs to sit down. He doesn't care if it makes him look old, he needs to sit down. His legs feel like they're on fire; he can feel how red his face is. The sweat is pouring through his greying hair, making it stick to his forehead. The headache from the thumping music is now so familiar that he hardly notices it. He can scarcely imagine his life without it. He goes to the bar first. Another bottle of beer. Expensive, but he doesn't care. It's all that's keeping him going right now. Winter is just drunk enough to keep his patience. Just miserable enough not to be angry. He finds a little empty table off to the side and sits at it. Long gulps of beer. How many bottles so far? Who cares?

Occasionally the movement of the dancers in front of him will create a little gap through which he can see her. She's still dancing with the same man. The friends they arrived with have all splintered off in other directions; some have already left. Winter has tried to keep up with her, to stay close. Even that has been to no avail. Some young buck with a head full of styling gel and big ideas danced his way across to her. He didn't even have to say anything. He just started dancing close to her. Winter stuck around for ten humiliating minutes and then went for a beer.

There are men in the business who know how to handle slick young men like him. They would let him dance away with the young lady all he wanted. They would wait for the man to leave the club, and follow him out. Then they would kick the shit out of him. Put him in hospital. Scar him for life. That would get the message across. They were no doormats. He is. This kid—twenty-two or twenty-three—walked up to his girl and made him look pathetic. It made him angry. Another bottle of beer. Back to the table. He hasn't felt this anger rise in him before. The more he drinks, the more convinced he becomes that the anger is a good thing.

A couple of dancers move away. He has a good view of her now. She's pressed up against this young man. He's whispering in her ear. She's laughing. She has her arms round his neck, dancing as if they're the only ones in the room. They look like young lovers. His hand moves down. It rests on her bottom. She doesn't appear to notice, still dancing. She's still moving her back end as if his hand isn't groping it, Winter thinks sourly. How many people here know that she and I live together? How many people have I been humiliated in front of? Again. Hardly the first time. A man half his age. Making her smile in a way that he can't.

He wants to get up, to go over there. Say something? Maybe. Maybe just pull her away from him and make her dance with her partner for a change. She wouldn't understand. She'd say he was making a scene. She'd say that he was humiliating her. Him humiliating *her*. What a laugh. She'd say it, though. And she'd believe it. How can they not be exhausted? He just wants to go home. Another bottle of beer. Expensive. Complain? Nah, just drink. Obliterate everything. Destroy the world and then you don't have to be in it any more. Let them have their fun. Let them have their world.

There is no fun for him. No place for him. What time is it? He can't remember to look at his watch. Timeless.

Someone comes across to the table. A woman. Not as young as Zara. Not as pretty. This woman is in her thirties. She's trying too hard. Her hair dyed to within an inch of its life. A tan that certainly wasn't acquired courtesy of the Glasgow sunshine. She's dressed in clothes that Zara would wear. It flatters Zara; her body's more attractive than the little clothing that covers it. That isn't the case for this woman. Less is more doesn't apply.

'You on your own?' she asks Winter, sitting down beside him. She looks sympathetic. She looks desperate for affection.

Winter puts his hand out and presses it on top of hers. Be a gentleman. A woman who cares. It doesn't matter if she's not perfect. Why did you ever think you deserved perfect? Why did you kid yourself that you could keep perfect?

The woman talks for a couple of minutes. She isn't as drunk as he is, but she is drunk enough that it takes her two minutes to realize that he's barely capable of speech any more. She sighs. Another bust. He had looked sweaty, but presentable. A man of an age that she might appeal to.

'I'm gonna go,' she says to him, patting his hand.

'No. Go. Not you too. She treats me that way. Not you.'

The woman sighs again. Another complete loser. She really can pick them out of a crowd. It isn't even a joke any more. Oh well, one consolation: she isn't the most pathetic specimen in the place. There's always someone worse off.

Had he fallen asleep? He isn't sure. It feels as

78

though something has changed. Time has leapt ahead without him. No, couldn't have been asleep. How could he have slept with that noise? Not possible. The woman has gone. A woman came across and sat with him. Now she's gone. Or had he dreamed that? A nice woman. A woman who cared. It must have been a dream. There was no such thing in his life. Only when he slept. Perhaps he had slept. He looks across the dance floor. Is Zara kissing him? Both his hands are on her backside. Winter gets up from the table. Go over and say something. Go on. Tell them both what you think. Give that little shit a good thrashing. Make him look pathetic, instead of you. Let her see that you're every bit as much a man as that little prick. The bar is closer. One more bottle of beer.

He has no idea of time. He knows that he needs to go to the toilet. He gets up and looks about. Strobe lighting. His legs are weak. He sits back down. He can hold it until they get home. Surely it won't be long until they go home. What time is it? If only there was some way of finding out. People are dancing in front of him. He can't see her any more. She'll still be there. Dancing all night. Dancing with another man. Kissing another man. She will take the other man home. Winter knows it. She will insist on taking him home. Back for 'drinks'. As per bloody usual. This time he'll say no. This time he'll put his foot down.

18

His name is Stewart. She doesn't know what his surname is. They had gone over to the other side of the dance floor and found a seat. They sat for ten minutes, chatted. He seemed nice. Not as stupid as most. He bought her drinks. He ran his hand up her leg. She let him. After dancing again, it was he who suggested they go home.

'Sure,' she was saying, 'we can go back to my place. I live with someone, but he doesn't mind. I'll tell him you're coming back for drinks. He'll go to bed. He's over there. Come on, we'll get him and get a taxi.'

Zara is leading Stewart across the floor by the hand to the table where she had seen Winter. She had seen him go over there nearly a couple of hours ago. He had been drinking a lot, and he doesn't hold his drink well these days.

He looks pathetic, sitting at that table by himself, surrounded by beer bottles. He looks like a sad old man, sitting in the wrong establishment. He's an embarrassment to her. He looks half-asleep. She sits beside him and nudges him aggressively.

'Lewis, this is Stewart, he's coming back to the house for drinks. It's time to go. Get up.'

She looks up at Stewart and shakes her head. He sympathizes. This pretty girl is living with a drunkard. No wonder she needs to cut loose and enjoy herself. He probably treats her like dirt. Drunks are so selfish. The old man mumbles something. He's obviously trying to sound forceful, but he manages a sentence that contains only vowels and some spit.

'For God's sake,' Zara says loudly. 'Help me with him, will you?' she asks Stewart pleadingly. Helping is the decent thing to do.

He's nearly able to support himself, he just needs to be pointed in the right direction and occasionally rebalanced. Stewart walks on one side of him, Zara on the other. She seems angry; it seems to Stewart that the promised entertainment probably isn't going to happen now. She hasn't said so, so he stays with her. Besides, how would it look if he left her with this drunk and didn't even make sure that she got home okay? You have to have some standards. A taxi is pulling up alongside them. Zara helps Winter get into the back. She leads Stewart round the other side and they get in. Stewart finds himself between the two of them. He's looking at this Lewis. He's not as old as he had seemed in the club, but he's too old for Zara. Perhaps they're not a couple. Perhaps they just live together. Best not to pry. The lives of others.

'He okay?' the driver's asking, looking back at Winter. He's worried that he might throw up.

'He's fine,' Zara's telling him forcefully, and she gives him the street name.

As they're driving through the city centre, Stewart is watching Winter. The older man is struggling to stay awake. He seems determined to stay awake, but also determined not to look at any of them. His half-open eyes are staring out the window, his head bobbing slowly up and down. What a dreadful thing to have to live with. Then Stewart's feeling her hand on his thigh, just moving up and down, nothing more yet. He turns and looks at her. She too is staring out the window, not apparently focusing on anything. She seems serene. She seems unaware of where her hand is. Then it moves up, and it's on his crotch. There's a light grip, and a massaging. She's still staring out the window. The promised entertainment remains a solid promise.

The taxi pulls to a stop in a pleasant suburban street. Being stuck in the middle, Stewart has no idea where they are. His mind has been occupied by other things. The taxi driver looks back over his shoulder and tells Zara what they owe him. She pulls a twenty from her bag and flings it at him, opening the door as she does. She seems in a bad mood. Yet she seems eager not to let Stewart go. Some women are odd like that. She's probably under a great strain with her drunken partner. It's bound to make her a little irrational.

Zara comes round to the other side of the car and opens the door. Winter almost falls out. She grabs him roughly. Stewart has got out her side of the car and has come round to help. Together they get Winter on his feet out of the car. As soon as they close the rear door, the taxi pulls away.

It's slow progress up the garden path. Winter seems less steady on his feet than before. The cold night air isn't sobering him at all. If anything, it's making him more sleepy. They reach the front door.

'The key, Lewis,' she's barking at him. 'Where's the house key?'

He's mumbling something in response. They're not obviously words, just groans. She's reaching into his pockets, stuffing a hand in and rummaging. He's making a noise now, trying to resist. She finds what she's looking for, and mumbles a string of swear words as she unlocks the front door. She shoves him inside, Stewart doing his best to hold onto the man before he falls over. Now that they're through the front door, she doesn't seem to care at all.

The front door shuts. Stewart's still holding Winter. Zara puts the key on a little table in the hall. She turns and looks at them.

'You don't need to keep holding him; you can just dump him on the floor if you want.' It's said with scorn. She obviously hates the man. He must treat her terribly.

'I don't want to do that,' Stewart is saying. 'Is there a bed or something?'

She sighs deeply. She must go through this a lot. 'Yeah, upstairs. Come on.'

The journey up the stairs is long and arduous. Winter seems unwilling to go. He's trying to push Stewart away. He wants to go back downstairs. He can't resist. They get him up. Well, Stewart gets him up. Zara does nothing but lead the way. Poor girl.

Someone puts a light on. The bedroom. They're in the bedroom. Winter seems to react. He knows. He stops. He manages to summon the strength to push Stewart away. He's trying to shout, but he isn't as loud as he obviously thinks he is. He slurs some words in an incoherent dribble. Had they listened closely, Stewart and Zara would have heard the word 'humiliation'. They would also have heard the words 'last time'. They didn't, because the words are so badly broken by the time they make it into the open. They fall from Winter's mouth and disappear from the world. It sounds like nothing more than a drunken ramble. It's embarrassing to hear a grown man speak that way.

Then Winter does something quite unexpected. Despite being apparently unable, he takes a swing at Stewart. It's limp, pathetic. It misses by a couple of feet. It comes with a guttural growl that suggests vomit is close behind. Winter falls forward. Stewart reaches out and grabs him by the coat, struggling to keep him on his feet. He looks at Zara. He sees her look at Winter, look down and pull a face of disgust. Stewart looks down at Winter. He appears to have wet himself.

'Put him on the bed,' Zara is saying, 'just put him on the bed and leave him.'

Stewart is lying Winter down on his back, trying to be careful with him. 'Will he be okay?' he's asking now, as he joins Zara in the doorway.

'That's his problem,' she's saying as she switches off the light.

They're downstairs now, in the living room. Stewart is unsure about what happens next. He's standing in the doorway. Zara's gone into the living room and across to a drinks cabinet. She's pouring out a glass of whiskey for herself, not asking Stewart if he wants one. She downs it in two gulps and then closes the cabinet.

'God, I really need this now,' she says to him, and pulls her top over her head. As she's unclipping her bra, she's nodding for him to come into the room. Stewart starts to undress, his enthusiasm rebuilding. She's quickly removed her short skirt and underpants and is moving across the room to help him.

84

19

Calum and George are sitting in the car. Sitting in silence. They know what they have to do. It's a matter of patience now. Calum is thinking it through, time and again, repeating the possible scenes in his mind. He's thinking of all the things he might have done differently. All the extra precautions he might have taken. He knows of others who go to such great lengths. He knows of one gunman who always wears shoes that are the wrong size for him on a job. If the police identify the footprint, they're not going to identify it as his. That seems like a good idea. Cops are always looking for shoe prints these days. One of their little tricks. Calum doesn't use it, though. Seems a touch excessive. Now he wonders.

George is impatient to start. He wants to say something. He wants to crack jokes to relieve the tension, but he knows that isn't Calum's way. They have different ways of dealing with the tension. That's okay. Calum's just sitting there, staring at the house, thinking things through. Fine. He's the one who has to do the dirty side of the job. George is sitting there, wishing they could talk. Wishing that the tension wasn't as high as it is. He doesn't like it that way. He wants something more relaxed. He wants a bit of a laugh. Probably because he's not intending to kill someone. He can afford to relax. He's there to keep all potential witnesses away from the act itself. His role allows some relaxation.

It's ten past one. A taxi turns into the street and

pulls up beside Winter's house. It stops. There's a little delay. A rear door opens. Two bare legs emerge. Then Zara, in her short skirt and little top. George inhales slightly. Approval. She walks round to the other side of the car. They're both hoping that only Winter will emerge with her. She opens the door. They can see a figure, but he's not getting out. Then another person gets out the same door she did. Damn! Double damn—it's a young man. He doesn't look too drunk. He looks healthy.

'Know him?' George asks. It's a small city. You see people around.

'No,' Calum answers. They're both glad they don't recognize him. They don't want him to be someone in the business.

The young man goes round to help Zara. She's obviously in charge. She looks disgusted with something. The young man helps Winter out of the car. He looks dead on his feet. He's been drinking more than is advisable. A drunk target. A target so drunk he can't possibly fight back. That good bit of fortune compensates for the young man being there. The taxi pulls away from them, leaving the young man to help Winter up the garden path. It's slow going. They reach the door. They can just see Zara reaching into Winter's pocket. They're almost out of sight in the doorway. She opens the door. They go inside. The door closes.

They wait. Silence. A light goes on—the downstairs hall. They wait. Another light. The stairs. Wait. The bedroom light. Then it goes off. It's been five minutes since they went into the house. Wait. The living-room light. Another three minutes. You never know what you're walking into.

86

You never know the right time. It's not judgement, it's a blind guess. Calum pulls his balaclava over his head. George follows. Calum pulls on a pair of thin surgical gloves. George follows. Calum opens the door of the car and gets out. He'll leave the car unlocked, keys in the ignition. Small risk, possibly a major time-saver. You never know when you might need to save those precious few seconds. George gets out of the car now. They're standing on the road. Each with a gun in hand, tucked against their side. Calum turns and nods.

They walk across the road and up to the door of the house. There's no sign of life in any other house on the street. Often people are watching. Often people are peering out from behind a curtain in the dark. The world is nosy. People notice things. A little old lady with insomnia and nothing better to do. No matter. The job has begun. No turning back. Calum knocks on the door. A steady knock. Loud enough to be heard inside. Not so loud that a neighbour will hear it. Not if they're asleep, anyway. The living-room light is still on. Nobody comes to the door. They can't afford to wait.

There's a danger with knocking. People hear the knock and correctly guess who's there. They run. You can't give them that much time. No more knocking. Calum nods to George. They both take a step back from the door. George raises a boot and firmly kicks the door, just around the lock. It shakes violently. He kicks again. The crack of splinters. The door bursts open, bounces against the wall. They go in quickly. Nobody in the hall. They can see along the corridor to the dark kitchen. A light. The living room. Calum pushes the door open, the gun raised. You never know what you're walking into.

George snorts, then stifles the laugh. Calum stands still, gun raised, checking the room around them. The young man is on his feet, naked, his hands over his crotch, trying to hide something that doesn't want to be hidden. Zara is getting up from the couch. Naked too, sweating. There's a gleam in her eyes, but a grim frown. She understands. She knows what's going to happen. Maybe she thinks it'll be worse than it will. Maybe she thinks they'll hit her too. The young man opens his mouth, wants to say something. Words can't make it from his brain to his mouth. Fear has put up a barrier between the two. A terror has gripped him. He's close to tears. Zara simply stands and watches, making no attempt to reach for her clothes. Calum glances at George, and sees his shoulders rocking up and down a little in silent laughter. You never know what you're walking into.

Then the young man does something stupid. Naked as the day he was born, he's trying to run for the door. That's a stupid move, but it's easily dealt with. George spends his entire working life dealing with people who try to run for the door. Admittedly the vast majority are clothed, but that only makes this easier. He has in fact dealt with naked people before. You charge in somewhere in the middle of the night to give them the fright of their lives. They stumble out of bed. Easy to deal with. As the young man takes his second stride, he's alongside George. He doesn't see the hand flash out. He doesn't see the gun gripped in the hand. He feels it when it smashes into the side of

88

his head, between the ear and the forehead. Suddenly the world isn't underneath him any more. He's sprawling sideways. He collides with the side of a chair and tumbles over it. Then he stays on the floor, whimpering.

George raises the gun. He has the safety catch on, but nobody else knows that. Zara crosses her arms and looks at the two men in black. She sighs a little. She's trying to look superior. Not an easy thing to do in her position. Calum looks her in the eye. Holds her eye. He knows that she's not going to put up resistance. She now just wants to get out of this night alive. The things that mattered to her three minutes ago mean nothing now. Now it's survival. Play nice for the men with the guns. Whatever they want. Anything is better than the bang of the gun. They mean business. She knows it because they're so calm. They've done this before. One of them is relaxed enough to laugh. Not hysterical laughter. Genuinely amused. The other is staring at her. Looking her in the eye. Judging her.

Calum looks at the man lying on the floor. He's breathing heavily, but he's not moving. Frozen with fear. Desperate to survive. There won't be any trouble from him, either. Calum can just see his legs and part of his back. He's hunched over. Wishing it would all go away. He came here tonight on a promise from a beautiful woman. Now this. Calum feels sorry for him, but a crack on the head is as far as it will go for him, provided he stays where he is. Just use some common sense, boy. He glances at George. He isn't laughing any more. He's looking at the man on the floor, making sure that he can cover both him and Cope. Professional.

There are many men in the business he would be worried about leaving alone in that situation. A pretty woman standing naked and compliant. A young man already battered and in fear of his life. There are many who wouldn't resist the temptation. Couldn't resist. There are many who would take it too far. Not George. He knows his job. He knows what he has to do. No messing around. Don't speak. Don't do anything you don't have to do. There for a job. There'll be ample opportunity to have fun in your own time, and without doing anything that you might have to feel guilty about later. That's why Calum can leave him alone in that situation.

Clearly Winter isn't in the living room. It's not hard to judge what's happened: the way they led him in; the lights going on and off. They took him upstairs. They dumped him in his and Cope's bedroom, and they came downstairs. They wanted to be alone. He was out of the way. On his own. Isolated. Ideal for the job in hand. Without saying a word Calum turns and makes his way out of the living room. You take nothing for granted. You never know what might be lurking behind every door. He expects Winter to be crashed out. He expects an easy hit. But he's not taking it for granted.

Up the stairs. Gun gripped, but not too tightly, don't cramp your hand. It's dark. Listen for any sound, anything suspicious. Winter may have heard the door being kicked open. If he did, then he's had two minutes to prepare for you. Time enough to grab a gun, if he's got one. Time enough to grab some sort of weapon and lie in wait. If he heard the door. If. Calum's at the top of the stairs. Pause.

90

Let your eyes get used to the darkness. Two doors on his left, one on his right. One directly facing him at the end of the corridor. No light from any. At least one door will be to a bathroom. At least two of the other three will be bedrooms. Work out where you are. The light that went on and off upstairs was on the front left of the house. So that should be second on your left. Should be.

Downstairs, George is staying silent. Alone with the two witnesses. Say nothing. Do nothing that could identify you. Take absolute care. He's been holding the gun up; making sure it's visible to Cope. He lowers it slightly; no need to strain your arm if there's no immediate danger. He's moved back three paces closer to the door, giving him a better view of the young man. Cope he expects no trouble from. She's still standing beside the couch, her arms crossed. She's made no effort to cover herself up. That ship has sailed.

She had started by trying to look defiant. Now she's trying to look bored by the whole thing. She wants to give the impression that she sees this sort of thing every day, no big deal. Not impressed. No fear. The harder she tries, the more afraid she looks. She is very pretty. George has made every effort to avoid the sort of women who hang around the industry he works in, but he can see the attraction of this one. He would have liked to tell her she has nothing to worry about, but he can't. Nothing that could identify him. Shame. He wants to tell the young man on the floor to stop crying and pull himself together, but that is also out. So silence. Enjoy the view. Hold your position. Cover the targets. Wait.

Second on his left. Calum pushes the door slowly

91

open. It's dark inside. Gun raised. Pause. If he heard you come in, he could be behind the door. Silence. Then a snort. A low, rumbling snore. The snore of a middle-aged, slightly overweight man, filled with alcohol. Calum's stepping slowly into the room, confidence growing. His gloved hand reaches out and finds the light switch. Winter is lying on the bed, on his back. His arms are stretched out on either side of him. He's snoring uncomfortably. There's an angry look on his face. Calum can smell the urine. He steps up to the bed, the gun held firmly at his side, and looks down on the target. Sometimes you get the feeling you're doing them a favour. You see the life they live, a snapshot of what they have to put up with on a daily basis, and you feel you're helping them.

Always do it differently. That's been Calum's approach. Some people shoot their target in the same place every time. Almost like a signature move. Why leave a signature? Sometimes Calum would shoot in the side of the head, sometimes the front, sometimes upwards from the chin or down from the crown. Sometimes you shoot a person once. Sometimes multiple shots are required. Sometimes you shoot them many times even when it's not required, just to give the impression of a desperate attacker. This time, with the target lying flat out, it's a simple choice. A single bullet, up through the chin. He won't even know it's happened. Winter groans and snorts pathetically. That angry look stays on his face. Doing him a favour.

Calum is pressing the gun up against the chin. There's a little loose flesh there. He pauses, turns his head slightly sideways and pulls the trigger.

The bang is always unsettling. It doesn't matter how many times you hear it. There's a puff of blood from the bottom of the chin. Winter's body jerks rigid and relaxes. Calum looks closely. There's no exit wound. The bullet has stayed in. There are times—when the bullet comes out—when you can retrieve it, take it away from the scene. Doesn't stop them working out what gun was used, but it slows them down. This time, nothing. He's stopped, looking down at Winter. Not a moment of reflection, just making sure. Dead.

They all hear the bang. Cope looks at the doorway, then looks away. She knew it was going to happen. It still hurts to hear it. The young man has gone silent. His worst fears are being realized. He thinks he's going to be next. George knows that the job has been done. Now, escape. He holds the gun up a little higher. He's a little more tense now. The escape is always the part that can go wrong. People hear the gunshot and react stupidly, put themselves in danger. The raised gun is a warning. Patience. So hard to have. The neighbours may well have heard the gunshot. You're no longer working to your own timeframe. He hears movement on the stairs. The last, illogical worry. What if it's Winter coming down the stairs after catching out Calum? George is looking over his shoulder, his eyes off Cope and the young man.

Calum walks out of the bedroom, switching off the light. He walks steadily. For him, the worst part is over. The target's dead. Now they need to get out. There's still the danger of being caught, but the danger to his life has almost passed. Down the stairs. George is standing by the doorway, his gun raised, looking back over his shoulder. Calum nods. Time to go. George turns and looks at Cope, makes eye contact. He means it as a sign that the danger is over for her. She thinks he's going to shoot her. Her eyes widen. Her hands fall to her sides. George is realizing the mistake he's made. Never mind. He turns and follows Calum out the front door, pulling it shut behind him. The door bounces against the frame, the lock broken.

20

In that moment she had thought she was going to die. When they burst in, she knew they were there for Winter. She didn't know who they were, or exactly what it was about, but she knew it was for him. His expansion plans had pissed off the wrong people. It happened. It was the threat of the business. She had been afraid, but not of being killed. They were so obviously professionals. They wouldn't shoot her if they didn't have to. When Stewart had made a run for the door, she had cursed him under her breath. Stupid. Unforgivably stupid. They certainly weren't going to kill him if they didn't have to, and yet he was encouraging them. Her fear was something else.

There are so many men in the business who are little better than animals. They have no care whatever for other people. The lives of others are playthings, to be ruined at their will. She was naked. They had the power. One of them went upstairs. The other stood and watched her. She knew he was watching her a lot more than he was

94

watching Stewart, even though Stewart had tried to run. He could have done anything. She couldn't resist. She wouldn't. He had a gun. He was a professional. Do what it takes to stay alive. But he did nothing. A real professional. Not an animal like so many others. These people were very good at what they did. She had worked out how professional they were by the time they left.

No words. The only sound, the whimpering of the naked man behind the chair. They didn't even have to ask where Lewis was. They knew. Somehow, they knew exactly where in the house he was. Perhaps they knew the layout. Perhaps they had been to the house before. Could they be people she had met? Possibly. She has met plenty of people in the business over the years. She didn't recognize them. Then the gunshot. She had been waiting for it, but it still shocked. Knowing that Lewis was up there, dead. He was the one she was most likely to settle down with. She had resigned herself to that. This meant starting again. Then the killer came downstairs, nodding to the other one. The other one turned and looked at her. Why would he look unless he had one last job to do? It was the one moment in the whole experience when she had thought she was going to die. Then he left. Safe.

Now it's just her and Stewart. He's still on the floor, silent since the gunshot. Zara turns and sits on the couch. She needs to sit down before she falls down. An exhaustion has taken hold of her, a weakness. She's not sleepy, but painfully tired. She wants to cry. She feels that she should. But there's nothing. There's emotion, but no tears. She catches movement out of the corner of her eye.

95

Could they have come back? No, it's Stewart. He's getting up. He looks pale; he looks like he wants to burst into tears. What happened to the confident young man who strutted across the dance floor and danced her away from Lewis? So full of himself. Gone.

Stewart stands up. He shakes his head. What's the right thing to say and do in these circumstances? He wants to know if he's safe. He wants to know if they might come back. He can't ask, that would seem callous. He mustn't be selfish. He has an image of the older man she was dancing with in the club. He had gone across to dance with Zara; he had been sure the man couldn't be her partner. Then she invited him back. Everything was fine. Better than fine. Now this. The worst experience of his life. And yet, somewhere in the back of his mind, a little voice is telling him otherwise. What a story. What a thing to tell the guys. Ploughing a beautiful girl, when two hitmen burst in and murder her partner.

'Are you okay?' he's asking her. He doesn't realize that he's breaking a silence. He's heard the sound of his heart thumping throughout this short ordeal. He's heard a ringing in his ears from the thump to the head that he took. It just seems like the right thing to ask.

Zara looks up at him. So pretty. 'Yeah,' she nods. 'They didn't touch me.'

The way she looks at him. She's not impressed with how he handled it. Stewart feels embarrassed. A man's dead upstairs, but he's concerned about looking pathetic in her eyes. He knows it's wrong, but it's how he feels. He walks to the couch and sits beside her. He puts an arm round her bare

96

shoulder, rubs it gently.

'It'll be okay,' he tells her.

The words mean absolutely nothing. He must realize how stupid it sounds to say it, she's thinking to herself. He's saying what he thinks he ought to. He doesn't know if it'll be okay. He doesn't care. He's only thinking about himself now. She looks at him. He's rubbing her shoulder. His hand is moving in widening circles. She sees that he's getting excited.

'You should put your clothes on,' she tells him coldly.

Stewart is getting slowly to his feet. Probably not a bad guy. Just not someone with anything useful to offer. Not any more. She has a feeling that she needs to be safe. She's not under any particular threat, but she wants safety around her. It won't come from him.

Stewart gets dressed quickly. Suddenly the selfish thoughts can't be pushed back any longer.

'Had you better call the police?' he's asking her. There could be a trial. Certainly a large police investigation. A man was murdered. He would be called as a witness. His name would be in the papers and on TV. They would ask him what he was doing there. It doesn't seem so funny any more. They would be laughing *at* him, not with him. This could even affect his career prospects. He would forever be associated with it. The panic that had consumed him earlier is coming back. Not as powerful, but more long-lasting.

Zara looks at him, and starts thinking. The police. They'll be here at some point. Maybe the neighbours have already called them. Think. Think clearly. What do you need to do? What can you do to salvage something from this? You have no money of your own. All you have belongs to Lewis. He won't want you to be left with nothing. How to get it out of the house? Stewart—he could be useful. Would he be willing? She could make him willing. She stands up, aware of her nudity. She walks quickly across to Stewart and throws her arms around him.

'You have to help me,' she says with a slight sob. She's looking up into his eyes now. She reaches up and kisses him passionately. His hands go round her back. One goes down to her bum. God, it's so easy.

Zara pushes him away. 'We have to protect you,' she's telling him, talking breathlessly in the passion of the moment and with her desire to help him. What a wonderful woman, even at a time like this. 'There's no evidence that you were here,' she's telling him. 'You could get out and nobody would ever know. You don't have to be dragged down by this.' It's so obviously what he wants to hear. He's nodding along. He thinks she's just wonderful. Thinking of him, instead of herself. What chance that he would ever meet a girl like this again? 'You can go out the back,' she's saying to him. 'Over the back wall, into the garden opposite. You go left and you're onto the next street. You'll be safe,' she's telling him, and they're kissing again. His heart is racing. This is magnificent. He wants to stay with her, but he has to get away. He turns for the back door. 'Wait,' she says, 'you can help me too.'

Stewart is standing in the hallway. Zara has run upstairs. She's told him to wait there. He watches her run naked up the stairs. His heart is still racing so fast that he can hear it. There's a dead body upstairs. The police are coming. He really needs to get out of there now, if he's going to get out of there at all. Maybe he should just go. No. She wants him to help. Helping is the right thing to do. This gorgeous woman. This woman who had to suffer a life tied to a drunkard. This woman who's just had to go through a traumatic experience. The least he can do is help her in some way.

Zara is upstairs. She opens her bedroom door and reaches for the light. She knows she's going to see something horrible. She knows she has to brace herself. She's seen terrible things before. You don't spend this much time in this business and not see a few things. She saw Nate beat a man half to death once. In an alleyway. When Nate was finished, the man's face didn't look human at all. His head hadn't even seemed the right shape. That guy had survived, though. Somehow. She knows she's going to see Lewis dead. She knows it might be gruesome. She cares about him. That's why this is different. She does actually care.

It isn't as bad as she expected. The smell isn't of blood, but of urine. The sight isn't bloody. A trickle runs from his chin, down his neck and disappears into his clothing and the bedding. It looks almost innocuous. If she hadn't known that it was a bullet wound, if she hadn't known that the killer was a professional, she might have thought he had survived. It looks like no more than a nick. There's no movement. She should have heard breathing. Something. There's a silence that makes her flesh creep. To be in the company of another person who makes absolutely no sound. The silence of death.

She shakes herself. No standing around. Don't waste time. If the police arrive now, you're in trouble. Naked in the room with the dead body. A lover downstairs. Drugs in the wardrobe. She walks briskly across and pulls open the wardrobe doors. The panel at the base inside the wardrobe pulls away in her hand. Underneath are two wads of cash, one bag of coke and a bag of pills that she can't immediately identify. Lewis knew what they were. He kept little of his supply in the house, often nothing at all, but he'd been having trouble with a peddler of his and had been left with excess. She doesn't know how much it's all worth, but between the money and the drugs, it's a few thousand. Zara has little else. She needs that money.

She puts it on the floor, and slides the panel back across the wardrobe. She picks up the cash and gear and gets out of the room, running now. Stewart is still at the bottom of the stairs, looking nervous. He sees that she's carrying something. His eyes widen.

'Please, Stewart, you have to help me,' she's saying to him. Pleading. Pathetic. 'If they find this in the house, I'll go to jail too. I need you to take this for me. Give me your address. I'll come and collect it from you. Just store it, for a little while.' She realizes she's going on too long. Saying too much. He can be persuaded. She's reaching up and kissing him again. 'Give me your address. I'll come round. I don't want to lose you too.'

She's beautiful. She's vulnerable. She needs you. It's a strangely wonderful thing, to be needed. Particularly to be needed by someone you want. She has suffered a lot at her man's hands. It's hardly a surprise to find that that drunk upstairs is a drug dealer as well. He must be a dealer. He couldn't have bags of the stuff for his own use. Stewart's drug use has been very limited, but he knows the difference between recreational amounts and a dealer's amount. There's cash too. A lot of cash. They look like twenty- and fifty-pound notes. There could be a couple of thousand there. Help her? She could name you, if you don't. She wouldn't, he's sure. Much too good a woman. But she could.

'Of course I'll help you,' he's saying, reaching down and kissing her again. She's handing him the bags and the cash, and he's stuffing them into various pockets, out of view. She's grabbed a piece of paper and a pen. He's writing his address. Is it wise? He can trust her. Those eyes. He can trust them.

'You have to go out the back,' she's saying, as soon as he hands her the piece of paper back.

'Yes,' he stammers. Thank heavens for her presence of mind, he's thinking, as Zara leads him to the back door. If it wasn't for her, Stewart would be there when the police arrive. She's saving him. Saving herself too. She's unlocking the back door.

'Go straight ahead, over the back wall, turn left and you come out on the next street. Don't draw attention to yourself.'

'Yes,' he's nodding. He bends down. She kisses him again. He steps outside and she closes the door behind him.

They're down the front path and across the road to the car. Calum drops into the driver's seat. He's turned the key in the ignition before George is even in beside him. They keep the balaclavas and gloves on. Keep covered until you're out of sight of any possible witnesses. The car starts and they pull away. Still silent. Guns out of view. Round the corner at the bottom of the street. Out of view of the house, out of view of the witnesses. Balaclavas pulled quickly off. More good luck. They've passed no cars in the short journey from the house so far. Nobody has seen them on the road in balaclavas.

'You have any trouble with him?' George asks. His voice is hushed. Unnatural. He's trying too hard to sound calm.

'Couldn't have been easier,' Calum's telling him. His voice sounds strained too. Trying to hide the fact that he doesn't want to talk. Always uncomfortable talking after a job.

'I didn't have any trouble, either,' George is telling him, having not been asked. 'After I knocked the guy down, he stayed down. She didn't move a muscle the whole time. Went quick. That was good. Don't know what either of them would've done if you'd been up there longer. Good job, though. Real clean.'

'So far,' Calum says quietly, concentrating on driving.

'Aye,' George is nodding.

A few minutes later. Still driving. Calum watching the road, George talking.

'Man, there was so much I wanted to say when we got in there. Jesus! There was so much goin' through my mind when I saw them like that.' George bursts out laughing. Calum smiles; one day he knows he'll look back and laugh. Not tonight. The job is still too fresh. 'The look on the boy's face. That was priceless. Man, he wasn't just scared, he was totally bummed. Did you see it, Cal? One second he's inside this gorgeous girl, next minute he's got a gun at his head. Christ! Poor bastard. Nobody should lose a shag like that. Can't believe she was with that loser Winter in the first place. Gorgeous girl with low standards. I like that,' George says, and he laughs loudly again. Calum is aware of the constant references to how attractive Zara Cope is, but now isn't the time to comment.

It takes eleven minutes to get to the drop-off point. He's not going to leave George outside his flat, that would be crazy. There's a risk in leaving him a mile away. He has to get back home with his balaclava and gloves, dressed all in black. That could raise eyebrows. George is good at this sort of thing, though. He does this in his work a lot. A lot of the jobs he does—beating and intimidations—are done during the night. He gets there and gets home again without being picked up. He needs no advice on how to do it, and do it well. That's why he's more relaxed. For him, the effort is over. The drop-off point is in a rundown part of town, an old industrial area with little industry left. Calum pulls up at the side of the road.

They won't see each other for some time. Certainly days, perhaps weeks. You keep your distance. You make sure people don't put the two

103

of you together. The police will have a vague description of body types. You keep yourselves apart. George opens the car door. It seems odd to leave without saying something, but what do you say?

'That was a good job, pal. Give us a call when the heat dies down.' He wants to say more, but he doubts Calum wants to hear more. Calum needs to change the car, get rid of the guns and get himself home before the sun comes up and people get out on the streets and notice him. Too much to do to hang around chatting.

'You did well, I appreciate it,' Calum is saying to him. It's the first thing he's said since they left the house that doesn't sound strained. The first thing that sounds genuine. George nods, and shuts the door.

He leaves George walking along a strange street in the dark. A strange pang of camaraderie. In the wake of most jobs Calum wants nothing more than to go home and be alone. There's a solitary streak in his nature that reigns after a job. Not tonight. Tonight he wanted to let George know that he appreciated the help. He felt a sudden urge to be in the company of someone. Anyone, really. Ageing, he decides. Pushing thirty, and suddenly wanting someone to spend time with. He has felt that outside of work. He has felt the desire to settle down, but has lived so entirely for his work that he's resisted the urge. Nearly two years since he had a serious relationship—just casual flings with random women since then. It's a curious feeling, as he turns the corner and George disappears from view in his mirror. He still feels his work is done more comfortably alone, but he needs more people

104

in his life.

There's much still to be done. Precautions must be taken. It used to be much easier. The older guys will all admit it. A more difficult job now than it's ever been. Used to be that you could dump things in bins at the side of the road. Not now. CCTV might pick you up. Bins aren't simply emptied into the back of a lorry, and the garbage then tipped into landfill. Most of the bins at the side of the road will have their contents sent to recycling plants. Got to be careful with that. He decides to hang on to the balaclava for now. Not in the mood to find somewhere safe to ditch it, this late at night. His rubbish will be collected on Monday. A risk to hold on to it that long. A risk to keep all the clothes he has on for that long. He's going to ditch them all. Maybe find something before then. See how the land lies.

For now, the priorities are the car and the guns. Guns first. The seller knows he'll return. He doesn't know when, but he knows. There's a process. Supposedly safe. Calum doesn't like it much, but it's what the man uses. Has been using it for decades, gets away with it. When you're finished with the guns and it's not a good time to knock on the door, you go to the house and into the back garden. You go up to the shed, pull away a small section of side panelling and push the guns in. You put the panel back in place. Then you leave. He checks the shed every day. He gets the guns, presumably puts them back in his loft. You go and visit him in the daytime, a day or two later, and he pays you for the guns you've delivered. He doesn't pay you what you paid him, but you get some of your money back. Calum doesn't like the system. What if someone follows him and checks the shed? What if someone's watching the runner's house when he turns up?

Forget all that. The priority is getting rid of the guns. Take them to the shed. Better they get found there than in your own flat. He drives to the house. Time is on his side. The beauty of Glasgow being a small city—you never have far to go. He stops down the street from the runner's house. He has his own gun in his pocket. George's has been in the glove box since they got into the car. Calum is taking it out, putting it into his other pocket. He can feel the surprising weight of them. He only uses guns for the job, doesn't like them otherwise. Doesn't like handling them or having them around. Can never get used to them. Never mind. He's getting out of the car.

He's across the street. Opening the side gate. Making sure it doesn't creak. Surely the runner is professional enough to oil the gate that his clients have to use. Surely a man of his experience wouldn't make such a rookie mistake. Silence. Along the back path to the shed. There's no sign of life in the runner's house. No sign of life on the street. No lights on. A little moonlight creeps through the clouds. Calum looks at his watch. It's now getting towards two o'clock in the morning. Things have moved quickly and smoothly. He'll be home by half past. Faster than he expected. He feels for the panel and pulls it open. There's a small gap behind, before you feel the inside panel that the runner's added to make the shed look untouched from the inside as well as out. Calum places the guns carefully inside and slips the panel back into place. It wedges in.

Now Calum's back in the car and heading for his brother's garage. If CCTV picks him up, then it will look odd, him returning a car to the garage in the middle of the night. Too bad. Nothing illegal about odd. Nothing wrong with driving at night. William will have parked Calum's car out on the street, in the parking bay in front of the garage. He'll have made as sure as possible that there's a space nearby. Calum will park the borrowed car in that space, slip the keys into the visor and get into his own car. Again the keys will be in the visor. Then he'll go home.

He pulls onto the street where the garage is. A quiet street, gloomy. Used to be full of businesses, full of life. Not any more. The garage, a warehouse and an army-surplus store. There are two people walking along the street. Damn! Can't be seen changing cars. Who the hell is out and about in this part of town at this time of night? They actually look like a respectable couple as he drives past. Calum reaches the end of the street and goes round the block. By the time he gets back, the couple are gone. He's pulling up in a parking spot along the street. He slips the keys into the visor and gets out. Glances round—nobody there. He walks along the street and casually opens the door of his car. He's starting the car up and he's driving home.

It all seems too easy. Calum suffers from a natural cynicism. When things go smoothly, he expects something to pop up suddenly and trip him up. There's no way it should have been that easy. The job he does should never be that easy. And yet, it often is. The majority of jobs he does are simple, effective, quick and trouble-free. Things

107

don't go wrong. There are no nasty little surprises lurking. There can be. It does happen. But the jobs where things go wrong are a minority, and quite a small one. They're life-threatening, but rare. As Calum is pulling up outside his own flat, in his own car, he's thinking that the job shouldn't be this easy. He doesn't deserve such an easy time.

22

First she memorizes the address Stewart gave her, then rips it into tiny pieces and burns it in an ashtray. If he's lying about the address, then she's lost all that she gave him. No, he's not that smart. Then she calls the police. She has to work herself up, get herself frantic for the phone call. The neighbours might already have called, and it's because of that fear that she has to call too. She doesn't want to have to explain why someone else has called, but she hasn't bothered. Don't waste time. Don't leave a gap that needs to be explained between the neighbours' call and yours. She's picked up the phone and taken it into the living room, pulling on some clothes while it rings. The woman answers, asks what service Zara requires. Now Zara's turning it on. Acting. It's not that she's not upset, not traumatized. She is, but she feels she needs to show it.

She's sitting on the couch, crying into the phone. She's clothed now. There are lies to tell, and they aren't going to be easy. The emergency worker on the phone is talking to her, twittering on. Being sympathetic. Trying to get information. She's trying to calm Zara, and Zara is playing along with that. But she's thinking. All the time the woman's talking, she's thinking about what she can and can't say. How far out of it can she keep Stewart? She can't deny that he was at the house, no matter what she told him. The taxi driver saw them. They'll look for the taxi driver, to ask him if he saw anyone in the area when he dropped them off. Admit that he was here. Helped her get Lewis to the front door, then left.

Don't admit that he came into the house. Tell them she got Lewis upstairs herself. Tell them she's come back down and poured herself a glass of whiskey when someone kicks the door in. One keeps her downstairs at gunpoint, the other goes upstairs. She hears the gunshot. Then they leave. She sits on the couch for a couple of minutes. Shock. Then she calls the police. It's a good story. It seems good enough. Convincing. She knows it's not that simple, though. She's heard so many people say that you can never think straight when you're under pressure and your heart is racing. She knows this is one such situation.

There's a knock on the front door. She hears it being pushed open, footsteps in the hallway. A voice, talking low to someone else.

'Someone's here,' Zara says frantically into the phone. She's making it sound like she's scared that the killer has come back. Making herself sound like the terrified victim. She knows it's the police. She knows it, but she doesn't say so until they appear in the doorway. 'Oh, thank God,' she says, a tone of exhausted relief. 'It's the police. Thank God.' The woman on the other end of the phone says something, but Zara isn't listening any more.

109

She hangs up the phone.

One cop she doesn't recognize. Young, self-confident, a little smug-looking. The other she does. The other is Paul Greig. A lot of people know Paul Greig. A lot more people know stories about him. Everyone knows that he's bent. She's met him a couple of times, but not in the last three or four years. He's always recognizable. Wiry, short figure. Black hair, always a little too long for him. A pinched face, mean-looking. And that scar. Running three inches down his left cheek, a bold red. Nobody knows where it came from, everyone knows him by it. It makes him look dangerous. It makes him look like a criminal in a cop's uniform. Something many people have accused him of being.

As soon as they make eye contact, she knows that he recognizes her. They met when she was with Nate. Nobody has a good word to say about the scarred cop, despite him helping many of them. He helped them for money; he cared nothing for their goodwill. Nate was always guarded about his comments regarding people in the business, so she didn't hear a lot about Greig. Knew he was bent, though. Knew he had done something to help Nate, at least once. Maybe she can play on that in some way. Maybe he can help to make sure that she isn't put under any pressure by the cops.

They know that Lewis is a dealer. Was a dealer. They'll want her to help them. Name names. Tell them where his money is. Tell them where his stash is. Tell them who his supplier is. Tell them who his peddlers are. Some of these things she genuinely doesn't know. Some of them she does, and doesn't want to share. You never want to be the person

110

who grasses dangerous people up. Doesn't matter that you're a woman. Doesn't matter that you're under pressure from the police after your partner has been killed. What matters is betrayal. Betrayal brings revenge. It has to. People must be seen to fight back. So you make sure the police don't ask you any awkward questions. That's where Greig could help.

Zara is moving forward and pushing herself against Greig. He's taking a step back, unwilling to be the sympathetic one. His young partner is better suited to that role.

'Oh, thank God you're here,' she's saying to him, not backing off. 'I was so scared. They went upstairs. I heard a gunshot. Oh God, I think Lewis is dead.' She bursts out crying again and leans into Greig. He's putting a hand on her shoulder now.

'Okay, you're okay,' he's saying, a little roughly. 'We're here now, it's just us.' He's turning and looking at the younger cop. 'Go upstairs—be careful.' The young cop nods and goes out into the corridor.

As soon as he hears the young cop's first step on the stairs, Greig is pushing her away and looking her in the eye. There's a cynical look, assessing her.

'You're Zara, right?'

'Yes, Zara Cope,' she's saying, still looking tearful. She isn't going to lie to him; she needs to persuade him to care a damn about her.

'Who's upstairs?' he's asking her now.

'Lewis. Lewis Winter, my partner.'

He's nodding his head. He knows who Winter is. He knows what Winter does for a living. He knows what's probably happened here.

111

'You used to be with Nate Colgan, didn't you?' he's asking her now.

Double-edged sword. Maybe he likes Nate. Maybe he owes Nate. Or maybe he hates Nate. Maybe he'd love to do something that would upset him.

'Yes,' she's saying, not sure of the consequences. He's nodding his head in answer.

The younger cop is already coming down the stairs, talking into the little radio hanging from the front of his jacket. Zara hears mention of a body, but she can't pick up what else he's saying. He stops in the corridor, and Greig is turning to join him. They want to talk without Zara hearing. Private conversation. Police matters. She stands in the living room. She's wearing the clothes she wore to the club; she knows she looks curiously out of place. It's a middle-class suburban house. It's a murder scene. She doesn't belong at either. She feels like she doesn't belong at either. Seems like she doesn't have a choice. Get herself out of this situation, and then think about what to do next. Life can't go on like this. Seems to be a downward spiral.

Greig comes back into the living room, telling her to sit on the couch. The young cop has gone out the front door, disappearing into the night. Greig sits beside her.

'My colleague has gone to look around the house,' he's saying to her. 'We need to make sure that there's no further threat, and he's going to look for any immediate clues. We want to get on their trail as soon as we can, catch them before they can dispose of evidence and whatnot. But then you know how these things work, don't you,

112

Zara?'

It's a very knowing question. She's looking at him. He has a little smile on his face, like he's enjoying this. Enjoying the power he has. He sickens her. She's shrugging her shoulders.

Greig scoffs a little. He leans forward, resting his elbows on his knees. 'You see, Zara, I know about you. I know about Winter, what he does. Did. I know that life's about to get pretty rough for you. I can help you. I can protect you from the worst of it. I'm sure you and me can come up with some way to help each other.'

He's looking her in the eye, still smiling. She's trying to work out what he's referring to. He's a crook. Not a surprise that he would want to take advantage of this for money. But is it just money? Didn't sound like it from his tone. She doesn't know of him using his position for sex, although he wouldn't be the first.

'What do you want?' she's asking him. You have to make sacrifices.

He's leaning back a little now. In control. This is his forte. 'I know what your partner did for a living. I find it hard to believe that he doesn't have money tucked away somewhere. Maybe in a bank account. You know what's going to happen to that money now? We're going to take it. Proceeds of Crime Act. Do you work, Zara? Do you have any money of your own tucked away?'

'No,' she's saying, 'I don't.' Just the money Stewart has. She's not going to tell him about that. If she can get the money Winter has in the bank as well, it'll be a bonus. There won't be fortunes; he never seemed to have more than just enough. Still, something is better than nothing. Greig can be bought with a share of the proceeds, which is a relief.

'And there's the house,' Greig is saying. 'If he's left it to you, you can sell it, keep the proceeds. Unless my bosses decide to confiscate it. Then you get nothing.'

She hadn't even thought of the house. Winter had a mortgage, but he hadn't paid a lot of it. He was always complaining about the cost, seemed to be struggling to meet it. Still, anything that can be gained from this. It seems wrong to be thinking about this. Wrong to be discussing this so soon. There is no other time. Now or never. It isn't that she doesn't care about Lewis. It hurts her that he's dead. She won't pretend that she had been in love with him. It had been something else. Comforting. Not perfect, but good. She hadn't been a perfect partner. She had cheated on him often. She had probably led him into trouble. She doesn't feel guilty—that was the relationship, and he knew it. He went into it with his eyes open. She had given him some happiness, and she regrets that she couldn't give him more.

'So, what do you have to say?' Greig is asking her, looking at her with a fierce expression on his face. He can see that she hasn't been listening to him. He's annoyed that she would allow herself to be distracted at a time like this. She's been around the business long enough to know better than that.

'If you can help me to make that happen, then I can make sure that you get your share,' she's saying to him. Her tone is annoyed. He has no right to be superior with her.

'Okay then,' he's saying. He sounds angry now. Regretting that he made the offer. He thought she knew better. Thought she was someone with the brain to be useful. Greig is standing up, looking out the window. 'Did Winter have anything in the house? Drugs? Cash? Anything that might incriminate you?'

'No,' she's saying, 'he never kept anything in the house. He was more careful than that.'

'Good,' Greig tells her. 'Means you don't have to try and get anything out. Now then, I can make sure that you're not put in a tight spot. I'll try to make sure you don't get asked any awkward questions about your role in Winter's work. Depends who gets the investigation. I can see to it that you don't lose all the money he had. Keep you on the straight and narrow. I won't be questioning you—it'll be a detective. Don't worry about it, though. I'll catch up with you when the time is right. You and me can spend some time together. So, tell me what happened tonight.'

23

Stewart turns to kiss her one last time, but she's already closing the door. She's right, of course; he has to be faster about this. It feels as though an eternity has passed since the gunshot. Since the neighbours heard and called the police. As he tiptoes carefully through the back garden, he has the presence of mind to turn and look at the neighbouring houses. No lights on. No sign of movement. That has to be a good thing. He's reached the back fence. A tall wooden structure, maybe six feet high. He's so aware of what's in his

115

pockets. As he pulls himself up and over the top, he worries that something might fall out. He might leave a clue behind. He might get himself into trouble. He might let Zara down.

He's in a dark garden. Hard to get your bearings, especially when you don't know the area. Trust Zara. She said to go left in the neighbouring garden. Go left and you come out on the next street. Trust her. He's going left, tiptoeing through the garden. Don't wake anyone up. Look at your situation, for Christ's sake. You're walking through a stranger's garden, with drugs and money bulging your pockets, having just left the scene of a murder. Okay, don't think about it. That's not a healthy thing to look at. Just makes you more nervous. He makes it through the garden and out a side gate. Onto the street. Well lit. Quiet.

Now he's a young man, well dressed, in a deserted suburban street. Stewart knows he must look conspicuous. He feels incredibly conspicuous. He's walking along the street, wondering what he ought to do. Does he get a taxi? There are none around, and he's not sure where to tell them to pick him up. Does he want a taxi driver to pick him up so close to the scene of a murder? Not really. His heart may be racing, but he's thinking clearly. He's excited. He's enjoying it. By God, he's enjoying it. Stewart chuckles to himself. He can't believe it, but this is fun.

There are no sirens. There are no police rushing to arrest him. He walks for what seems like an age, for what feels like miles, before he begins to gather a sense of familiarity. There are buildings that he's seen before. He looks at his watch and then looks away. He has no idea what time he left the house,

116

no idea how long it's been since the shooting. Safe to call a taxi? He knows he's nowhere near home. Home is a flat in the west of the city, shared with a friend. They've been pals since college. Both studied design. Both had wanted to get into the videogame industry when they started. His friend Tom, being much more gifted than Stewart, managed to get the job he wanted. Stewart, on the other hand, was stuck working in advertising. He only left college a year ago and hasn't given up hope.

There's a little bench built into a wall at the side of the street. Presumably for pensioners during the day, although why they would be there he can't fathom. It's an area of warehouses and business parks, bustling with work during the day. This is a Friday night, into Saturday morning, and there are only a few cars passing by. Stewart sits on the bench and finds a taxi-firm number in the phonebook of his mobile. He calls it, tells them where to pick him up and waits. Every car passing could be a police car. Every noise could be someone coming to get you. It's thrilling. He smiles to himself as the taxi pulls up at the side of the road.

Getting out of the taxi, into the flat. Making no noise. He doesn't want his flatmate to know that he has drugs and cash on him. It's not safe. Maybe, a couple of years down the line, it becomes a story to tell. Not yet. He trusts Tom, and doesn't want to get him into any trouble. Stewart makes his way carefully to his bedroom. Once he's inside, he feels the thrill depart and the exhaustion arrive. He's been living on his nerves for the last hour and it's drained him. There's an urge to lie on the bed in

117

his clothes and let the sleep take him. No. Resist. You still have to be careful, no matter how safe you feel.

Stewart empties his pockets, putting everything on the bed. He looks at the money first, because he knows what that is and can see its value. He doesn't count it all; the bundles of notes are mixed. He can get a good idea of the value, though. There's at least a thousand pounds in each of the two piles of notes, each held together by a single elastic band. Drug money. Dirty money. He's reluctant to handle it. He doesn't want to be associated with such a thing. Stewart doesn't earn a lot of money, but he isn't consumed by such a love of it that this money means anything to him. It doesn't mean anything to Zara, either. He's convinced she's not the sort of woman to be motivated by it. She wants rid of the money and the drugs so that she won't get into trouble.

The drugs. He doesn't know how much the bags are worth—he's never bought before. The few experiments he's had were all at someone else's expense. He quite liked the coke he took, he liked the buzz. He knew that if it was offered to him again he would take it, but he wasn't so enamoured that he's ever gone looking for it. Now there's a bag on the bed in front of him, and he hates it. He hates that he's stuck with it. He hates that Zara has been forced to go and get it to remove it from her house. It was haunting her. Threatening to have her put in jail.

He can't stop thinking about her. As he's looking around his bedroom, looking for somewhere to hide it all, he's thinking about her. He's thinking about her as he takes a shoebox down from the top

118

of his wardrobe. A pair of dress shoes inside. Bought for a wedding. Too tight, they left him with a blister on the side of his big toe. He's stuffing the money inside one shoe and the drugs into the other. Not a great hiding place, but it's only a bad hiding place if someone comes looking. If someone comes looking, then he has no prospect of hiding it all anyway. There's nowhere in the flat where he can make two wads of cash and two bags of drugs disappear. If the police come knocking, then there's no hiding.

Stewart's undressing slowly, relieved to be out of his clothes. Out of his clothes again. He thinks about Zara once more as he pulls himself under the sheets. He thinks about what he had been doing an hour or so ago. On that couch. Zara underneath him. God, what a night! He starts to laugh. Quiet. Don't let Tom hear you. Don't give him an excuse to ask any awkward questions in the morning. Silence from Tom's room. He lies back in bed, getting excited at the thought of Zara. Getting excited at the thought of the gunmen bursting in on them. He shouldn't be excited by that. That was two guys who could have killed him. That thought makes him recoil. Why is he excited by that situation? It's getting easier to understand why so many people are tempted into that sort of seedy life.

He runs his fingers through his hair. A pain shoots through him. It's the shock as much as the pain that catches him out. He had been hit over the head by one of the killers. It might have been a punch; he might have been hit with the gun. Good Lord, hit with the gun. It could have gone off. It could have blown his brains out. Shit! He carefully feels the bump. Doesn't feel like there's any blood there. No cut. Just a lump. He gets out of bed, puts on the lamp and gets a little shaving mirror out of a drawer. The bump isn't visible under his hair. He'll have a better look in the bathroom mirror in the morning. For now it seems that nobody will be able to spot it.

He's forgotten about his pathetic spell on the floor. Chosen to forget. That was an embarrassment. He let Zara down. He embarrassed himself. Still, nobody would know. Who would speak about it? The gunmen would surely never admit where they had been and what they had seen. Zara would never humiliate him by saying. He would certainly keep it to himself. As he gets back into bed and switches off the lamp, he's thinking about her again. Thinking about her naked at the back door, kissing him goodbye. He's not excited this time, but worried. Worried for her. Where is she right now?

24

She's sitting in what is known as the victim suite. Not an interview room, nothing so cold and formal. She is the young woman who has been witness to a terrible crime. You treat her with sympathy, with heart. You treat her in a manner she can't possibly complain about. There's a female constable with her all the time. Making her a cup of tea, asking her if there's anything else she wants. Keeping an eye on her. For her benefit, and for the benefit of the police.

'I'd like to change,' Zara says to her, 'I feel stupid in these clothes.' And she does. She's still wearing the clothes she had been clubbing in, and it seems even more ludicrous in that setting.

'I might be able to find you something else if you want, or we could send for something from your house.'

'All my clothes are in our bedroom,' Zara says quietly, and she starts to cry again.

Real tears. The shock of what's happened to her. The fear of what might happen next. The realization that Lewis is gone. Gone forever. What will she do without him? It isn't as simple as finding someone else. Lewis had been kind and patient. He had let her live her life the way she wanted. She had taken advantage of that, taken advantage of his nature. Perhaps unfairly. Where is she going to find someone else like that? There are so few in the business. There had only been two men in her life that she had ever felt any love for. One was Nate Colgan, but the love had been mixed with fear. The other was Lewis. With him, the love had been mixed with contempt.

The constable knows they're real tears. She's been round long enough to know the difference. Seen enough crocodile tears in this room. She knows when a victim is in shock as well, and that doesn't seem to be the case here. Zara Cope is handling the situation with admirable resolve, although the tears are flowing despite herself. The suite has a little kitchen leading into a living room. A couch, a TV, an air freshener. A desperate attempt to give the impression that you're in a safe and welcoming place. But you can never forget that you're in a police station. You can never forget that you're there to be questioned.

The door into the suite opens, a man walks in. Cheap suit, miserable expression. He looks surprised that he's having to work at this hour of the morning. Middle-aged, maybe mid-forties, maybe more. Maybe less. Depends how well he's looked after himself. Obviously a detective. Obviously just been told that this is his case. Get on it. Now. Gangland. Girl downstairs is a witness. Girlfriend of the victim. The gangland work can be exciting, but hard to get into. People build knowledge of it over many years. They learn who everyone is, what all the relationships are between families and organizations. It's taken him a long time to get into it.

Michael Fisher hates the fact that people see him as a stereotype. A cop obsessed with his job. Divorced. No kids. No distractions. Drinks too much when he's not working. Receding hairline, greying round the temples. Struggling to hold a little bit of weight off his stomach. He hates that that's the cliché. It's that much harder to be taken seriously. He doesn't want to be that way. He doesn't want to be a lazy character, plucked from the screen of a low-budget cop drama. He is what he is. He's a cop who enjoys his work. He's a man who hasn't found anything else in life that he cares about enough to be distracted by.

He walks across and sits on the chair opposite the couch. His first look at Zara Cope. Pretty girl. Very pretty. Dressed like a tart. Much younger than the victim. Her record is basically clean, although she's known. Been around a lot of criminals in her time. A cock-junkie. Chasing conquests. Looking for danger. Cheap thrills.

Stupid girl. He dislikes her already.

'Zara, my name is Detective Inspector Michael Fisher; I want you to just call me Michael. I'm here to help you in any way I can. Obviously I want to talk to you about what happened, but not until you're ready. I don't want you to talk until you feel ready, okay?'

Zara nods. They both know he's lying.

He wants to hear from her right away. Two reasons. Each one is dependent on her role. If she is an innocent bystander, a victim, then he wants to hear from her while events are fresh. Give people time to calm down and you give them time to forget. Get the first account fast, and you hear the things that really seemed important at the time. You wait, and what you hear are the things that seem important on reflection. You get it fast, and you hear what matters to the witness. You wait, and you hear what they think is important to you.

Then there's reason two. What if she's not an innocent witness? What if she's involved in some way, hiding something? Happens a lot. People have an insider. Someone to get them into the house. Okay, not this time—they kicked the door in. Someone to tell them where the victim is. Could be. Small enough house, though. The theory would hold more weight if there had been only one attacker, but apparently there were two. One to kill, one to keep her out of the way. So maybe she wasn't the insider. Maybe there was none. But maybe she took money to help in some way. Maybe she's hiding something. She might know who it was, but doesn't want to say.

People in that industry live so constantly in a world of fear that they don't think like normal people any more. They never grass. Never. Even if it's someone they love who's been killed, and they know the killer, they don't grass. The price could be death. First instinct, stay alive. They can be impossible to work with. That's why you question them quickly. You get them before they can put together a story. You get them before they can cover anything up. Winter was a dealer. She must have known. There's a lot that she's bound to know, and a lot that she probably won't want to tell him. Get at her fast and you can pick up a nugget from her, before she has the chance to think better.

'It's entirely up to you,' he says, putting a little bit of pressure on.

'I don't mind,' she says with a shrug. She's trying to look like she has nothing to hide, but she's thinking about a lawyer. If they're going to ask awkward questions, then perhaps she should have some sort of protection.

'If you could answer a few questions now, then that would help us,' he's saying to her. 'It'll help us get after the people who did this straight away. I won't ask you much, just the very basics.' Enough reassurance to gain her agreement, if not trust.

'Yeah,' she's saying, her voice a little hoarse from crying, 'okay.'

'Now, I just want you to tell me what you saw, what you remember. Don't upset yourself,' he's saying and realizing what a redundant comment it is. 'You know, just . . . er . . . tell me what you remember, as much as you feel able.' You have to treat everyone in such a precious manner. There are some who don't deserve it. She's one of them. The tart of a dealer. Please.

'We were out clubbing,' she's saying, trying to pick the right detail to give and the right detail to leave out. 'We came home in a taxi. Some guy shared the taxi with us. Lewis was drunk. The guy helped me get Lewis to the door.'

Already there's a hundred questions he wants to throw at her. Interrupt the silly bitch. Go on! Ditch protocol and ask the questions that might just nail a killer. Nope. Can't. You only end up getting hammered yourself.

She goes on with her story. She tells him that she got Lewis up the stairs by herself, that he was able to walk a little. She dumped him on the bed.

'I could hear him start to snore before I reached the bottom of the stairs,' she's saying. She rocks with another sob. The female officer hands her another tissue. Fisher already smells bullshit. Inconsistencies, and she's only just started. She needed someone's help to get him to the front door, but got him up the stairs herself? Come on. 'I came downstairs,' she's saying. 'I poured myself a glass of whiskey. I hadn't drunk nearly as much as Lewis had throughout the evening. I was sitting on the couch and I heard a bang. Sounded like someone had thrown something at the door. Then there was another one, and I heard the door smash open. God!' she's saying, and putting her head in her hands.

Maybe she's not acting, he's thinking to himself. If she is, then she's good. Got it down to a fine art. Acting or not, she can't be trusted.

'They came in. They were dressed all in black. They both had balaclavas on. They both had guns. One of them stayed downstairs and pointed the gun at me. The other one went straight up. It was like he knew where he was going. I don't . . . I don't know how. He was up there . . . I don't know how long. It felt like forever. Might have been two minutes. I heard the bang.' She's pausing for a few seconds, seems to Fisher like it's for dramatic effect. 'Then he came down. The two of them just left. I don't know what happened next. I remember sitting on the couch. Then I went for the phone.'

It all seems simple enough. Two men force their way in—one to cover the witness, one to make the kill. The story rings true.

'Can you remember anything about them that might help us?' he's asking her now. 'Height, weight, accent, anything.'

'They didn't talk,' she says. 'Neither of them said a word.'

Professionals.

'The one who went upstairs was taller than the one who stayed with me. Quite tall. Over six foot, I would guess. I don't know exactly. The other one was, I don't know, average height, I suppose. They both seemed normal. Not fat, or anything. I don't know. God, I wish I could help more.'

She tells a good story, and he's pushed her as far as he feels able. One last question. Just one.

'Miss Cope, do you know of anyone who might want to kill your partner, anyone who might have a grudge against him?' Of course she does. He was scum. He was a dealer. There will be people who wanted him out of the way. She'll know, and she'll say nothing.

'I have no idea,' she's saying, with a predictable little shrug. She's keen on the little shrugs. Keen on making herself look like some little bimbo who found herself in the wrong place at the wrong time.

'Okay, Miss Cope,' he's saying to her now, 'that'll do for now. You try and get some rest; I'll see you later on.'

25

To the scene. There's nothing else to get out of her. Fisher has what he needs for now anyway. It was a professional hit. Very professional. They knew exactly what they needed to do, and they did it without a single hiccup. Didn't even speak a word. Most of the idiots who try to set themselves up as killers are just dreamers. Small brains, big ambition. They see these things in the movies and they think it's all so easy. They go in all guns blazing. They shout their mouths off. They want credit when they get it right. They want to be celebrities. They get caught. The depressing truth is that the gunmen who get caught are the shitty ones. The talented ones know how to avoid that fate. Talented ones, like these two.

Nearly four o'clock in the morning now. Fisher gets out of the car and takes in the street. Not hard to see how they did it. Sit in the car somewhere down the street. Watch them come home. Wait five minutes. If she takes him upstairs, she switches on the light in the bedroom. Then switches it off, goes downstairs and switches on the light in the living room. They know how many people are in the house, and they can guess where each is. Easy. Going to need to get a hold of the taxi driver. He might have spotted something. And this guy who shared the taxi with them. Might be interesting to find out who he is. Could be very interesting.

They kick the door in. Does that tally? He's thinking as he walks up the front path. If you know it's just the two of them in there, and one of them's downstairs, do you need to kick the door in? Surely they guess that he's upstairs and she's down. So you knock, don't you? You knock, and when she answers, you force your way in. That's how they tend to do it. Make as little noise as possible before you fire the gun. That's the way the pros try to do it. She said the first she heard of them was a bang on the door, like someone throwing something at it. The first kick. Then they kick it in. Doesn't sit well with their professionalism elsewhere.

Into the house. A forensic team already there. A DC comes across and shakes his hand, tells him where to find the body. Fisher nods, but doesn't say anything. He's trying to see what they saw. They come in the door, go straight to the living room. She's there, drinking a glass of whiskey. There's a glass on the cabinet on the far side of the room. A single glass, he notes. Okay. So one of them stays with her, pointing the gun at her. She stays there, not moving. Not speaking. And the second one goes upstairs.

Fisher makes his way up the stairs. The body is still in the house, going to be moved in the next hour. Single bullet wound, he knows that already. There's a smell as he walks in through the open bedroom door. Piss. The figure is lying on the bed. Not a lot of blood. A little has run down the side of his neck from a wound under the chin. Sort of thing you see when someone kills themselves with a small handgun, he's thinking. The man's pissed himself. Before or after being shot? Wasn't from fear anyway—no way he was awake when he was killed. Not unless there's a second wound that he can't see. He must have been lying like this when the killer entered the room. May have pissed himself after he was shot. It happens.

He looks more closely at the man. Typical middle-aged small-time dealer. A little overweight. Not too handsome. If his knowledge of Winter is correct, then not a big player. Not a big earner. Surprising that he has a house this decent. Surprising that he has a girlfriend who could obviously do better. Need to find out more about their relationship. Find out how long they've been together, what sort of life they lived. He's looking round the room. No sign of any struggle. Even if you're pissed, you fight for your life. He was already unconscious. All the killer had to do was put the gun to his head and pull the trigger.

'Bullet's still in there,' one of the forensic team says to him, breaking his train of thought.

Taking in the room. Two wine glasses on the dresser, one empty wine bottle. She hadn't mentioned that. Need to find out about that. He can see that the forensic mob want him out of their way. They have their scientific wonderment to be getting on with, and he's blocking the path to the body. Fisher steps back to the bedroom doorway. So the killer kills. Then what? You turn out a light when you leave a room. Did he? Need to find that out as well. Find out the ID of the first cop on the scene, get some proper detail. Don't rely on a report. Get it from the horse's mouth. Few people write with the same sense of detail as they speak. You don't get the mood of the place and people

129

from a report.

Back down the stairs. His mate standing just inside the living room. The living-room door is directly opposite the bottom of the stairs. His cohort hears him coming down the stairs, no need to speak. They leave. Back out the front door, back to their car. Did they have a driver? Could be looking for three men rather than two. May not have felt they needed one. They didn't. Textbook job. Easy. You avoid using a third man if you can. The pros make sure they use no more people than is necessary. Probably no driver. Can't rule it out, though. Got to talk to that taxi driver, and the guy who shared the taxi.

Fisher is standing out on the front doorstep. Breathe in the cold night air. Did any of the neighbours hear the gunshot? They're all up now. Lights in every house. Nosy bastards peeping around curtains. Heard the sirens, heard the chatter. One of them might have something interesting to say about their deceased neighbour and his girlfriend. One of them might have seen a strange car in the street. Sort of place where people notice that sort of thing. Sort of place where people have nothing better to do. If one of them hears the gunshot and runs to a window, they might have seen the killers leave. Might have seen what car they got into.

Hard to catch a pro. Relying on a lot of unreliable things. Give her a few hours, then question Cope again. Find out what club they were at. Get CCTV from there. They might have been followed home from the club. Slim chance, but worth the trouble. It'll help them to ID the taxi driver who took them home. That'll help. She won't know who it was. Don't trust the taxis. Too many of them tied up in the criminal business. Find out who the driver was. Find out if he might have tipped people off about movements. Then question the guy who shared the taxi. Is he involved in the criminal world? Was he there to make sure Winter got home safe and sound? Get him home pissed. Make the hit that much easier. Possible.

Not a lot more that he can glean from the scene. The first thing he'll do is find out who the first cops on the scene were. If they're still on shift, then have them come and see him. If not, get them as soon as they're back on tomorrow. Not urgent enough to warrant getting them out of bed if they've already gone home. They'll have filed reports. That'll do for now. Only for now.

Fisher is driving back to the station. You never know how these investigations will pan out, but it already feels like a long shot. As the police become more professional, so do the people they're up against. People learn how to avoid all the new tricks they develop. More and more, the ones they're catching are the dregs. They get the occasional good one, but that takes so much more work than it used to. Smart lawyers make life difficult. The police spend so much time on that one good catch that they lose sight of other targets. Fisher has become convinced that the approach is wrong. They need to better target the people at the top of the tree, forget about the gunman halfway down.

26

It's after ten o'clock when Calum wakes up. He often sleeps late. He still feels the exhaustion of last night. It was after four when he finally got to sleep. Most people don't sleep at all after that sort of job. The adrenalin won't let them. They stay up, they do things. There's not a lot that can be done in the middle of the night. Perhaps those with girlfriends have something to do, he's thinking. And then he's thinking about what sort of girlfriend he could have in his life. One who understands what he does for a living. One who knows the business. Otherwise he would have to try to hide it all from her. Impossible. It would have to be one who knows the business, and he doesn't want the sort of woman who knows the business.

It's the buzz after the job that catches a lot of people out. They go and do something that draws attention to themselves. A lot of people get caught by drink. They can't sleep; they can't slip back into a proper routine. They go home and they open a bottle. Deadens the nerves. Helps them get to sleep. A necessary part of the job, they say. It becomes a bottle after every job. Then they're using it more often—a tonic to cope with the work they do. Every time their nerves jangle they go for a bottle. Before too long you can't even do the job because of your dependency. Not a mistake Calum will make. He doesn't drink. Not at all. He just copes. No great secret to it. No great skill. Just deal with it.

He's getting out of bed and going through the same routine he goes through almost every single day. Toilet. Brush teeth. Shower. Breakfast. Something light. He's not in the mood to eat. Not in the mood to do much. It's the comedown. An inevitable consequence of the highs of the job. Something else a lot of people don't cope well with. The higher the buzz from the job, the steeper and more damaging the comedown when the buzz wears out and it's back to life as you knew it. Some people chase that buzz. Some do a lot more jobs than is safe. Again, not Calum. Studied. Methodical. Keep the jobs spaced safely apart; don't do too many or too few. Don't get too high during the job, don't get too low afterwards.

It's a solitary job. If you want to do it well, then you must learn to work alone. You must learn to live alone. You must be a solitary person. The best gunmen all are. It gets harder as you get older. The need to have other people around you. The need to be a part of something bigger than yourself. So far, that's not an issue for Calum. He's used to being alone, used to living alone and working alone. This job required a second pair of hands, so he used George. Usually he works alone and is more comfortable that way. He's lived alone since he was nineteen years old. He's had girlfriends, some who stayed over, but he has never allowed a relationship to reach the point where they expected to stay over every night. No danger of them moving in. He needs space. Needs it to the extent that he now worries he can't live any other way.

You see a lot of them in the business. Guys in their forties and fifties, chasing younger women.

Not just chasing them for sex. They look like dirty old men, but there's more to it. They want a younger woman they can settle down with. They want a family. They want all the things they avoided earlier in life. To hell with the risk—life isn't worth it any more if they can't have the things they want. It's a chilling thought. You work hard, take risks and make sacrifices when you're younger, and all you end up with is a craving for the things you sacrificed. There are so many of them. Of course, those old guys won't admit that they were mistaken in their youth, but it seems obvious.

He's sitting at the kitchen table, dressed and eating a bowl of cereal. Thinking about the usual things gunmen think about when they find themselves with time and opportunity to think after a job. What did I do wrong? Were there any mistakes that might catch me out? What are the police doing right now? What are the other people involved doing right now? It's impossible not to think about the consequences when they're so monumental. A lifetime in prison. He's never been inside. Knows some people who have. Hears the stories. Some bad, some terrible. Mostly about how crushingly boring life is. How you'll want life to end, because carrying on is too tedious for words. His one consolation is that he's good at coping with boredom.

No mistakes. No obvious mistakes anyway. Take nothing for granted. Try to remember every detail. No mistakes. The police? It's possible to find out how their investigation is progressing, but it's better not to. There's danger in asking questions. People will wonder why you want to know. Better to stay silent and glean what you can without asking. Sometimes they make it easy for you. A murder is likely to get some reporting, certainly in the local media. But it won't go big these days unless the police want it to.

A lot of gangland killings don't get reported on the national news. Not newsworthy enough—niche story. If the police make an issue out of it, then it is reported. The police do a public appeal; ask people if they saw anything. Then it is reported. Then the journalists flock around and speculate about death, destruction and the moral collapse of society. They link one crime to a number of others. It becomes a good story. You don't want that. You don't want the killing that you carry out to be the one the media latches onto. You don't want it to get a name for itself. The 'something' killing. Once it has that profile, you have problems. Potential employers don't like working with people whose crimes gain notoriety; even if the crime itself was no better or worse than any other gunman's.

There are two reasons the police go to the media. One is that they have nothing. They have no clues, no leads, nothing that can point them in the right general direction. They need help. Desperately. They go begging for clues. Sometimes people see a police appeal on the TV and decide that they remember something. Sometimes that something can lead to a conviction. The begging is worth it. The other reason is that they have something very specific. They have a clue that they know will nail the killer—they just need other people to see it. Maybe a piece of clothing, an accurate description. Something. They put it on TV and they know that people will recognize it.

Then they get the name they need.

If it makes the news, then he'll read about it, or see it. If not, then he waits. Typically you hear nothing for some time. Sometimes you never hear another word about it. You know the police are investigating, but if it's obviously gangland, and the victim is obviously scum, then the motivation to catch the killer is slighter. The police won't admit it, but they want to help victims who deserve their help. They'll say they never differentiate. They're human—they differentiate. They want to help people who have been treated appallingly and don't deserve it. Their emotions lead them towards the undeserving victims of crime. They're human. That's their weakness.

So you hear nothing, and the investigation is wound down, and nothing happens. Other times you get cops who chase after you for years, but they have nothing to go on. They might even suspect the right person, but they can't find the evidence they need to take it to court. It's infuriating for them. They think they know who did it. Everyone keeps telling them the same name, but it's all rumour. They have nothing that they can put before a jury. You simply can't go before a court with a hunch. There's a lot of cases like that. They're damaging because you don't want to be a gunman with a cop looking over your shoulder.

The first two weeks. That's when there's nothing but uncertainty, and worry. You're thinking about what everyone else is doing. You're wondering how close to you the police are. You're worrying that this might be the crime that tips you over the top. You go from being off the police radar to being in their sights. You become the target. It's almost bound to happen at some point. Calum tries to be as careful as he can, but one really smart cop might come along and catch him out one day. Technology may move forward and catch him out, not just on one job, but on every job he's ever done. He's met people who committed crimes twenty years ago, thought they'd got away with it, and are now terrified that the police will reopen the case and catch them with modern technology. 'Modern technology' have become dirty words to some in the business.

He's wondering what the others are doing. He won't be able to find out. George will be going about his business as he always does. He'll be making sure that he does nothing to suggest he ought to be in hiding. Jamieson and Young may or may not know that the hit has happened. Sometimes they find out within a few hours. Word goes round, police contacts tell people in the business, and they find out. Sometimes it takes an age to find out. The person's body isn't discovered as soon as you would expect. The police keep things under wraps. For some reason your employers don't find out for a couple of days. They just have to trust. So do you.

The key is not getting twitchy. You trust them not to bottle it; they trust you to do the same. You don't call them up to find out how things are going. You don't get in touch to let them know you've done the job. Such is the job. Silent trust. They will find out at some point that you carried out the hit, and that you did it about as well as it could be done. They'll know, they'll be happy, but they'll keep it to themselves. You don't go near them for at least a couple of weeks. Maybe longer. Depends on the developing situation. If there's heat, then you might not go near them for a month, and even then only through a third party. You have to get paid. Established people like Jamieson don't screw you over on the money. If they do, and word gets out, then who wants to work for them in the future?

The last thing they want is you calling them or turning up to see them. What if the police check phone records? So, Mr Jamieson, why did Calum MacLean telephone you the day after he murdered a man? The police have their link. They know who ordered it. Your stupidity brings down many powerful people, who won't forgive and forget. They could be watching you. They could be watching Jamieson. You must be careful, and give them nothing. So you sit tight. The clock ticks. The world goes on around you. You do nothing.

27

Fisher is run off his feet. That frantic period, in the immediate wake of a killing, when there's so much to do. This is the bit he enjoys. You can see it in his face, in his mood. He's loving this. He knows it won't last, for one thing. He'll either catch the killers, the investigation ends and he goes back to more mundane things while he waits for the next one, or the investigation will run out of steam. Depends on how good they are. Depends on how good he is. For now, though, there's everything to do. Revel in it. Immerse yourself in it. This is what makes it worthwhile.

He's on his way to meet Zara Cope again. She slept at the station last night, she's still there. Just a few more questions, little things. Find out what club they went to, for one. Get CCTV, if there is any. Find out what taxi they took home, what driver. Find out who the other passenger was. See what these people have to say for themselves. He already knows who the first plods on the scene were. One of them was Paul Greig. Jesus fucking Christ! That crook seems to be able to stick his nose into places it shouldn't be, even when he's just doing his job. Fisher knows him well enough to know that he shouldn't trust him. Not one single damned word. Okay, Greig hasn't done anything wrong in this case, yet. Wouldn't put it past him, though. There are cops who are paid to be the first on the scene, remove any evidence left behind. Fisher knows it happens. Wouldn't be surprised if Greig was one such cop. It's always worth being suspicious when that lying bastard is first on the scene. Why has nobody complained about him yet? Why in hell hasn't he been kicked out of the force?

Back in the station. Little bit of paperwork. Boring, stupid paperwork. A report about the contents of the house waiting for him. Nothing deemed suspicious by the detective constable who looked around. No drugs found. Little bit of money, but just loose cash. Nothing that would raise eyebrows. Going to take longer to work out the other details. How much money does Winter have in bank accounts, and can we prove that it came from drugs? Difficult with a dead guy. Difficult if he didn't leave any easy evidence behind. Initial search of the house suggests that he didn't. Disappointing. Someone else will decide

139

what happens with his assets, and whether they can be taken.

As he walks down to the suite where Cope's stayed the night, he's annoyed that he has nothing to throw at her. No drugs. No suspicious documents. No suspicious money. Not a huge surprise. A dealer of Winter's experience would know how to be careful, would know how to hide the things that need to be hidden. They plan for the worst-case scenario. Doesn't get worse than this. If there had been drugs, he would have her over a barrel. He could ask her whatever he wanted. Put the pressure on. Get some proper detail from her.

People would scowl if they knew how he was thinking. He knows what people make of his attitude. You mustn't be so aggressive towards the woman. She's a witness. She's a victim. She had a gun pointed at her. You must treat her with the sympathy that she deserves. Bullshit! Complete bullshit. She's the girlfriend of a drug dealer. She lived with the man. She knew that he was a dealer, a peddler of filth. She went along with that. It's inconceivable that she doesn't know some detail about the business he was involved in. Names. Dates. Amounts. She'll be sitting on all sorts of information. Smart little girl. Knows that she can't give too much away. Knows what's safe for her and what's not. If something had been found, then he could dangle it over her. Not now. Not yet.

He's knocking on the door and waiting outside. The female cop answers it, nods to him, invites him in. He can't remember her name. Not important. Cope is sitting on the couch again. Dressed properly now. Someone must have brought her clothes. No family with her. There usually is, morning after something like this. People rush to comfort.

'How are you feeling this morning, Zara?' he's asking her. He sounds like he's concerned. He's not. Years of practice.

'Okay, I guess,' she says with a nervous shrug. She looks afraid. She is.

'There's just a few little questions I want to ask you about last night,' he's saying to her. 'A few details I need to know, then we can let you go. Do you have somewhere you can go to?' he's asking her, presuming she knows that the house is out of bounds for a few more days.

'I'll find somewhere.'

He's trying to put on his sympathetic face. That's just for form. He suspects she's smart enough to see through it. You don't live the life she has without learning what a liar looks like.

'I should ask you if you would like a lawyer present, before I continue,' he's saying, 'although, of course, I'm only going to ask you a few wee questions about what you saw. You're just a witness. But if it would make you feel more at ease.'

He's presenting it as if it's the most reasonable thing in the world, but she knows it would make it look like she has something to hide. 'No, it's okay,' she's saying, her tone attempting to suggest that she doesn't think a lawyer is at all necessary. Why would it be? She's done nothing wrong.

He's nodding, looking at the sheet of paper he has in front of him. Doesn't look, from where she's sitting, that it has much written on it.

'Before we begin,' he's saying, 'is there anything

141

you remember from last night, anything that you want to tell me?'

She's shaking her head. He made it sound like he expected her to have something new to say, but she doesn't. 'No. No, nothing. I've thought about it. A lot. But there's nothing.'

'That's okay—it was just in case anything had come back to you,' he's saying. He's trying to sound like the consummate professional, the sympathetic copper, but there's an underlying tone that he can't disguise. She'll probably notice, he's thinking to himself, but he doesn't much care. He never solved a case by sucking up to a dealer's bit of skirt.

Down to the useful stuff. Oh, how he wishes there was something better to throw at her than this. Maybe there will be. Maybe the people who are examining the laptop found at the house will discover something that incriminates her. Anything at all would be nice.

'Zara, I need to know what club you and Lewis went to last night. Can you remember the name of it?'

'Er, yeah. Heavenly, in the city centre. Do you know it?'

'I know of it,' he's saying. Big place. Should have proper CCTV. That could help.

'We go there now and again. Just to unwind. Just a night out. You don't think they were there, do you? You don't think they followed us?'

'I really don't know,' he's telling her.

She's not as tearful as she was the night before. Understandable. Appropriate. If she's performing, then she's judging it well.

'I wonder if you know the taxi driver who took

you home? I need to talk to him, in case he saw anything on the street after he dropped you off. He might have noticed people, or a car.'

'I don't know,' she's saying, shaking her head.

'That's okay, it was a long shot. Did you call him, or was he just waiting outside for random pickups?'

She's running a hand across her forehead. 'I think he was just outside. I don't remember calling. I think he must just have been outside.'

'That's fine. The club should know who waits outside regularly. I can find out from them.'

So far so good, she's thinking. No lies. Nothing to trip me up. But there's one more. She knows he's going to ask about Stewart, and she's going to have to lie. This is when she has to be at her most cautious. The danger is real. If she's seen to be evasive or difficult, then they'll get twitchy, they'll start to press her. Once that happens, she's in trouble. She's a suspect.

'The last thing I wanted to ask you about was the man who shared the cab with you. Do you know the man? Do you have a name for him? An address, perhaps, where I could reach him?'

'No,' she's saying, shaking her head. 'I'd never met him before last night. I think I danced with him earlier in the evening. He was leaving at the same time we were. That was it.'

Fisher is nodding. 'Okay, Zara, thanks for that. I think the forensic team will be at the house for at least another twenty-four hours, perhaps longer. We'll let you know. If you have nowhere else to go, then you can stay here another night. I'm sure that would be fine.'

She's sitting on the couch, thinking bitterly

143

about it. She has nowhere else to go. Her friends are all fair-weather ones; she wouldn't turn to them in an emergency. She's had almost no contact with her parents in the last eight years. They're bringing up her daughter, and they seem happy to do it without her getting in the way. They have more contact with Nate than they do with their own daughter. Nate. An appealing prospect. She would feel safe with Nate. Would he want to see her? They haven't spoken for almost a year. He's always polite, respectful. There's always that underlying danger with him. The fear. No. Get the money from Stewart, use it to get a place of her own. There must be somewhere she can rent. She'll sell the house, if the police don't take it. She's not going back there.

28

John Young is in a pub when he hears the news. It's half past ten in the morning, and he's not there for a drink. One-third of the pub is owned by the Jamieson organization, and it appears to be the only third that isn't making any money. It's remarkable that the other two owners would try such a thing. That they would think they could get away with it. But then, some people are stupid. They came to him because they were in debt. In debt to bad people. They made Young an offer. One-third share in the pub to make the debt collectors go away. He took it. The pub had the potential to make money. Easy money in a legit business that could be used to filter more ill-gotten

144

cash.

This is Young's area. He picks out the right businesses to invest in. He's the one with the head for this. So when it goes wrong, it reflects on him. He doesn't like things that reflect badly on his judgement. Who does? The pub is making money, as he was sure it would. They were cleaning bad money through it, as he thought they could. A call from an accountant had suggested that the money the pub was making was not being split evenly between all three parties. Remarkably the two other owners, who still run the place, handling the day-to-day stuff, think they can screw Peter Jamieson.

They will get one warning. Just one. The pub's a useful place to have, and Young doesn't want to have trouble with it. Kicking the other owners out and taking it for themselves would mean trouble. It is the next step. If they really think they can hide money from the people they ran to in the first place, then they're kidding themselves. They need to understand that. Make them understand. If they try it a second time—which very few ever do, having already been warned—then they will be punished appropriately. They only have their share in the business because Young did a deal with the debt collectors. He didn't pay the full amount owed, but the other owners don't know that. All they know is that they owe him.

He called them up early this morning, told them they needed to have an urgent meeting. Told them that he had worrying news for them. Told them he'd had an urgent call from his accountant and there were things that needed to be worked out. He worded it to sound like he wasn't blaming

145

them for anything. His tone made it perfectly obvious that he was. Now he's at the pub, and he's brought Neil Fraser with him, just as a little reminder of how angry he is. Neil is a thug. He's not one of the more sophisticated hardmen that Peter Jamieson employs. A man like George Daly, for example, is a hardman with a brain. Reliable and decent. Neil Fraser is a thug. Big muscles, small brain. Big mouth, small words. Big presence to have sitting beside you when you confront these people. Useful as a warning.

The meeting is everything Young expects it to be. The two men play at being mortified. Two middle-aged Glaswegians, trying to pretend that it's all the fault of some accountant they hired to look after the books for them. They assure him, repeatedly, that they're as angry as he is. If not angrier, in fact. They mutter about making sure their accountant pays the price, all the time glancing at Fraser. He's under strict instructions to sit there, keep his mouth shut and look mean. It's an easy part to play, and he's playing it better than the pub owners are playing theirs. Young rounds it off with the warning that he can't allow this sort of thing to happen again. Nothing against them, of course, but he can't have his business mistreated. If it happens again, then he'll have to take serious action. No word on what that serious action is. All very friendly.

'We totally understand, John, totally,' one of them is saying to him. He's letting them off the hook, not demanding back every penny that was stolen from the Jamieson organization. They're grateful for that too. It doesn't occur to them that the pub's principal purpose for Young is money

146

laundering, but then it's not clear that they've yet worked out that he's laundering drug money through the business. He hopes that if they have realized, they'll be bright enough to continue to ignore the fact.

'I feel like we've been mugged here,' the other one's saying, 'and by our own accountant. Goes to show, eh, you can't trust a soul.'

The conversation descends into the usual pit of excessive mock-outrage that you get from people caught with their fingers in the till. John sits and lets them play it out; they'll feel better for having said it all. He slowly turns the conversation round to local news. People in a pub hear it all, often before most other people do. Sometimes you find out some very relevant things. Like this morning.

'Heard there was a shooting last night. A fellow who comes in here now and then. Drugs. Probably had it coming.'

'Yeah, who's that?' Young's asking.

'Name's Winter. Ah've chucked him out of here before, when I thought he was doing a drug deal. Can't have that. We have a reputation.'

You sure do, Young is thinking to himself. Winter must have refused you a cut. He doesn't say it, though; no need to antagonize.

'Got shot, huh?'

'Aye, in his own home. No surprises, the way he's been carrying on.'

'How so?'

'Been running around like Flash Harry lately. Got himself a wee girlfriend, half his age. Pretty thing, was in here with him once. Stuck up, but pretty. He's startin' to dress young, go to nightclubs, live the flash life, you know. Tryin' tae keep up with his girl. You got tae act yer age. Must've been showin' off his money one time too many. Pissed off the wrong person, or somethin'. Drugs. They all end up dead in the end. Serves 'em right.'

Young leaves them to their moralizing. The chant of the hypocrite. If they threw Winter out of the pub, it was because of money, not drugs. That pub's been used by dealers over the years—it's that sort of pub. The owners turned a blind eye. The dealers cut them in on deals done on their premises. Maybe they give them a little supply of their own to be getting on with instead of cash. Winter obviously decided not to. His margins were probably too slim to allow for anyone else getting in on the deal. Everything points to the fact that he was struggling. It's what made him so attractive to someone wanting to get in on the market. An easy lure. The sort of person that a smart prick like Shug Francis would target.

He's meeting Jamieson at a flat that Peter owns. Not a company flat, a personal one. Down by the river. Lovely view. Very few people know he owns it. A private little place where he can indulge himself now and again. They're sitting in the kitchen, Young tutting that his friend is still in a bathrobe at twenty past eleven. He doesn't honestly mind. Jamieson's the sort of person who needs to relax now and again. Needs the occasional blowout. Can't function well without it. Does nobody any harm.

'I hear Lewis Winter was shot dead last night.'

'Yeah?' There's a brief hint of relief in his voice. It's been dragging on.

'Apparently. At his house. Don't know anything

148

else about it. Find out in due course. No word of anyone being caught, anything going wrong. Just talk about it happening, people saying that Winter had it coming. All talking about him being a dealer. Talking about his younger woman. Talking about him living the high life and attracting the wrong attention.'

'Uh-huh,' Jamieson's nodding. There's nothing else to say. Until they know more detail, he can show no greater concern than that.

They both know that nothing went wrong with the killing. If it had, that would be what people were talking about. It wouldn't be a story about Lewis Winter being killed; it would be a story about Calum MacLean being arrested, with Winter being reduced to an afterthought. A shame for him perhaps, but the perpetrator is more glamorous news than the victim. The victim only gets his moment in the spotlight when the perpetrator is nowhere to be seen. So it went well. They're not complacent. They assume it went well because there's no evidence to the contrary. Time may change that opinion.

Young leaves Jamieson to his amusements. Call it a day off. Jamieson doesn't get many. Young gets fewer still, but that's through choice. He's built his life around his work—there's little else to do with his time. Holidays are of no interest to him. The things that tend to occupy so much of Peter's spare time hold little interest, either. No interest in golf or horse racing or even snooker. He plays only because Peter insists on having someone to play against. So life becomes work, work becomes life. And he loves it. It continually thrills him. It tests him every single day. It tests his judgement. It tests his intellect. It tests his nerve. It may have its downsides, but they are hugely outweighed by the good, in his mind.

29

A DC has been given the job of assessing the possibility of claiming Winter's assets under the Proceeds of Crime Act. It's become a big deal in the force—getting as much as you can from the criminal. An extra punishment. A chance to raise more money. Tough to get anything from a dead guy, though. Rarely happens. Usually only comes from the living who have been convicted, and even then you rarely get as much as you should. You have to be able to prove the link between the asset and the crime. Greig knows that his suited colleagues struggle to do that, and knows they'll struggle in this case. There was nothing at the house to prove that Winter paid for his assets through crime, and Cope won't be stupid enough to hand it to them on a plate.

The DC's name is McGowan. Greig's searching his memory. Little fat guy. Middle-aged. Decent fellow. Easy to talk to. Greig will keep an eye on the situation, but he doesn't expect to have to do anything about it. Eventually everything will be handed over to Cope, presuming that nobody else has been named in a will, and he'll get his cut. Money for nothing. Might not be nothing. If McGowan gets excited about something and tries to make a grab at Winter's belongings, then he'll have to step in. A quiet word.

Now he has a meeting with the DI in charge of the day-to-day investigation into the Winter murder. The DCI will be looking over his shoulder, acting as the face of the investigation, if it comes to that, but most of the donkey work will be done by Fisher. Fisher hates him. Greig knows it. Fisher doesn't make much of an effort to hide it. Strange, because they have a lot in common. Both coppers who've made sacrifices for the job. Both coppers who work harder and longer than most others. Okay, Greig is thinking, maybe Fisher doesn't have his sense of realism. That comes from being on the streets. You learn what can and can't be done. You lose the fantasy that all crimes can be solved, all criminals stopped. You learn to take advantage when the time is right. That's not bad policing. Bad policing is doing nothing at all. Bad policing is trying to do things that you know can't be done.

Fisher is waiting for him, along with Marcus Matheson, the young cop he was on duty with last night. They're upstairs, sitting at Fisher's desk in the open-plan office. Greig says hello to a couple of the other detectives as he makes his way across to them. He's been around the station a long time. He's part of the furniture. There's nobody there that he hasn't worked with on some case or other over the years. They all know him. He knows what most of them think of him. You don't last as long as he has without being self-aware. Some recoil from him. Some are convinced that he's part of the problem rather than the solution. Others are smarter.

Greig sits at the table alongside the young plod. He can see the look in the detective's eyes; he

151

knows what Fisher is thinking: why the hell do they put impressionable young coppers under the wing of a disgusting crook like Paul Greig? They do it, Greig is thinking, because not everyone is as naive as you are. Not everyone believes that you have to be an angel to fight crime. People understand that the first big step in beating the criminals is understanding them. You have to know who they are. You have to know where they live and work. You have to have a feel for the environment. A hard thing to teach. Greig is a good teacher, and the people who matter know it.

'So you two were first on the scene at the Winter house. Tell me about it.' Fisher leans back in his chair. He's been short with them, but they won't care. A lot of people think he's a prick, and he doesn't care. They know he's a good copper. They know he's honest and straightforward.

'Not a lot to tell,' Matheson's saying. 'We get there, the door is open, lock broken. We go in. The girl is downstairs, on the phone to the operator. She hangs up, comes over. She was obviously terrified, maybe thought we were more trouble. You could see the relief when she saw us.'

The first and only report of the shooting came from Zara Cope. None of the neighbours heard it. Apparently.

'Then what?' Fisher's asking.

'I went upstairs to look around, PC Greig stayed downstairs with the witness. I went up, looked in a couple of doors before I found the bedroom. Opened the door. Smelled the urine. Put on the light.'

'You put on the light?' Fisher interrupts.

'Yeah, I put on the light. It was pitch-black in

152

there.'

So the killer did stop to put the light off on his way out. He wasn't sure why that should matter to him, but it did. A real pro. The sort you rarely catch. The forensic team were already checking prints they'd found at the house, but Cope had told them that they had a lot of people round to the house. Friends. There had been one friend round that day. Worth checking.

Fisher pauses for a few seconds, thinking about it. Thinking about how the killer is unlikely to have gone bare-handed, but you never know what you might get.

'That important?' Greig's asking him, deliberately breaking his train of thought.

'He wasn't killed in the dark. Guy didn't turn up with night-goggles on. The guy had to put the light on to see Winter. Then he put it off again on the way out. How did you find the witness?'

'She was in shock,' Greig's saying. 'Obviously. Terrified out of her wits, I'd say.'

'Uh-huh. She didn't say anything in those first few minutes—anything interesting?'

'She hardly said anything at all. What she said was just gratitude that someone was there.'

How Fisher wished that Matheson were there by himself. He could talk properly then. He wouldn't have to put up with Greig interrupting him all the time. Fisher would be able to take the young cop aside and get a real sense of the atmosphere in the house. Get a sense of Cope's attitude. It might also be interesting to know how she and Greig interacted.

'You know that nothing was found at the house,' Fisher is saying.

'Nothing like?' Greig's asking.

'No drugs. Little money. Nothing of any great value in proving that Lewis Winter was a drug dealer. We all know he was. Did Zara Cope show any worry about hiding anything? Did she mention anything?'

'Not a thing,' Greig says.

Fisher's thinking again. Apparently, Greig's thinking to himself, Fisher can't think and keep a conversation going at the same time. Has to stop and make a show of it.

'How far away were you when you got the call for the shooting? How long did it take you to get to the house?'

'Four, five minutes,' Matheson says with a shrug.

If he could find some discrepancy. He knows Cope was on the phone to the operator the whole time. She was still talking to the operator when these two arrived at the house. But how long did she have before she called? That's the crucial point. Surely one of the neighbours heard the gunshot. If just one of them could put a time on it.

Fisher thanks them for coming up, lets them go on their way. Greig isn't sure what the hell it was all for—the detective didn't gain anything from it. Sometimes you can just tell the way a case is going to go. Unless Fisher can find some sort of dead-cert evidence that points to Winter being in a feud with someone, this is already going nowhere. To Greig's trained instincts, it has the distinct whiff of an investigation that's decomposing faster than the victim. No evidence found at the scene that can ID the culprits. No eyewitness who can ID the culprit. No evidence to say why the murder took place. All that exists so far is conjecture about Winter being a

154

dealer. He was a dealer, but knowing why someone might want to kill him doesn't tell you who did it. It's not impossible that Fisher might catch the people who did it, but it's already looking less than fifty-fifty.

It's not his concern. The killers, the victim—they're for Fisher to entertain himself with. This case seems to hold little importance, as far as Greig can see. Falling into conjecture of his own, he works it all out. Lewis Winter has got hold of Zara Cope. He wants to keep hold of her. Who wouldn't? He starts living the high life to keep her happy, throwing money around. Maybe he borrows cash. Maybe he takes on a lot of gear from his supplier, on the promise of future sales. Maybe the sales don't come, the supplier doesn't want his gear back, he just wants money. Winter doesn't pay, so he gets a bullet. Or maybe he was fighting so hard to make more money for Zara that he strayed onto patches where he wasn't welcome. Typical dealer death.

Greig's interest is in Cope. She's still at the station. Due to leave in the afternoon. Been interviewed, told every tale she has to tell. Seems to be dealing with the whole thing pretty well. Not obvious yet what she's going to do with her life. Seems like she was pretty tied up in Winter. Bad move. The guy was a walking disaster zone; girl that smart should have noticed. Now she's got nowhere to run. The cop looking after her has already put it around that the girl has nowhere to go. Going to dip into her meagre savings to pay for somewhere. Won't go back to the house. Meagre savings. He finds that hard to believe. She must have something.

30

It's the middle of the afternoon. It feels like she's been in that police station for days. They've told her all the right things. You can go back to the house tomorrow. Don't want to. You can rest assured that we don't think there's any threat to you. Never thought there was. If there's anything we can do for you, please come and see us. I won't. If you remember anything—no matter how insignificant—that you think can help, get in touch. I definitely won't. If anyone contacts you regarding the murder of your partner and tells you anything that might be of any interest to us, let us know. Wow, you people really don't know how this world works, do you? She didn't say these things to them, of course. She nodded along. She was polite. She was the pretty little victim. The tragic case with nowhere to go.

There was a grain of truth in that. She feels tragic. She has nowhere to turn. How can you get this far through life, twenty-eight years, with good looks and a decent brain, and still have nobody to turn to? It doesn't make sense to her. It should be easier than this. Fine, deal with it. No moping around. No feeling sorry for yourself. You still have to make sure that you get out the other end of this with as much of a cushion as possible.

First step in that is going and seeing Stewart, and getting what she gave him. She's not in the mood to deal with him. She can picture him pawing at her already, but she doesn't have a choice.

The address she knows by heart. If he's lied to

her and their paths ever cross again, then she won't be responsible. By God, she isn't in the mood to be pissed around by some self-adoring little dweeb, just out of nappies. She walks away from the police station for twenty minutes. There's an instinctive paranoia. It's fed into you by the industry she's lived within for nearly a decade. You get used to thinking of the police as the enemy. You get used to thinking of an enemy as someone sneaky and underhand. Zara can't shake the feeling that the police might be watching her. Someone following in the middle distance, just close enough to see where she goes and who she talks to. Not impossible. It's obvious that Fisher doesn't like or trust her. But she can see nobody out of place behind her.

She's calling a taxi. What are the odds that it's the same driver? Slim. It isn't; this guy's much younger. She gives him the street that Stewart gave her. The guy drives. He makes idle chit-chat. She wishes he would shut up; she's trying to listen to what's being said on the radio. It's a local radio station. There's a news report. She can't hear what they're saying. It doesn't sound like there's anything about the shooting. It's maybe a little soon. Tomorrow, probably. If Fisher decides to go to the media. Maybe he'll keep it all under wraps. Some sort of evidence that he wants to use.

The city rolls past her as she sits in the back of the taxi, thinking about it all. She wants them to catch the people who did this. In her heart, she wants them to pay for what they've done. Okay, Lewis wasn't perfect. No angel. Their relationship was hardly perfect, either. It was theirs, though, and nobody else has the right to take it away from them like that. Not perfect, but could have been for life. Now, in the blink of an eye, it's all gone. The future has gone. They had no right. But her head tells her that she doesn't want them to be caught. If they're caught, then you'll never be able to put all this behind you and get on with your life. They'll tell about Stewart. She'll fall into the hole she's dug for herself. Head rules heart. Stay professional, you murderers, and stay free.

The taxi pulls up in a street she doesn't recognize. Respectable. Old houses, pre-war. Large. Probably all split into flats. An area full of the aspiring. The first step on a property ladder that will lead to something much grander. Good for them. She's walking along the street, looking at numbers on gates. She finds the right one. Well-maintained front garden. At the front door there's a buzzer with four buttons. Four names. She knows she's looking for Flat C. It has the names Macintosh and Shields on it. Which one is Stewart? She presses the buzzer.

He sounds almost breathless through the intercom. Tells her he'll be right down. Through the glass in the door she sees a figure bounding along the corridor to the door. He opens it. He's grinning. Then he stifles the grin, realizing that it's not appropriate for the situation.

'Come in. Come up. It's so good to see you. How are you?'

Stewart sounds so enthusiastic, no matter how hard he tries to sound sympathetic. He's been living on his nerves. Sitting at home all day, waiting for the buzzer. Will it be the cops or Zara? Please be Zara. It is. She looks dowdier than she did. No make-up. Plain clothes. Still beautiful.

158

The intoxication of the moment guarantees that, anyway.

He takes her upstairs. He shows her into a sparse but clean flat. Nice, but obviously little lived in. Occupied by two people with better things to do than stay at home. Lucky them.

'My flatmate's not here. Just the two of us,' he's saying nervously. Maybe that sounds like a come-on—say something else. 'We can talk freely.'

She's sitting down at the little kitchen table. He's sitting opposite.

'Okay,' she's nodding. 'That's good. Did you get back okay last night, no trouble?'

Bless her. She's been worrying about him. 'Yeah, fine, no bother at all,' he says, aiming for nonchalance. Better not tell her that he was thrilled by the whole thing. Now's not the time.

She looks nervous. She's trying not to look fed up, but he can see it in her. What do you say? So many firsts. First time he's been in this situation. First time he's felt this way about a woman. But then, how much of that is real, how much is the thrill? Most of it's the thrill. She's pretty, but he's aware enough to know that it's not her that he's falling in love with.

'So, what do we do now?' he's asking. He's aiming for sympathetic. He's aiming for conspiratorial. He's aiming to keep them together.

'Did you manage to keep what I gave you?' she's asking. Down to business.

While he's disappeared off into another room, Zara's taking the opportunity to have a look round. Maybe Stewart's earning reasonable money. Maybe he's not such a bad option. It's a boyish flat. The flat of young men who live like

159

young men. Still, potential. Maybe nothing long-term, but useful for a little while. No. Don't settle for clinging to short-term measures. Don't fall into any port in a storm. You have to do better. The only way to get a better life is to aim for something better. He's coming out of the bedroom with the wads of cash and bags of drugs in his hands. He seems to think she's going to take them as they are.

'Do you have something I can put them in?' she's asking, not bothering to hide her incredulity.

'Oh, yeah.'

Is it a good thing or a bad thing that he doesn't know what he's doing? Good that he's not likely to try to cut in on business, get involved. Bad that he might not realize the gravity of his situation. She decides she's going to spell it out. He's coming back in with a shoebox and a plastic bag. He begins packing it all into the shoebox for her, and she starts to speak.

'Stewart, you do understand how serious all this is?'

He pauses and looks at her. 'I heard your partner being shot dead. I don't suppose it gets more serious than that. I ran away from the scene of a murder with drugs and cash. That's serious.'

'Good. It's important that you realize that this isn't something to make light of, joke about with your friends. This is the sort of thing that you don't talk about at all. You need to understand what the consequences will be if you do run off at the mouth.'

He pauses as he's putting the lid on the shoebox. That sounded a little bit threatening. Is she threatening him to keep his mouth shut? He's looking at her quizzically. She looks back, maybe

160

guessing what he's thinking.

'I'm thinking of you, Stewart,' she's saying to him. 'Me too, I admit, but you have to be very careful now. If the police find out that you were ever there, they will lock you up. You could easily get a couple of years for what you did. I don't want that. I don't want to think of you suffering because you wanted to help me.' There are little tears forming in the corners of her eyes. 'I feel like I've lost so much. I just want to protect the good things that are left.'

He's getting up and rushing to her, throwing his arms around her as she breaks down. He's hugging her, telling her all sorts of comforting things that matter little. It sounded so impressive. It sounded like she was throwing herself at him. Like this was going to be a long-running thing. That would be good. He realizes that he does want to be with her. Not just because she's pretty, but because of the life they could live together. The thrills. More nights like last night. Sex, guns and going on the run. That's exciting.

That sounded a little stronger than she intended. She's laying it on too thick. She needs to keep him happy for a while, to make sure he doesn't make life difficult, but she shouldn't lead him in directions that she has no intention of going in herself. This isn't going to be a relationship. In an ideal world, this will be the last they see of each other. That'll be tough to pull off. He seems a little too interested to just let it go. She's going to have to be gentle with him. Be careful. Always good advice.

She's pulling herself away from him now.

'I'd better go. I have a lot to do.'

'Oh. Where . . . uh . . . where are you staying?'

'I'm going to rent somewhere for a few weeks, then take it from there,' she says, before she has a chance to realize that a lie might be the better approach.

'Well, you could stay here,' he's saying, brightening as he speaks. 'I'd love to have you here. It would be a great place for you.' He doesn't believe that, but he wants her to stay.

She's already shaking her head. 'No, it's not a good idea for us to be seen together so soon. People might ask questions.'

Her instincts are better than his, he must concede that. She's thinking more clearly, not rushing into things. She's considering the consequences. She's getting up and heading for the door. He's walking behind her, trying to think of something to say that will make an impression. It doesn't feel like he's handled this meeting especially well. Say something.

'I want to help you,' he's saying, not knowing where he's going to go next. 'I like you a lot. I want to protect you. I want to be there for you.'

She stops and looks up at him. 'That's sweet,' she says and reaches up to kiss him briefly on the mouth. Then she's out the door.

31

The Heavenly nightclub. Do they have a sense of irony when they name these places? Maybe they realize that their clientele are all pissed when they turn up, so they can't judge their surroundings. It'll be dark inside at night anyway—that hides the multitude of heavenly sins. Fisher walks along the edge of the dance floor to the bar. Someone's cleaning behind it. He hasn't seen anyone else since he came in. Noticed the CCTV cameras on the outside, though. Good start.

'Excuse me, I'm looking for the manager,' he says brusquely. The stout woman behind the bar looks at him and then points towards a door across the dance floor.

Who does she think he is? She didn't even ask. Maybe she recognized that he's a cop. He hates that. Some people pretend they can spot a cop a mile off. He doesn't believe it. Never has. The cleaner has probably been told not to ask questions of those who come looking for the manager. Never mind. Across the floor and through the door, into a dingy corridor. It doesn't seem like a building that's had a great deal of money spent on its upkeep. That's a concern. First thing to suffer when money is tight is often security. Maybe those cameras don't even work.

He's walking down the corridor slowly, inspecting everything, when someone emerges from a room ahead. The man stops and looks at him. Surprised, obviously. Not happy to see someone in the private area of his club.

'Can I help you?' the man's asking. Trying to sound hard. Trying to sound like he's not in the business of helping people. Fisher encounters this a lot.

'I hope so. Detective Inspector Fisher, Strathclyde Police. I'm looking for the manager.'

'You found him.'

'Is there somewhere we can talk?'

163

The man knows Fisher isn't here to arrest him; he wouldn't be by himself if he were.

'Aye,' the podgy little man nods, 'this way.'

Do I know who the manager of Heavenly is? Fisher's thinking to himself. No. Should I? Maybe. He looks like someone with something to hide. Balding, short in the arse, chubby, mid-thirties at the most. Many people in his business have connections they shouldn't. A lot of others fear the police because they don't want their place getting that sort of reputation. Might be nothing.

'What's your name?' Fisher asks him.

'Adam Jones.'

No bells are ringing. Fair enough. Off the hook. For now.

Into a little office. Small and cramped. Whitewashed walls, a single small window high up on the wall. It feels like someone converted a toilet. Not a sign of a luxurious establishment. He's been in the offices of club managers before. He can't remember one like this.

'Last night a man named Lewis Winter was shot dead in his house. He was here at the club before he went home,' Fisher says.

'Okay,' the man nods needlessly. Trying to show off how casual and relaxed he is. Trying badly.

'I want to have a look at your CCTV. The killer may have been here too. We'll want copies of everything you have from last night. Everything.'

The manager leads him along the corridor to another room, the security room. There are two tiny monitors on a rickety table, and a chair in front of it. That's the extent of the security room.

'The footage from last night should be here,' the manager's saying, picking up tapes from the table.

164

'Obviously we keep everything, just in case. Cameras go on when we open, off when we shut. Expensive stuff, ya know. Very expensive.' He's shoving a tape into a machine and switching on a monitor. 'What time was yer man here?'

'I don't know,' Fisher tells him, and ignores the sigh that follows. He knows roughly when they arrived, and roughly when they left, but that's not the point. It's not them he's looking for. It's the people near them. It's the man who shared the cab with them.

Fisher sits in that little room for more than an hour. He fast-forwards through long sections of video. He picks them out when they arrive. He watches the footage of the night and gets a new impression of the relationship between Winter and Cope. They arrive with others. They dance together for a while, but he looks absurdly out of place. Hard to spot an older person there. She starts dancing with a younger man right in front of Winter. Treating him like shit with legs. Getting close to this young man.

The rest of the hour is taken up in watching Zara Cope dancing close with a young man, looking to all the world like a couple. Winter is sitting by himself. A lonesome figure. Downing bottle after bottle of beer. Numerous questions are flitting into Fisher's mind now. They can wait. First priority is picking out anyone at the club who seems interested in Winter. Nobody stands out. A woman, apparently desperate, goes and sits next to him. The pictures aren't good, jumpy and at a distance. They look like they're talking. Eventually the woman gets up and walks away. It takes Fisher a few minutes to realize that Winter is asleep at the

165

table.

Nearly an hour later—after half past midnight on the security-camera clock. Club should be shut at midnight. Cope and the young man she's been getting happy with walk across to Winter. She's talking to him. She's sitting beside him. She's helping him up. Struggling. The young man steps in. It looks like young siblings carrying their embarrassing father to the exit. They go out through the hall. Fisher marks the time. A quarter to one. He ejects the tape and finds the one for the doorway CCTV. The manager has long since disappeared, leaving the detective to his own devices. Said he had a lot of work to do. Probably gone to call the owner. Remember to check who the owner is too.

The doorway tape in the machine. Fast-forwarding. He's given up on looking for the killers. Long shot that they would have been there. Probably waited at the house. That makes the taxi driver and the young man who shared the taxi more important. First problem. Damned club. Bloody idiots. Whoever's in charge of their security wants shooting. The camera doesn't record a wide enough area. You can see the doorway and most of the pavement outside, but you can't see right up to the road. It's too close. He won't see them getting into the taxi. Shit! Why the hell have they got the camera focused on so small an area? Ah, easy enough to guess. They don't trust their own door staff. They want to keep an eye on them. Hard to blame them for that.

Not as good as he hoped it would be. Interesting, though. The three of them come out of the club and onto the pavement. Zara hails someone, presumably a taxi. The younger man helps Winter across to the taxi and they move out of view. Can't see the taxi, can't see who gets into it. They shared the taxi with a young man who just happened to be leaving at the same time as they were. That's what she said. Coincidence; not someone she knew. Random stranger—don't know his name. Nope, not buying that any more. She was lying about this much at least. Look at Winter. Jesus, look at him. He can hardly stand.

Think about her story. They share a taxi with a stranger. He helps her get Winter to the door, then leaves. She gets Winter all the way up the stairs, along the corridor and onto the bed by herself. No fucking way. Not a chance. Look at him! He can barely stand up. If the young man wasn't helping him out of the club, he would have been face-first on the pavement. Lying bitch. You did not get him all that way by yourself, not in that state, not a wee girl like you. Someone helped you. The young man. He came into the house. Had to. He came into the house, and yet he's nowhere to be seen when the plod arrive. Fisher rewinds, gets a shot of the young man, mostly the back of his head. That could be our killer. More than a stranger.

Fisher goes looking for the manager. He finds him in his office, on the phone. The manager hangs up when he enters without knocking.

'D'you have a list of the taxis that wait outside to pick up your customers?'

'Aye,' Jones is saying, reaching into the drawer of his desk. 'Your lot made us draw up a list, keep a watch on who uses the place.'

Your lot. Charming. The manager passes a list across to him. At a glance, he sees nothing that stands out. There are taxi firms that he knows are owned or controlled by organized crime, but he sees none of them on this list.

Fisher shoves the list into his pocket. He looks at the manager, sitting looking back across the desk at him. Looking nervous. Looking at the tapes, wondering what's been found on them.

'I'm taking these tapes with me. They're important. I might send someone else round to have a word about a few other things I happened to notice while I was here,' he says and leaves the office. It's an idle threat. If the club was open past its hours, then that's for the plods to deal with. He might send someone to warn them about it, though, so that they can bitch about the positioning of the security cameras while they're there. Yeah, that's not a bad idea. Make them see that they need to have a better view of the outside.

Back to the station. Give the tapes to someone with the time to go through them in detail.

'Find out who the guy leaving with them is. Try and spot anyone else that might stand out.' They won't spot the killers. That's too much to ask for. You never know what might come up, though. They might spot someone talking to Winter or Cope that he didn't spot. They might find out that the younger man has connections. A bit of luck. That's what he needs. Luck. Now the taxi driver. Find him. He can add to the picture. The picture of Cope and the younger man.

A thought. A grim thought. Cope wasn't treated as a suspect. She was a witness and she was a victim. There was no pressure to make sure that they knew where she was going next—people assumed the house where Winter had died. Maybe not. Maybe she goes somewhere else and he has no way of getting to her at short notice. Fisher stops in the middle of the office.

'Someone get me that plod that was looking after Cope.' He's worried. She's a suspect to him. She lied to him repeatedly when he interviewed her, and he now has the proof. She's hiding something, and that's something he wants to find. First, Fisher has to know where she is.

32

His phone jingles in his pocket. He takes it out, looks briefly at the screen. A text from Shug Francis. Greig puts it back in his pocket, unread. Standing outside a newsagent's, waiting for his colleague to come out with a bottle of water. Walking the beat. Reassuring the public. Utterly tedious. Largely pointless. Catching criminals whilst walking the beat is very rare. Being in the car, you get the call and you're there that much faster. You have a better chance of actually catching criminals. This is just a way of being uselessly visible, letting the public see your pretty face.

His colleague comes out, hands him a bottle. Surprisingly warm day. Busy Saturday afternoon. The shops are busy; it reassures the owners to see you popping in and out. Stops them complaining, that's the main thing. Walking along the street, not saying much. Not on the beat with young Matheson today. They've given Greig an older cop to work with, which seems pointless. A cynical guy, obviously bored with his job. Doesn't seem to treat it with a lot of respect. Needs to realize that this is a vocation. He won't last much longer. Mind you, he's lasted long enough already. Amazing how some people hang on.

Plod through the day. Hot and dull. Nothing happening. No big incidents, nothing of much note. Hot Saturday, though, so there'll be a lot of unpleasant work for the nightshift. People drinking all day in the heat. People falling over, falling off things. People knocking each other down. Men trying to impress women by knocking lumps out of each other. Men trying to have their own way and knocking lumps out of women. Lot of ugly domestics on a night like this. Greig hates domestics. Tricky business. Better avoided. He's glad when the shift's ending and they can wander back towards the station. Out of the uniform, into a T-shirt. Maybe go for a drink before he goes home? Nah, better go home, check that text.

Into the flat. He has a casual girlfriend, but it's very casual. Hasn't spoken to her for a few days. That's how his relationships go, and it's how he likes them. It's always been that way. He needs space—he feels everyone does. That's where relationships go wrong, when someone intrudes on the space of the other. No desire for marriage, no desire for children. Love the job. Enjoy the life. Don't spoil it. Don't let others spoil it. Well, that's obviously harder to do. It's that thought that leads him to take his mobile phone out of his pocket and look at the text.

Come round and see me when you can. That's all it says. Innocuous, you would think. Greig knows better. He knows that Shug doesn't ask him to pay a visit unless it's urgent. He wants Greig to come and see him as soon as he gets the message. Greig texts back. *Just finished shift, still want me to come round?* He hopes not. It might have been urgent in the afternoon, but not important now. Better always to try and keep your distance. Doesn't matter how good you are at this sort of thing—you don't want to be seen too often in the company of people like Shug. The phone gives a little rumble. He checks the text. *Yes* is all it says.

He hates visiting Shug. Hates visiting anyone in the business. They ought to know better than to ask him. His relationships with people inside the criminal industry are important. They help him to be a better copper. People find it hard to get their heads round that. They think that no cop can have any relationship with any crook. Not true. Knowing them makes it easier to know who's up to what. His relationships with career criminals have brought him a wealth of information that he has often put to good use. Those relationships have resulted in some very serious criminals being put behind bars, but there are some who don't want to admit that. Some, like that stuck-up prick Fisher, want to believe that policing means there must always be a 'them and us' attitude.

People think Shug is a nice guy. Everyone who knows him considers him a harmless and charming character. Obsessed with cars. Obsessed with them. Loves racing them. Loves fixing them up. Seen as a wee bit of a crank. There are some who genuinely think he's only in the business because of the cars. He has a string of garages, all round the city. People steal cars, take them to the garage. They get resprayed. They get retagged. All distinguishing marks—like the engine block number—are filed down and removed. A false service history is created. The car is then driven south and sold across the border somewhere. Doesn't do it too often. Not enough to raise undue interest. Not enough ever to be a crime wave. Shug's smart about it. The best car man in the city.

But he's smart. People forget that. People think of him as a harmless geek and forget what he's actually doing. He's running a lucrative business within the criminal industry. He's been running it for more than a decade, since he was in his mid-twenties. It takes a smart man to start that young and last this long. It takes a ruthless man to ensure that he has no competition. People think Shug has no competition because others think it's too hard to set up and run a car ring. There's some truth in that. It's a tough thing to do these days, car security being so good. Others have been tempted, though. Money to be made, and only one competitor in the market.

That's where Shug's reputation has served him well. Nice guy. Charming geek. Hard to imagine him doing anything worse than nicking the occasional car. His people don't use violence. They steal cars—that's it. They don't car-jack. They do no harm. Except to people who try to muscle in on their business. They've driven people out of the city. Out of the industry. They've used some tough cookies to do the work for them. Violent work. Ruthless. As soon as he knows you're making moves on his patch, Shug sends people round to wipe you out. Greig's not sure if he's ever had anyone killed—doesn't think so. Wouldn't put it past him, though.

172

Greig turns a blind eye and a deaf ear to these things. Shug is one of the criminals that the city needs. The least of all available evils. If others get involved in the car racket, then they might get ambitious, might start using violence. People break into houses just to get the car keys these days. That's something to be avoided. Only tends to happen here with opportunists: burglars who stumble across the keys, or junkies getting desperate. Shug keeps things simple, reduces the amount of work that the police have to do. It's crime management. It's why Greig is involved with people like Shug. No violence. Keep the number of stolen cars down. People are insured. It could be worse. That's the point. It could be a lot worse.

Greig pulls up outside the large house that Shug owns. A big double garage. It has two cars inside it, another two on the driveway. His network of garages creates the kind of credible front that allows him to live a good life without questions being asked. Greig parks his Mondeo on the street and feels rather insignificant. He doesn't know a lot about cars, but the two on the driveway are both worth good money. One is a BMW M5, the other one he thinks is a TVR Tuscan. He knows Shug has a Ferrari California, but it's obviously in the garage. The most expensive two get the protection of the garage. He walks to the door and rings the bell.

The door is answered by one of Shug's mates. There's a bunch of them that hang around with him, and have done since they were at school. They were all petrol-heads together, and have been together since they were teenagers. Now they all help in the business. A close-knit group. Close enough to treat like family, to trust like family. It's what makes Shug's operation so strong. The chubby bearded fellow—the stereotype of a car nerd—nods for him to come in. There's no conversation; the man knows this is business. Greig follows him into the house. Expensive, nice place. The garage is Shug's; the house is his wife's. She too has expensive taste. Nice, kindly woman, apparently. Another boost for his image.

He's led through to what's been previously called Shug's office. It's a loose term. Maybe some work is done in there, but it looks a lot more like a large playroom to Greig. He's said that to Shug before, and got a loud laugh in reply. Shug's full of laughs. Doesn't take anything too seriously. He admits it. His kids have a playroom, so why shouldn't he?

'Paul, come in, take a seat,' Shug's saying, on his feet and offering a hand. Always friendly. Always on first-name terms.

'What's up?' Greig's asking. Time to get down to business. No messing around; not here to be friends.

There are two other men in the room with Shug, plus the friend that led Greig in. Shug nods and two of them leave the room. Now it's Greig facing Shug and his right-hand man. David Waters, known to everyone as Fizzy. Another jolly fellow. Another with a tough core. Those two are sitting on a leather couch against one wall, with Greig in a swivel chair opposite. It feels relaxed, as it's supposed to. But he wouldn't be there if they were relaxed. A criminal doesn't invite a cop to his home if he's feeling relaxed about life.

'I wanted to ask you about a crime that

174

happened yesterday sometime,' Shug's saying to him. 'A friend of mine. I'm a wee bit upset about it.'

The Winter hit leaps immediately to the front of Greig's mind, but he pushes it back. Implausible. Nothing to do with Shug. Must be something more innocuous. Something that Greig isn't aware of, flown under his radar. That happens a lot. What look like little crimes to a guy like Greig feel like something big to a guy like Shug.

'Lewis Winter was shot dead in his house,' Shug's saying, and Greig is struggling to hide his surprise. 'Looks like a professional job. What do you know of it?' It's asked with a tone filled with innocence. A friend asking about a friend. Asking a cop that he doesn't think has anything to do with it.

How much does Shug know? Why does he care? Does he know that Greig was first on the scene? Might do, if he has another cop on his books. What does that matter? Why should he care a damn? Is Shug trying to muscle in on getting a share of the Winter estate? No. No way. That ain't Shug. He doesn't push his luck. Not ever. He doesn't muscle in on areas that don't concern him. Never been involved in a crime beyond the car ring. Something to do with Zara Cope? Nah, not that, either. He's a loyal husband, everyone knows that. Gives a wide berth to all those cheap temptations. So what?

'I didn't know you knew Lewis Winter,' Greig's saying to him. It's the only way—go straight for an answer. Normally he wouldn't, but he has a deal with Cope and he doesn't want it falling apart because of Shug. He's asking awkward questions only because there's money in it for him.

175

'I knew him,' Shug is saying. Not happy to be asked, but not surprised. 'Wouldn't say I knew him well, but I knew him a wee bit. Heard he got hit by a pro. I'm concerned about it. I feel like I need a wee bit more detail on the subject.'

Greig's nodding along. Fair enough. You know a guy, he gets hit, you ask a few questions. But you don't send everyone but your right-hand man out of the room. You don't drag a cop round to your house at the first opportunity.

'He was hit by a pro,' Greig's saying, 'no doubt about that. Textbook. Very well done. I doubt they'll catch the guys who did it. Guy leading the investigation is DI Fisher. Good copper,' he says grudgingly. 'If there's no clue to find, though, you don't catch the guy.'

Shug is nodding. He doesn't know what sort of facial expression he should have. He doesn't know what Greig would expect of him. He goes for poker-face. Give nothing away.

'You said guys? There was more than one?'

Greig's nodding. 'Two-man job. One to keep watch on Winter's girlfriend, the other to do the killing.'

It's turning into a curiously nervous conversation. Each man seems to be trying to hide much from the other. They both know it.

'Do you know much about the case?' Shug is asking him. 'I'd like as much detail as I can get.'

Greig's nodding, playing along. Still unsure what Shug's motives are. 'I know Winter and his girl were out clubbing. They came home. Winter was pissed out of his skull. She dumps him upstairs, goes back down. Two guys kick the door in. They don't say anything, they're well covered up. One

176

goes upstairs and shoots him. He was passed out, they say. Wouldn't have seen it coming. Certainly didn't put up a fight.'

The last question. The one that matters most. 'So, do they have any idea who might have done it? Do they know what it was about?'

Greig's shrugging his shoulders. A little petulance in response to what feels like a stupid question. 'Drugs, obviously. Winter was a dealer. Sooner or later he was going to upset the wrong person. That's how it goes in that business. You're always playing with fire. We're not aware of any other reason that someone might want him dead.' He's pausing. 'Are you?'

Shug's shaking his head. 'No, no. I suppose that's what it probably was.'

Greig's making his way back down the path to his car. Not concerned with looking at the cars in the driveway any more. Concerned with the man who owns them. Why the hell is Shug Francis interested in the death of Lewis Winter? It shouldn't matter. Out of his sphere. Not his problem. But he's making it his problem. You start asking questions about a dead guy, and people start to think you're somehow involved. Shug knows that, Greig's thinking as he gets into his car. He knows that by asking questions he's getting involved in something serious. Something that goes beyond his comfort zone. Greig's driving along the street and a worrying thought is settling in his mind. Shug is involved. Somehow he's involved in the death of a dealer. Either he had him killed, or Winter was killed because of him.

33

Who do you go to? You can't do it all by yourself. You have two bags of drugs that are worth some money, but you must get rid of them. You have to find a buyer quickly, before someone catches you out. The money you put in a bank. You set up a new account. You don't hold onto it, though, that's the worst-case scenario. You can't be found with unexplainable money. So you need help. You need someone else to go to the bank and set up the account for you. You need someone else to take the drugs off your hands. The police won't be far away. They'll stay close for some time. They'll want to speak to you regularly, every time they turn up a new piece of evidence.

Sitting in a strange flat. Looking at a bleak future. Picking out the people who could help. Zara knows people. She hasn't spent so long hanging around these men without knowing who matters. She could go to someone near the top of the tree. A big mover. They could give her protection, but what does she have to offer them? Herself? No, she's not offering, and she's realistic enough to know it wouldn't be enough. They're not going to risk getting involved in a murder case just for her. The drugs aren't worth enough for them. The information about Lewis and his contacts that she could give them wouldn't be worth enough. It has to be someone more easily impressed.

There are many of them. The industry is full of the impressionable, the deluded and the easily led.

It's never hard to find someone willing to take a risk. A pretty girl, the chance of making some money—there are plenty of men who would be suckered by that. Stewart? No, has to be someone inside the business. He took the drugs and cash, but that was then. He needed to get out of the house to protect himself. Selfish. She was standing naked in front of him. Easily led. He's a last resort. It would be easy if it were him. An innocent mind. A blank canvas. Perhaps. Just perhaps.

Someone in the business. Someone who would know how to handle this. Two people spring to mind. Two people she knows would help. Each sends a shiver through her, but for different reasons. One is Marty Jones. A pimp. A loan shark. A scumbag of the very lowest order. He's sniffed around her a couple of times in the past. He'd have no problem handling the cash and the drugs. He's well connected. Does a lot of work for Peter Jamieson. The prospect of working with him is sickening. She knows what he would want in exchange. Maybe worse than that. Maybe worse than just sleeping with him. He sends a lot of women into the world of prostitution. High-class parties for rich arseholes. Good women. Women who had no intention of falling into so dark a world. No, the price would be much too high.

The other option is scarcely more appealing. Nate. Nate Colgan. The father of her child. The man with whom she spent years of her life. A man she loved, to a point. A man she feared in the extreme. He never hit her. Not once. He just hit everyone else instead. A cold man of terrifying brutality. He seemed emotionally dead so much of the time they were together. Just glimmers that there was a human heart in there. A practical man. He gets things done. That's why so many people hire him. But they're all afraid of him too. That's why he never lasts anywhere. Why no relationship he's ever had has lasted. He fears himself. He never said it, he would never be that open, but she saw it in him. He fears what he might do, and what he might do to someone he loves.

It has to be Nate. She knows that he'll help. He won't ask for anything in return. She's given him a daughter he loves and visits every weekend. That buys her the help she needs. She's asked nothing of him until now.

Getting the shoebox. Out of the flat. Along the road to the bus stop at the corner. Taking the bus to the east end. Funny how people drift apart. For so long she had been afraid of splitting with Nate. Afraid of his reaction. But he had known it was time. He accepted it. She had thought he would try to keep in touch, try to win her back. But no, that hadn't happened, either. He had let her go. Almost as if he didn't much care any more.

Now she's going to him for help. As she walks up the path to the door of his terraced house, in an ugly part of the city, she's wondering if he'll even want to help. Surely. They have a connection. She's looking at her watch. Nearly ten o'clock at night. It's dark. There's the familiar noise of kids shouting in the distance. He might not be at home. There's no doorbell that she can see, so she knocks. She waits. Nervous. Wishing she'd made more effort with her appearance. Would that matter? It's not as though she has anything he hasn't seen before. What if he has a girlfriend? She has no idea. He might have a woman in there with him. She knocks on the door again. This is feeling like a bad idea. The idea of manipulating Stewart to help suddenly appeals more. A harmless character. A decent human being. He likes her. He revelled in the occasion. He could be persuaded. A light comes on. The door opens.

Nate's standing there, looking back at her. That stern face. Handsome, but never inviting. His expression doesn't change when he sees that it's her. Is he happy to see her? Who could guess from that look in his eye? Just looking at her, as if he's judging her.

'Hi, Nate, it's me, Zara.' She says it with a giggle. That's nerves, not flirting. He's not susceptible to flirts, and she knows it.

He nods his head. 'You'd better come in,' he says and steps aside. It's funny, he looks the same as ever, but he sounds older. He'll be thirty-five now. He always had the blunt, dark and slightly lined look of a man in his early forties. A man of the world. A man who knows things worth knowing. His voice is a little gruffer now. More strained.

Into the house. Into the living room. Zara stops. Toys on the floor. A doll's house with little animals in it. A little stable with plastic horses. She looks back at Nate as he follows her into the room.

'I've just put her to bed,' he's saying without concern. It all seems easy to him, but it scares Zara. Would her daughter even recognize her? She doesn't want to find out. 'I've got her for the weekend. Your parents are on holiday. Lake District. Back on Monday.'

'I didn't know,' Zara's saying hurriedly, letting him know that she's not here to see the child.

'I didn't imagine that you did,' he says, and she

181

spots that familiar edge to his tone.

He's a very intelligent man. Reads books in his spare time. She always thought him an intellectual. Speaks very well for a man of his background too. All that adds to the sense of intimidation that he provides. He nods to a chair, an instruction to sit. He does the same.

'I heard about Winter,' he's saying. He's keeping his voice down, doesn't want his little girl woken for no good reason.

'Word travels fast round here,' she's saying with a sigh.

'It does.' He says nothing else. He's putting all the pressure on her. He has an idea of why she might be here, but he doesn't see why he should make it easy for her. Let her explain things. Let her do the hard work.

She's usually so confident. Even when she's not, she's usually so good at faking it. She's looking at Nate and wondering why she can't manage to fake it now. She used to be able to, even with him. So what's changed? It's because he doesn't care. When they each cared about the other, she could control him. Not any more. Time has taken him outside her reach.

'I'm in a wee bit of a corner,' she's saying. 'I don't know what's going to happen to the house and the money Lewis had. I won't get it soon, if I get it at all. I have some things,' she's saying, and she pats the large handbag on her knees. 'Some cash. Some . . . merchandise. I need help with it. I need help from someone I can trust. Otherwise I have nothing to live on.'

He's sitting and listening to her, but he's not reacting. There's no change in his expression.

Nothing. It's as if he wants to make her suffer. Does he even know how to behave properly with people any more? So much time spent intimidating.

'You want me to set up an account, sell the drugs, put the money in the account.' Not a question, a statement of fact.

'Yes. I need your help with this.'

'You have no one else who can help you?'

'No,' she says in a whisper. She knows he's not asking in order to humiliate her. He's asking her because he'd rather she turned to someone else.

Zara sits and waits for him to say something. She thinks Nate wants her to go somewhere else because he doesn't care about her. She's wrong. Very wrong. He wants her to go somewhere else because he does care about her. He still loves her. He assumes that he always will. But she's bad news. Not for him; he can handle her and, indeed, far worse demons than her. But she's bad for Rebecca, their daughter. His first responsibility is to her. If Zara comes back into his life, then she comes back into Becca's as well. He doesn't want that. He wants better for his little girl. But he can't just leave Zara to the wolves. There are so many people in this business who could take advantage of her, if he doesn't help.

'What have you got?' he's asking her, leaning forward to see.

Zara takes the shoebox out of her bag and opens it. Two wads of cash, two plastic bags. Coke and methamphetamines. She places them on the coffee table.

He's looking, and nodding his head. 'Okay. Leave it with me. I'll set up an account on Monday morning. Get the money safe, as quick as possible. The rest will take longer. I'll find someone safe to sell it through. You won't get full value, not for a one-off provision. You'll do all right out of it, though.'

She's nodding enthusiastically. 'I get that, but anything would help. Right now I've got next to nothing, so . . .' She trails off in a shrugging embarrassment.

There's a moment of silence. As far as Nate is concerned, this meeting is over.

'When will I?' she says, pointing to the coffee table.

He shrugs. 'Say, a week Monday. Come round then and I'll let you know how it's gone. You might want to leave the money in the account for a couple of months, until you can be sure the cops aren't watching you. Aren't watching the account, either.'

'I don't think they are watching me. I'm a witness. I'm not a suspect.'

Nate looks at her. There's a little hint of disgust in his expression, but only a hint. 'You're the girlfriend of a dead drug dealer. They will be watching you. You know things they want to know, and they'll keep watching you until they know they can't get anything from you.'

He's showing her to the door, giving every impression of a man fed up of her company. When he closes the door behind her, she finds herself out in the front garden, unsure of how she feels. She's glad to have his help, but his warning rings in her ears. The police will be watching you. The spectre of DI Fisher looms somewhere in the city, and she has a horrible feeling that she's not going to be able to shake him off. Nate knows these things. As Nate closes the door he pauses. Zara, back in his life. Help her, and then let her go. She's so entirely selfish; once she's been helped, she'll be gone again. Keep her away from Becca.

34

Phoning round taxi firms, finding out who was working the club on Friday night. It feels like plod's work. It's being in the office that does it. Fisher hates being in there. Some detectives love it. Some hide away in the office, scared of going out among the people. Clinging on by their fingernails. Desperately hoping to survive until retirement and pension. How they made it this far, he cannot fathom.

First couple of calls draw a blank. Third call, and success. Yes, they had a couple of people working that area. Yes, they regularly do. Yes, they can give him the numbers of the two drivers who might have carried those passengers.

Half eight in the evening. Neither driver is apparently working tonight. Fisher calls the first. Gets a grumpy reception. Would rather be doing this face-to-face, but he needs to find the right person first. Fellow says no, he doesn't remember picking up a young couple and an older man. Goes off on a rant about a fat woman being sick in the back of his car, and a young couple behaving like animals. Feral scum, he's saying, and then something about not having any shame. The police need to do something about it. Fisher hangs up.

185

His patience with people who aren't useful only goes so far. He rings the second man. Better reception. More polite.

'I'm looking for the driver that picked up a young couple and an older man from the front door of Heavenly at about twelve forty-five.'

There's a pause, the cogs are turning. 'Yeah, I think I remember that. Yeah, I think that was my pickup. The older guy was out on his feet, the other two weren't so bad.'

'I'm glad I've caught up with you. When can you come into the station to have a word with me about them? You see, they were involved in a crime not long after you dropped them off, so I'd like to chat about them. It shouldn't take long.'

Another pause. People are always reluctant to get involved, even when they've done nothing wrong and they know they can help. 'I suppose tomorrow. Any time after four tomorrow.'

Fisher arranges it. That's for tomorrow. What about tonight? Find the cop who was looking after Cope and kick her right up the arse. He was sure Cope had suggested that she wasn't going to go back to the house. She had left the station and gone off the radar. The useless plod had said that Cope was planning to go back to the house in the next few days. Bollocks! Now he has to find Cope. Time to put her under a little pressure. Catch her while she's still feeling the nerves of the incident. She's a liar. It's just a question of what she's lying about. No progress on an ID for the younger man, either. People looking into that. Find out if he's in the industry. Find out if he's a potential killer.

A stroke of luck. Putting out calls to a few contacts working in hotels didn't throw up

186

anything, but the first call to a rental agent hits the target. Magnificent. Cope's taken a little flat in the west end. Nice place, cash up front. So she's got a little bit of money from somewhere after all. Easy to find her. Get out of the station. A chance to get some almost-fresh air. Out into the city, onto the street, where police work should be done. He's falling into an idealistic mood as he gets into his car and pulls away from the station. Found the taxi driver. Found Zara Cope. Two little strokes of luck, just need a third to get the young man. And Zara can provide us with that.

After a fashion, he finds the flat. Hidden away, built-up area. Nice little street, though. Small flat, but respectable enough to command a respectable price. He's knocking on the door. Nothing. He rings the doorbell, waits thirty seconds. Still nothing. So he's knocking on the door again. There's no sound coming from the flat, no sign that there's anyone at home. The poor little wretch, with no money and no one to turn to, suddenly has money and places to go. Don't jump to conclusions. That's reckless. That's what gets good coppers into trouble. No assumptions.

She made it sound like she would struggle to find help, but she still has family and presumably some friends. There was one friend at the house before they went to the club. So someone could easily help her out with cash. Her parents are alive and looking after her kid. There's the father of the kid. Nate Colgan. Apparently they're not in touch any more. Shame. Fisher would love to be able to take Colgan on with something concrete. Get that evil bastard behind bars, where he belongs. One day. For now, it's time to set a little test for

187

Miss Cope.

Knocking on the neighbour's front door. Wait thirty seconds. The door opens. A suspicious old woman looks out. Excellent, just what he was hoping for. Some gossipy old biddy who'll make a big deal out of everything.

'Excuse me, dear, my name is DI Fisher, Strathclyde Police. I'm looking for the young woman who's just moved in next door. Do you know if she's in?'

'I don't. I don't. Is she in trouble?' she's asking, and her eyes are getting a little wider. A bit of scandal. A lovely bit of juicy scandal to tell the world about.

'Not necessarily, no. But can you do me a favour? When you see her, let her know that I was round.'

'I will,' the old lady's saying as Fisher is turning away and going back down the stairs.

That old crow will spend the rest of the night with her ear pressed up against the inside of her front door, waiting to hear her new neighbour come home. She'll be out there talking to her, first chance she gets. That'll let Cope know that she's been found. Then it'll be interesting to see how she reacts to that. Does she run? Does she feel the breath of the law on the back of her neck and flee the flat? It would prove that she has a lot to hide. Maybe she sticks around and waits to see what happens next. Tries to bluff it out. Her sort often do. Think they can get away with just about anything. Not this time, love. This time you're going to pay the price for your misdeeds.

35

It feels distant already. It feels as though the precise details are fading in his memory, to be replaced with an overview. It doesn't matter. Calum's never going to tell anyone the story of what happened. The only people who might ask would be Jamieson and Young, but they won't. They know better. There are some in the business who tell their employers every last detail. There are some employers who want to know everything. That won't happen here. Too much professionalism. All Jamieson and Young want to know is that it was done, and done well. They want to know that it won't come back on them. If they know that, they're happy.

A quick shower, then breakfast. Something heavier today. Feeling like normal already. Amazing how quickly normality intrudes. Used to take many days to fight down the nerves, but not any more. Now it's hours. Soon there won't be any at all. Is that a good thing? Probably not, he's reflecting as he works in the kitchen—probably better to have a little edge. Once you think you've got nothing to be worried about, you slip up. No taking it easy. Stay alert. He remembers talking to Frank, more than a year ago now. Frank told him that even now he gets nervous before a job. If he didn't, he would quit.

You quit when you stop feeling nervous, because you're no longer able to work out the risks. Happens to people. You become blasé. It's a job. You go to work and you do it and you don't even consider the risks any more. That's downright dangerous. There's another problem, though. You get older. You become more aware of your mortality. You become more concerned about the things you're missing out on. Suddenly you're not nervous, you're just scared. Then you definitely stop. Then you're going to make a multitude of mistakes that are going to cost you your life. But a deadening of nerves seems more likely to Calum. He's never been truly scared on a job.

Sitting at the breakfast table, reading a Sunday newspaper. Flicking through it, looking for the one story that matters. There it is. A little sidebar. No pictures, no big headlines. Man murdered in Glasgow. Killed in his own home. Lewis Winter, forty-four. Killed after a night out. Police looking for information. Suspected links to organized crime. And that's about the sum of it. Winter's life and death, reduced to a little side column on page twenty-three. Maybe a hundred words. It's not much to call a life.

It reassures Calum. The mention of organized crime is just there to reassure the public. It's drug dealers killing drug dealers, so you have nothing to worry about. Most people will read it and think: who cares? The world's better off without him. Let them all kill each other. The only people who'll be terribly concerned will be the people living on his street. For everyone else, it's one less scumbag in the world. No description of who carried it out. Most likely because they don't have one. Certainly nothing reliable. The naked guy wouldn't have been able to give a description anyway. Cope might have—she was calmer. But even so, they took every precaution.

190

He's feeling good about what he's read. A standard piece about a drug dealer being killed. The police with no specific requests for information. No descriptions issued. He'd be more concerned if there hadn't been anything at all in the papers. They would be holding back information for a reason. That would be unsettling. So far, so textbook. Still, he must be cautious. Sit about the flat, doing nothing that he wouldn't ordinarily do. Keeping an appropriate distance from the people that matter. A boring consequence of the job. Into the living room, sitting down in front of the TV, letting time die around him.

It's the afternoon when the phone rings. Mute-button on the TV remote, picks up the phone.

'Hello.'

'Hi, Calum, it's Glen Davidson—long time no speak.'

Alarm bells are going off all over the place. Loud and constant. Why the hell is Glen Davidson calling him? Glen Davidson is a gunman. Freelance. Kills, and often kills rough. Good at covering his tracks, but a nasty bastard. He's been lucky to stay out of jail. Big fellow, been around the business since he was a kid, because of his father. It's the family trade. Calum's crossed paths with him a couple of times, knows him to say hello to, but nothing more than that. They've never done a job together. Calum wouldn't want to do a job with him. Not trustworthy.

He's paused longer than he should have. 'Glen, how are you?'

'Not bad, not bad. Keeping the wolves from the door, you know how it is. How's tricks with you?'

Weird to hear him being so chummy, like they're pals. Calum's remembering all the stories he's heard about Davidson. About his temper. That woman he put in hospital. Someone said that a girlfriend got pregnant and he punched it out of her. Might not be true. No evidence. He's the kind of gorilla that these stories attach themselves to.

'Same old, same old. What can I do for you?'

In other words, say something to justify phoning me. Piss or get off the pot. This is becoming a nervous call, and Calum doesn't like that.

'Are you keeping busy?' Davidson asks.

Calum pauses. An offer of work? Why would Glen Davidson be looking for someone else for a job? Maybe to go along as partner, but he wouldn't look to Calum as a first port of call for that.

'Run off my feet,' Calum's saying. 'Haven't got a spare minute in the day.'

'I hear that. I'll leave you to it. We should go out for a drink sometime, in the future.'

'Sure thing,' Calum's saying, knowing it'll never happen.

Now he's pacing around the flat, thinking about the call. Paranoia is a terrible thing, but it doesn't mean they're not out to get you. In this business, paranoia has been known to be a lifesaver. Glen-bloody-Davidson. It's worth being nervous about strange phone calls from him. Worth being nervous about him at any time. The TV's still on mute. The F1 cars are going round in their merry circles in silence. The rest of the world has ceased to exist for Calum. It's now shrunk to a size just big enough to fit him and Glen Davidson.

Look back through your history. Have you done any work with Davidson or anything that might step on his toes? No, never. Always kept a safe distance. You always keep distance from other gunmen. You don't get in their way, they don't get in yours. Unwritten rule. Maybe he wanted you to help him on a two-man job. You have a good reputation amongst other gunmen. They know you can do the job. They know you can be trusted. No, not likely. There are so many other people Davidson would turn to first. One of them would have said yes before he got to Calum. Davidson's been in the business long enough to have better options than Calum.

There's that one horrible, ugly, looming possibility. He was laying down a little test for you. He wants to know if you've done any job recently. He thinks you might have been behind a job and he wants to find out for sure. It could only be Winter. What reason would that ape have for investigating Winter's death? They weren't working together, as far as you know. Or maybe they were. Maybe they were working for the same person. Maybe this person that Jamieson hinted was planning to work with Winter has found out. This person employs Davidson. Dear Mr Davidson, please find out which of the people in your business hit Mr Winter. Then what? Do they just want a name? They might want revenge. They might want to send a message to Jamieson.

So what do you do, hotshot? The temptation is to rush and tell Young or Jamieson. They'll need to know eventually. Not yet. You don't know anything yet. All you know is that Davidson called you. You don't know why. Don't leap headlong into assumptions. Never clever. Don't contact them until you need to. You're putting two and two

193

together and coming up with a range of numbers. It might be innocent; it could be that Davidson's looking to make new connections. People do that. They call you up out of the blue because they think they might want to use you in the future. He might be trying to position himself. Maybe make himself look important by working with as many other gunmen as possible. It might be that he wants to get close to Jamieson. People can see that he's the coming man, so they want to work for him. Davidson knows you've worked for Jamieson in the past, so maybe he knows that you're working for him again.

It may be that he's on the way round to kill you. He calls you up and works out that you've recently done a job. He knows that you're at home. He's going to guess that a pro of your quality won't have a weapon in the flat. He knows you live alone. Easy target. A fast answer to Jamieson. We stepped on your toes. You killed our man. Look how quickly we killed yours. Impressive, aren't we? Found out who did it and killed him off, inside a couple of days. This is what you're up against, big fellow. You're up against people who know how to get the job done.

Most gunmen wouldn't want to rush a job like that, but sometimes you don't have a choice. Sometimes you go where you're told because the alternative is no job at all. Sometimes the alternative is worse than that. So you go and you rush it, and you make the best of the circumstances you encounter. You don't enjoy it, but that's how it has to happen. Sometimes it's the only way. This might be one of those occasions. For Davidson's employers to make the best impact on Jamieson, they'll want you dead as soon as possible. Calum's over at the window, looking out into the street. Just like one of those pathetic old lags who have been in and out of jail, living on their nerves, terrified of every sound and shadow.

Wait. Pause. Think about this a second. Does the person employing Davidson even want a war with Jamieson? Maybe not. Maybe they want a good patch to sell gear on—everyone does—but that doesn't mean they want a war. You get people who invade another person's patch only because they think they can get away with it. They think the guy they're pissing off won't bother fighting back. Too much effort. Too much risk. Bigger fish to fry. People try their luck and fail. Jamieson hits Winter to send out the message. The message is learned and the people back off. Then why have Davidson call you up at all? Damn, can't get away from that.

It's scary and nervy because it's unexpected. They should have warned him that this could happen. They should have said what level of threat this job carried. Maybe they didn't know. It wasn't entirely obvious that they even knew who Winter was planning to work with. Stop pacing the flat, for God's sake, you're tiring yourself out. Sit down, calm down and think rationally. You need to get a message to Jamieson somehow, let them know that they ought to be concerned. You find an indirect route, let them know, and then see how it plays out. You stay vigilant, but you don't do anything stupid.

36

He presses the button on his mobile to hang up and looks across the room. 'Yeah, it was him all right. No doubt. Thought it would be. I'll bet Frank MacLeod recommended him for it. He's always thought the sun shined out of that boy's arse.'

Shug, sitting on the couch in his den, nods his head. 'Okay, so we go after this MacLean. I want it done quick. I want people to know it got done quick.'

Davidson is shrugging. 'Sure. I can do it tonight—makes no difference.' He's pausing; there's something else he wants to say. He's picking his words because this is virgin territory for him. Shug's new to this, might not know how it works. But he's got money, and he could be a regular employer, doesn't have a gunman of his own. Guide him through it, carefully. 'Thing about MacLean is, he's always been freelance. If he's still freelance, then hitting him isn't going to harm Jamieson, you know.'

Shug and his right-hand man Fizzy are the only others in the room. Fizzy's said almost nothing beyond hello. Shug's watching Davidson, nodding in the right places, seeming like he's taking the advice on board.

'You don't think we should go after MacLean?' Shug's asking.

'That ain't what I'm saying,' Davidson is saying sharply. He's in danger of talking himself out of a job here. That won't do at all. 'No, no, I'm just saying if he's freelance, then you can't expect

Jamieson to fall apart over it. But he might not be freelance. Might be on a short-term contract sort of thing. What with old Frank being out of commission. I bet Frank picked MacLean as his replacement. You get rid of MacLean, and that's Jamieson down to third choice. Does make him look weak, like he can't hold onto a good thing.'

Shug's still nodding in all the right places. He's noted how quickly Davidson changed his tune when the possibility of losing the job came along. All about the money. No friendship here. No bond. Not someone he's ever going to feel comfortable working with. Fizzy was right, they should have found someone they liked and trusted and taken them on full-time. Too late now. They need to act quickly, and Davidson is the best option available at short notice.

'You can do it tonight?'

'Sure,' Davidson is shrugging, making every effort to look nonchalant. 'I'll be keeping it as simple as possible—nothing too clever. Get in, get him dead, get out. Shouldn't be too tough. Just need to make sure he's at home first.'

It's a lesson. Getting the right people is important for every job, even if it's just a one-off. You don't just grab the easiest available person; you plan ahead so that you have access to the best when you need them. They'll get better at it, with experience. Jamieson had Frank MacLeod for many years, and when Frank wasn't available, he knew immediately who to go for. The benefit of being an insider. In the future they'll research it better, get a better option than Davidson. They'll be insiders too.

'So you know how you'll do it?'

'Oh, aye,' Davidson says, hinting that it's a stupid question. 'Break the lock, get in fast, catch him in his bed. I'll go about two in the morning. I'll use a knife. Quieter. With any luck, nobody will find him until late tomorrow, maybe later than that. As long as I get away unseen.'

It's a spur-of-the-moment decision. Davidson will hate it, Fizzy too, but Shug can see he wants the money. Lead him into it. He'll reluctantly accept.

'You know this MacLean at all?'

'A bit,' Davidson's saying, and there's a sneering look on his face. 'Don't think much of him. I mean, I'm sure he's good at the job, but he's a stuck-up little prick. Met him a couple of times, hardly said a word, behaved like he was better than me. That's his way. Supposed to be a quiet little smartarse. A lot of people like that in a gunman, someone with no mouth. Fair enough, I can see why they would. Makes him seem a safer bet. Means he's hardly got any friends in the business, though,' Davidson's saying, enjoying the sound of his own voice. 'That's one thing you don't have to worry about. Won't be a queue of people wanting revenge.'

He's stopped talking now that he realizes how long he's gone on. Shug saying nothing. Looking across at him, a thoughtful look on his friendly face.

'I want Fizzy to go with you,' he's saying out of nothing.

Davidson's shocked, but he does a respectable job of hiding it. Fizzy, on the other hand, doesn't. He's turned his head and half-raised a hand before he controls himself, but at least he hasn't said anything.

'You sure that's wise?' Davidson's asking, keeping it friendly. 'I'm guessing he doesn't have a lot of experience at this. To be honest, I don't have much experience of working with a spare wheel.' There's a patronizing tone in there. Shug hasn't done things like this before, so he needs to be told. It's to be expected that he should make a few little misjudgements; he just needs to be steered right.

There's a little smile running across Shug's face. Davidson's seen it before in others. It's a smile that says I'm right and you're wrong, and even if I'm wrong, you're going to agree with me.

'I'm not saying that he should go in with you, not at all. He picks you up, drives you to MacLean. You won't find a better driver than Fizzy anywhere. You go in and do the job. Fizzy drives you back to wherever you want to go. It would make me feel more comfortable. It would make the whole situation a little clearer to me. Give me a better understanding. I know it's unconventional, but I don't think it'll be any problem, will it?'

It's a question that demands a quick answer. 'No, I guess not,' Davidson's saying. They both know it's because Shug doesn't trust him. It's an unpleasant start to a relationship.

First thing, kill MacLean. Easy enough. Just a kid. Might be good at the job, but he doesn't have Davidson's experience. Killing him is the easy bit. The aftermath will be more difficult. Jamieson will want to be seen getting revenge. That scheming bastard John Young will come up with something. That's who Shug should be going after. Stop pissing about further down the food chain and go for the right-hand man. That would make Jamieson look vulnerable. Instead, it's a short-term replacement for Frank MacLeod. And when Frank gets back, guess who his number-one target will be. That's the bit to worry about. Frank is still one dangerous hombre. Shug could be worth it, though. Take Jamieson's patch, build on it, watch the money roll in. Could be very lucrative.

Out of the house, back in his own car. Cursing Shug Francis. This could be so much easier if Shug would listen to good advice when he got it. But no, he has to be like all the others. He has to be the boss, and only his opinion is allowed to matter. Whoever heard of the boss's right-hand man going along on a job? It's a bloody embarrassment, that's what it is. As long as Fizzy stays in the car, doesn't get in the way. As long as he doesn't drive off without Davidson and leave him stranded. No reason why he would, but you don't trust easily in this business. If he's going to make money out of Shug in the future, then he's going to have to earn his trust, get pally with him. Boring.

37

The taxi driver is a fucking idiot. Knows nothing. He can remember picking them up and dropping them off, but it seems like he's the only person in the world who drives with his eyes shut. He's obviously bullshitting. Fisher struggles to keep his patience in check. The guy knows that a serious crime has happened, that it's to do with the underworld. He's keeping his mouth shut, in case he says anything that gets him called as a witness. Nobody wants to be seen going into court to act as a witness against gangland people. Fear of reprisals. People keep their mouths shut even when they might hold the key to a case.

Chances are the taxi driver didn't see anything. Pros like these gunmen wouldn't have done anything that might draw the attention of the taxi driver and his cab's occupants, but still, you hope. One interesting thing he does say—and even that's largely by accident—is that the young couple seemed very much a couple. It hadn't occurred to the driver that they were anything else. They were close. They were together. They didn't seem, Fisher gleans from the conversation, like the sort of couple who would break apart at the front door. Seems like Cope had found herself a little playmate, someone more energetic than her usual decrepit partner. The other thing the driver says was that, as expected, the older guy looked pretty smashed. Didn't look like he could stand up by himself. A few pieces of ammo to throw at Cope.

The plod who had been looking after Cope comes upstairs to see him. She knows that Fisher is in a monstrous mood with her, but that's frequent and expected. She's convinced she has done nothing wrong, and she's sure that she now has the ammunition to prove it.

'Zara Cope called the station, looking for me,' she says, just a little smugly. 'Wanted me to know the new address she's taken. Little flat somewhere, away from the scene. Called me up without prompting.'

'No, she didn't,' Fisher's saying as the plod passes a piece of paper across the table with the address on it.

'Excuse me?'

'She was prompted.'

Another visit to her. This time to find out about her little bit on the side. Who the hell was he? She's opening the door of her flat. Minimal make-up. Hair tied back. Simple, casual outfit. Very pretty. But scum. Total scum.

'Nice to see you, Miss Cope. How are you feeling?' Fisher's asking. He hopes she can spot how little he really cares. She's smart. She will.

'About as well as can be expected. Would you like to come in?'

'Please.'

Small flat. Basic furnishings. It looks, and feels, short-term. He's found a place to sit down and he's making himself at home. No need to wait to be invited.

'I want to ask you some questions about the young man you took home with you. I want you to tell me who he is and where I can find him, and I don't want you to lie to me.' He says it sternly, but matter-of-fact. He's not looking for a screaming match here. He's giving her a chance to be straight with him for once. Fisher can't help but feel that he's showing more generosity than her behaviour has earned.

'I don't . . . I don't know what you mean,' she's saying, and she's sitting opposite him in the cramped living room. But she already looks rattled, and she knows it.

'I mean that you lied to me about your relationship with this man. I mean that you know who he is. I mean that I'm fed up of you thinking you can string me along. Do you understand how that makes you look, in the light of what's happened?'

202

This time she really does want to cry. It won't do her any good, though. Quite the reverse, with this hard bastard. Don't give away more than you absolutely have to.

'You've obviously got the wrong end of the stick somewhere, Mr Fisher.'

'DI Fisher, and I know what I've caught a hold of. A liar. You and this young man were practically inside each other's underwear at the nightclub. You went out to the taxi. You didn't just bump into him because he was leaving at the same time you were. You met him in the club, you got close, you invited him home. Hey, I'm not judging you and your old man—whatever you two got up to with consenting adults in your own home is your business—but I hardly . . .'

'How dare you,' she's shouting. 'How dare you speak about Lewis that way. Whatever we got up to? You cheap and nasty bastard.'

Okay, that went too far. Trying to avoid a screaming match, but letting your temper get the better of you. It happens. Now rebuild the bridge and try again.

'Okay,' he's saying to her now, trying to find a tone that sounds contrite. 'I accept that I went too far. It was wrong of me to insult Lewis that way. But you were not honest to me about your relationship with that young man, when we spoke at the station. I've come here to ask you to be honest with me. I don't think it's necessary for us to do this at the station, because I think we can find the right answers without taking it that far. What d'you say? I want you to start again, and tell me everything you can about that young man.'

She's nodding her head. All right, he doesn't

know much, just that they were heavy in the club. You can still talk your way out of this one. 'He was just some guy in the club,' she's saying, talking quietly. 'He came over and we started dancing. He was nice. He was cute. We got close. I'd had a lot to drink. We'd been drinking at the house before we left; I had a few more at the club. I don't . . . I remember leaving. Lewis was really drunk. He helped get Lewis out to the front. I hailed a taxi. This guy got in with us. I didn't invite him, he was just imposing himself. We went back to the house. At the front door I told the guy it wasn't going any further. That was it. I had to persuade him. He didn't like it. He thought he was on a promise. That was it.'

Still lying. Still fucking lying. What is it with this girl? She doesn't seem stupid, but maybe you're misjudging her. Maybe it's your fault, Michael Andrew Fisher. Maybe you overestimated her from the start. Just another dumb slut. Fine, time to shoot her down. He's leaning back in his chair, going for the stern and disapproving look that he does so well.

'So tell me what his name is.'

She's sighing, putting her head in her hands. 'I don't remember. I really don't. I think it was Sean. It was something like that. Sean. I don't remember. I was drunk. He said it in the club. It was loud, and I didn't really care.'

She really is something else. You can see why so many men fall for her, you really can. There's something rather sexy about devious women; it's what makes them so dangerous.

'You dance with this guy for hours. He goes home with you. He thinks he's getting some action.

You turn him away at the door. You don't even know his name.'

'I don't,' she's saying, carefully allowing a little defiance to return to her voice.

'Thing is, I have witnesses saying you and this young man were still acting very much like a couple after you left the club. That you and he were still close.' Okay, that's exaggerating what the taxi driver said, but let's see how she reacts.

'Well, your witnesses are liars. I'm not sure I spoke a word to him from the time we left the club to the time I told him to go home.'

Last throw of the dice. You don't have enough to take her in anyway. You don't even know why she's lying to you. It looks like she might have known what was going to happen, maybe was even involved. No evidence. You might have visited her too early.

'You say you got Winter into the house by yourself?'

'Yes.'

'You got him up the stairs by yourself?'

'Yes.'

'Along the corridor and into the bedroom by yourself?'

'Yes.'

'And yet when he left the club he could hardly stand up. I happen to know that when he reached the house he could hardly stand up.'

'He could stand up. It wasn't easy, I never said that, but I got him to the bed by myself.' Defiance, real and strong.

Leave her. Just leave her. You don't have enough. Not yet. She knows that she's under pressure, though, and you know that she's likely to make a mistake because of that pressure. As soon as she does, you'll be there.

Back to the station. Get a couple of plods up. Going to need a little bit of help finding this guy. Nobody seems to know who he is. Need a couple more bodies to get out on the street and see what we can find. Start by interviewing people at the club. Pick a couple of plods. Bollocks to whoever's due to be on duty tonight. Bollocks to whoever the desk sergeant recommends. You need people you can trust. Get a couple of good coppers. Young, willing to learn to do things the right way.

PC Matheson and PC Higgins standing in front of his desk. They both look like kids, but that seems to be the way of it. Both good young coppers. Both coppers who need to be taken in the right direction. Fisher knows Matheson is the better of the two. He knows that he needs to learn a few good lessons, having probably picked up a multitude of bad ones from that dickhead Greig. He's heard good things about Higgins. Conscientious, decent, a proper copper. It would be nice to have a couple of plods that he can rely on. Call for them whenever he needs the help, and know that they can be trusted. Push them up the ladder.

'Okay, you two; I want your help finding a man in connection with the Winter murder. This is the fellow we're looking for,' he's saying and passing a picture across the desk.

He gives them their instructions. Go to the club, question people. If this guy's been there before, then someone might just recognize him. They're both nodding along, happy to be involved in something on this scale. They know it's an opportunity for them. He tells them they can go now. Matheson turns and walks out of the office with his copy of the picture taken from the CCTV. Higgins stays. He looks nervous.

'Something the matter?' Fisher asks him.

'I was given a tip-off, sir, and I don't know if it relates to this case or not. It might, it might not. I certainly think it's worth passing on.'

'Okay, go on.'

'Shug Francis.'

Fisher pauses. He's sitting in his chair, thinking about the name that's just been thrown at him. He knows who Shug is. Owns a chain of garages. Everyone knows that he moves stolen cars and parts through his garages. He's a crook, but the cost of proving it wouldn't be worth the reward. Tame stuff.

'Shug Francis?'

'I was told,' Higgins is saying nervously, 'that he was moving up in the world. I was told by a contact that he was worth keeping an eye on. At the time I wasn't sure exactly what it was all about, but then this happens. I think, maybe, I was tipped off because people on the street suspected this might happen. I wouldn't trust my contact much— lowlife, but still.'

Fisher is nodding. The boy might be onto something. Shug wants to move into drugs, so he needs to get rid of people like Winter and take over their patch. It's possible. Not the most likely cause, but worth remembering. 'You did right to tell me.'

38

You always get a warm welcome. Everyone is treated as a friend. How much of that warmth is real, only Frank ever knows. He has a policy, though: welcome them in, treat them as friends and listen carefully. Might not sound like much, but it has helped keep him at the top of the game all these years. Everyone who knows what Frank does for a living also knows that he's the best. Well, was the best. He isn't anything any more. Now he's an invalid. Temporary invalid. That's what he keeps telling people. Had his hip done. Coming back stronger and better than ever before. He has to say that. He listens carefully. He can detect the doubt in others.

Calum is ringing the doorbell. He waits a while. How does a cripple answer the door? He doesn't. The lady who's been sent round to clean up for him does. She lets Calum in, without even asking who he is. Good God, woman. Calum's shaking his head and smiling as he enters the living room, knowing that Frank's going to be mortified. The idea that this stout little tyrant is going to let people in uninvited . . . A man who's carried out as many jobs as Frank has over the years does have to be careful, and this isn't careful. Still, how could she know?

'Calum, good to see you, wee man,' Frank's saying, reaching out a hand and shaking his head at his help. He's sitting in his comfy chair, with one leg resting up on a cushioned stool. The whole leg looks ramrod-straight, and Frank looks older than he ever did. Frank plays it like the jolly old man, happy to see a young colleague come and visit, but he'll be on the alert already. He knows Calum isn't the type for social calls. He's here on business.

'Thought I'd come round and see how you're getting on.' Calum is lying. This is just the typical preamble, making sure the woman is out of earshot before anything else is said. 'You look . . . like a guy who just had his hip done.'

Frank's laughing. 'I feel like a guy who's just had his hip done.'

The woman says a goodbye to Frank, tells him she'll be in later to make his tea. She seems awfully rough, but when you're in Frank's position you must take what's given.

'So what's happenin', kid?' the old man asks, reaching for a packet of sweets that have been placed out of view of the carer.

'Maybe nothing. Maybe bad things.' It's a strange thing. You spend your whole life and career making sure that you never spill the beans about your work to anyone. You train yourself. You work hard to make sure you never talk. Yet there's a person out there that you can't help but talk to. Calum knows he can trust Frank. He knows there's nothing he's done that Frank didn't do thirty years before him. Frank has that rare skill of being easy to talk to.

'There's always bad things goin' on. What now?'

Calum pauses. He has to get the message to Jamieson. 'I was sent on a job. Got the job done, nice and easy. No loose ends. Nothing that could come back on me. Then I get a phone call from Glen Davidson.'

Calum can see the look on Frank's face. He

209

hates Davidson. Hated his father before him. With good reason, although it's never been entirely clear to Calum what that good reason is.

'He calls me up this afternoon. He asks me if I'm busy. What can I say? I have to admit that I am. Then he plays nice, and that's the end of it.'

Frank seems to have forgotten about the chocolate he's holding. He's staring off towards the window, contemplating things that he has no intention of sharing.

'He wanted to know if you'd been working recently,' Frank says in a low growl.

'Aye. I figure he wouldn't turn to me if he had a two-man job—way better options.'

'Not better, cheaper. But you're right; he wasn't fishing for a friend. Looks like he's fishing for info, and that ain't a good thing.' He's nodding his head. Frank knows what he's going to do. He's going to make sure that Young finds out about this as soon as possible. He has that tingling feeling that he gets when big moves are afoot. The excitement starts to build. You know you're going to be busy. You know there's going to be a lot happening. The thrill of the job.

Sitting with his leg up. A cripple. This industry isn't an equal-opportunities sort of a place. No room for elderly cripples. They only get in the way.

'You know that Peter's told me to take a few weeks in his villa in Spain when I'm able to get up and about,' Frank's saying now. Time to move the conversation along towards a friendly conclusion. The message has been given. Calum knows what he has to do. He's a smart boy. Frank's always respected him.

'I didn't know that. That'll be nice—a bit of sun

on your back for a wee while.'

'Aye, air-sickness, sunburn, poofy drinks and a hairy wee lassie to keep me company, then back to work. I'm lookin' forward to it.'

Back at the flat, Calum is riddled with paranoia again. There's nothing more to do. Get a weapon? No, never. Don't go down that road. Don't ask for trouble. You don't know there's anything to be afraid of yet. You know what's happening right now. Frank is calling up John Young and passing on the information about the Davidson phone call. He and Jamieson will better understand what the threat is. They might sort things out. Have a sit-down and talk with whoever is behind this. Get them to call off the dogs. We already killed one of your guys, don't make us kill a whole lot more, that sort of conversation. It works, sometimes.

This could be the start of a war. The start of something big. Frank had that far-away look in his eyes, the sort that implies something impressive is on the horizon. The old guys like this sort of thing. It's all they have left to live for. Not good if you want to live for a lot longer. Could be nothing. Could be a little flare-up between people testing each other out. Even if it is war, it may not have an awful lot to do with you. You've fired the first shot, now you stand back. Jamieson is smart enough not to overwork one of his better options. So you might have little to do. The threat right now is from Davidson. The next move for Jamieson and Young may be to get rid of Davidson. High-profile move. Comes with more risk than Winter. A well-connected man. Not well respected. Certainly not liked. Could be a good way of slapping down whoever's standing up to them, though.

211

A dim light in the corner of the room. Curtains drawn. Keeping the volume of the TV down. He tries to play a game on the PS3, but his nerves won't let him. Too much pausing every time he hears a distant sound. No way to play. Beginning to hate himself. He's never been on the receiving end like this, but he's dealt with threats before. You've been in the business long enough to handle this better. You know you've done what you can. You know there's little else to do but go about your business as you normally would. Get rid of the clothing you used to hit Winter. Get some money back from your runner. Keep your head down. Play it straight.

39

The club's loud, but there aren't many people there. A few stragglers going in and out, but they look like they emerged from the rough end of hell even before they went in. Only the dregs are clubbing tonight. Matheson and Higgins are standing in the foyer, asking everyone who comes in whether they recognize the man in the photo. It's boring work. It's unpleasant work. There are a lot of unpleasant people around. A surprising number who see the police as their enemy. Matheson's never been able to understand that attitude. One drunken halfwit even spat on Higgins' copy of the photo, in protest at being asked to help. Matheson threatened to arrest him, Higgins was more forgiving. Should have arrested him.

Higgins seems like a decent enough fellow. Matheson's heard a few people speaking well of him. Even Greig had good things to say about him. Plus, Fisher hand-picked him for this job. If he can impress those two opposites, then he's worth knowing. Didn't expect him to be this quiet. You hear about a copper doing good work, you expect him to have a mouth. You expect him to be pushy and determined—that's how most stand out. Not this one. He's keeping it quiet and polite at all times. Greig once told Matheson that Higgins came from a family on the other side. Bunch of crooks, apparently. Petty stuff, but still, not good people. You wouldn't think so to meet the boy. He seems like good people.

'Excuse me, sir, could you have a look at this photograph and tell me if you recognize the man in it?' Standard question. The standard response is infuriating. People stop and stare at the picture. They make it look as though they're really concentrating, because they want to make a good impression on the man in uniform. They stare at it, and slowly begin to shake their head. 'No, officer, no—don't know him.' You say thank you, and you let them get on. It's a nonsense. If you know the person, then you know him when you look at the picture; you don't have to spend thirty seconds trying to look intense in order to work it out.

The manager's been out into the foyer twice in the last hour. He wants rid of them. They're scaring away the customers. It won't do to have a couple of uniformed officers welcoming his regulars into the building, even if it is a slow night.

'We'll be here all evening if we don't get anything,' Matheson took great delight in telling

213

him. He nodded miserably and left them to it, presumably praying that someone would give them some information that they could rush back to the station with. They went in to see him when they first arrived. On Fisher's orders, they told him they were going to spend the evening at his club. They warned him about respecting his opening hours, and not to stay open late. They also warned him about his security cameras at the front of the club. He needs one to cover the whole pavement out there. Fisher had said the manager was a prick, wanted the fear put into him, but he seemed relieved more than anything. He had obviously thought he was in for more legal trouble than that.

'Excuse me, sir, can you have a wee look at this photograph?' Matheson's asking a young man. There's two young men and two young women. The women look a little ragged to Matheson. The young men are obviously not of discriminating taste when it comes to temporary relationships. 'Do any of you recognize this man?' They stop and look at it. The women give it a glance and shake their heads; at least they're not messing around. The two men pause a little longer. Always the men. Who are they trying to impress?

'Is that . . . Aye, it is. That's Stewart what's-his-name. Christ, what's his surname? He's Tom's flatmate. You know the guy,' he's saying to his mate.

Turns out his mate, tipsy though he may be, does know. 'Macintosh, that's his surname. Like the jacket. Aye. Shares digs with Tom Shields. Tom works with Harry. D'ya know Harry?' he's asking Matheson.

'No, but do you know where they live?' He wants

to hurry them along; it sounded disturbingly like the conversation was heading for a Tom, Dick and Harry joke.

'Oh God, I dunno the address. I got Tom's number on ma phone, though. Ya wan' it?' The man seems to be getting drunker as the conversation goes on. He's losing the will to hide his pre-clubbing drinking.

They have a name, they have a mobile number (albeit for the wrong person), and at the station they'll get an address. In the car on the way back Higgins puts in a call to Fisher, giving him the details. Before they get back Fisher will know what history this Macintosh character has. There's a good mood between the two of them. They were given a job—an irritating, uninspiring one—and they delivered. It may seem like very little, just getting the job right, but they both want to impress Fisher. He's the sort of detective who can get you moved up the ladder. The sort who can bring you in on more cases that count.

Upstairs at the station. Fisher is walking around in circles, looking irritated. He sees them come in.

'Good, you're back, let's go. I've got the address. Come on, both of you.' He's marching past them. Often it would be two detectives who went, but Fisher has monopolized the investigation and he calls the shots. He works with whoever is most useful to him, and if that's not a fellow detective, then that's just too bad. That's why you want to impress him.

'Doesn't have a history, but you never know,' Fisher's saying from the back seat of the car as they speed through the streets. 'He may be our killer, and he may still have the weapon. Let's

215

move fast and hard. We'll see if we can't catch him by surprise. I think Mr Macintosh is going to have a few interesting things to say to us.' You can hear the excitement in his voice. Loving it.

At the front door of the building. A buzzer. The front door locked. Damn! Fisher finds Macintosh's name on the list and presses the buzzer for the correct flat. Pray it's the flatmate. Better chance of him playing straight.

'Come up,' the crackly voice says. That's it. That easy. He's obviously expecting someone else. He's obviously in for a surprise. The buzzer goes. Fisher pulls the door open; Matheson and Higgins follow him in. A well-lit staircase up to the first floor. A well-maintained building. This is not a grotty little flat. This is home to the middle class. It doesn't feel right to Fisher. This isn't a gangster's flat.

A hitman doesn't live with his buddy in a comfy area. Not unless the buddy is in the business too, and he wouldn't have let them in without checking, if he was. Could be a couple, of course, but that sort of thing is still kept largely hidden in the criminal world. Not a liberal-minded bunch. Happens, though. They just keep it quiet. So Macintosh probably ain't a hitman; doesn't mean he's not a killer. Up the stairs and round the corner. Two doors, one on either side of the corridor. Two front doors. Fisher is walking over to the correct one when it's pulled open. A young man stands looking down at a mobile phone. 'You took your time. Col was already phoning and he . . .' The young man stops the moment he sees the cops.

He's standing still, looking like he's never seen a policeman before in his life. He looks scared, which is good.

'My name is Detective Inspector Fisher. You are?'

'Erm . . . Tom. I'm Tom. Tom Shields. Is there something the matter?'

'Could be, Mr Shields. We're looking for your flatmate, Mr Macintosh. Is he home?'

'No, he just went out. Just to get money, though. We're just going out for a few drinks. Just . . . What's going on?' Now he's really scared. It's not idle speculation any more; he knows there is something wrong.

'You might be able to help us, Mr Shields. You can answer a few questions.'

They're sitting in the flat. Fisher opposite Shields at the kitchen table. Matheson and Higgins are standing nearby, waiting for orders. They don't have a warrant to search, just to arrest. They'll have a search warrant within thirty minutes. Then they'll turn the place upside down.

'Friday night. Were you in Mr Macintosh's company?'

'Erm . . . Friday night, no. We went our own way. I had a date. Nice girl. He went clubbing, I think. I don't know.'

'He did. Did you hear what time he got home?'

'No. I had a . . . late night. Well, early morning. You know. I wasn't here when he got home.'

If this wet drip is in the criminal business, then the criminal business is going to hell in a handcart. Life would be very easy if they were all as pathetic as this guy. Terrified. Eager to please. Ready to tell whatever truth is necessary.

'Has Mr Macintosh told you anything of what happened on Friday night?'

217

'No,' Tom's saying, 'he hasn't. Not at all.' Then a pause. 'Did something happen?'

'Has Mr Macintosh been behaving any differently since Friday night? Have you noticed anything?' Fisher's asking in a way that makes it clear that Tom has no right to ask questions of his own.

'No, not that I've noticed. I haven't seen him that much, but . . . I don't think so.'

Then the buzzer goes again. Shields is looking at the intercom, panic-stricken.

'Let him in,' Fisher is saying, 'don't say anything.'

Shields walks across to the intercom and presses the buzzer. He doesn't say anything. Just one flatmate opening the door for the other. No big deal. He's walking back across and sitting at the table. He looks on the verge of tears. He has no idea what his friend has got himself involved in, but if it involves a detective and two uniformed officers then it must be bad. Was there something he could have said to protect his friend? Is there anything he's already said that's likely to get his friend into further trouble?

Too late. A key in the door. Stewart pushing it open. Talking as he pulls the key from the lock. 'Stupid old woman in front of me, don't think she even knew how to use a cash machine. Why do they have cards if they . . .' He stops when he sees the uniforms.

'Stewart Macintosh?' Fisher asks. He's getting up from the table, while Matheson and Higgins move in behind Stewart to ensure that he can't make a run for it.

'Yes,' he says in response. In that one word,

218

there's acceptance. Like he knew this was coming. It's almost as if he was expecting it.

The detective arrests Stewart. He's not just looking for a witness; he's arresting him as a suspect. This isn't just to ask a few questions. Jesus!—he just used the word 'murder'. They want to talk to Stewart in connection with a murder. They're arresting him over a murder.

'Stewart . . .' Tom says, and then pauses. The cops are opening the front door, ready to take him out. 'What's going on?'

Stewart looks back at him. There's a broken look in his eyes. He's got mixed up in something that's overwhelmed him. He looks heartbreakingly guilty. He says nothing.

'Is there anyone I should get in touch with?' Tom's asking.

Stewart pauses. 'No.'

40

It's dark. The room seems to be spinning. Fear in everything. Underscoring it all, the death of the thrill. It had all seemed so wild. Otherworldly. Now it's intruded into reality and his stomach is lurching. He can hear it making little noises. Didn't happen instantly—it's taken the car journey to the station and being booked in to realize what happens next. Throwing your life away. Shocking everyone who knows you. The reality has become inescapable, and the reality is no fun at all. The little part of Stewart that enjoyed this has shut its mouth and gone to lie down in a dark corner.

Sitting in the interview room, waiting for a lawyer to arrive, Fisher's been treating him like a killer. It scares him. He doesn't want to go to jail. He doesn't want the consequences of the thrill. Living like a villain is fun. Being treated like one is not.

The door opens. A lawyer comes in. Bearded fellow, mid-forties. He looks angry already. Fisher, sitting across the desk from Stewart, turns and looks at him. The lawyer can't see it, but Fisher rolls his eyes. Not impressed with the new arrival. The bearded man walks over and sits next to Stewart.

'I'd like a few minutes alone with my client, please,' he says to Fisher. There's history there. Not happy history. Fisher is sighing and getting up from the desk. 'And I do hope you haven't mistreated him already. I know how enthusiastic you can get.'

Fisher scoffs as he reaches the door. 'Don't worry; I've treated the precious little lamb with the utmost respect.'

Just Stewart and the lawyer now. 'First of all, my name's Norman Barnes. Second of all, you would appear to be wrapped up in a whole lot of trouble. They have you on suspicion of being involved in the murder of Lewis Winter. Now, I want you to be completely honest with me. If we're going to get you out of here, then we need to know how to fight this.'

Stewart's nodding. Involved in a murder. That could be a life sentence. The thrill is dead, it's funeral-brief. Time to be honest. Time to minimize the damage.

'I wasn't involved in the murder. Not really. I was there, though.'

He's thinking about Zara as he talks to the lawyer. Where is she right now? Does she think she's safe? He's letting her down by talking to the police. He's betraying her. He knows how it works on TV and in the movies. The man comes up with some clever story that protects the beautiful girl from the police. He ends up going to jail instead of her. Jail. No. She's beautiful, and thrilling, but she's not worth jail. Nobody is worth that. Surely she'll understand that a relationship as fledgling as theirs can't justify a jail term. He might go to jail anyway. But he has to be honest.

It takes a few minutes, but he tells Barnes everything. The lawyer writes copious notes in shorthand as Stewart talks. He sits with one hand to his mouth, the other writing, looking at the paper all the time. Stewart reaches the end of the story.

'Okay. Stewart, have you any police record?'

'No, none. I've never been involved in anything like this before. This was a complete accident.'

'Good. You see, a judge is going to hear that and he's going to wonder about you. Does he need to punish you, or does he need to put you on the straight and narrow. You see, if you have a record, he'll believe there's something darker behind this. If you don't, then he might believe that you've been naive. He won't send you to jail, ruin your life, over this.'

Send you to jail. Ruin your life. It could happen. It's all in the hands of others.

'I think the best thing you can possibly do,' Barnes is saying, 'is tell DI Fisher everything you just told me. Tell him the whole truth. What you did was a crime. You fled from a murder scene.

221

You handled class-A drugs and possibly drug money, although they'll have to prove that's what it was. You withheld information about a murder. They're all serious. Even a generous judge might feel obliged to put you behind bars for a few months. Your best bet is to give them everything you have. You get a positive report from the police, and the judge will look favourably on you. That's as much as you can hope for right now.'

He wants to cry. Barnes has left the room to make a phone call. A DC has come in to sit opposite him. Fisher has gone upstairs to get some paperwork. Fisher took great delight in telling him that the two uniformed officers were already going back to his flat to look for any evidence. They would be ripping the place apart. Fight back the tears. Barnes has warned him. Fisher is a bully. He'll try to intimidate you. He'll try to browbeat you into confessing to things that didn't even happen. Don't let him. Tell him only what you told me. Tell him only what you know to be true. If he asks you anything you're uncomfortable about, then you say nothing. If you pause, I'll step in. The lawyer is good. Comforting. But Stewart still wants to cry.

Fisher comes in and sits next to the DC. Doesn't say anything. He's just sitting there, looking across the table. The boy looks emotionally wrecked. He looks ready to spill his guts. Still, got to watch out for the lies. He has no record. His back-story is convincing. College-educated, working for a respectable company. If you can call advertising respectable. The hairy-faced lawyer comes back in, ready to be a nuisance as usual. Always looking to pick a fight. Always keen to make himself the centre of attention. So many of these lawyers are media whores these days. They're a bloody embarrassment.

'Okay, Mr Macintosh, shall we begin?' Fisher says, not bothering to wait for a response before switching on the tape recorder.

He goes through the formalities. He introduces himself and DC Davies, introduces the suspect and his lawyer. He tells Macintosh that, as well as the tape recorder, they will now be switching on the camera in the corner to record the interview.

'My client would be happy to tell you everything that happened on Friday night,' Barnes says, before Fisher can even get a question in. Fisher looks at him and glares. That forest-faced prick is enjoying undercutting the detective. Fine. Have it your way.

'Would he really. Well, Mr Macintosh, why don't you press ahead and tell us what you can.'

Stewart is pausing. Not for dramatic effect, just a last-ditch effort to think of a version of events that doesn't incriminate Zara. Or at least doesn't incriminate her any more than is necessary to keep himself out of jail.

'I was at Heavenly, the nightclub. I saw a girl I liked. I went over and started dancing with her.'

'This was Zara Cope?'

'Yes, Zara. She was dancing with an old guy; I didn't think he was her partner. He went away; we kept dancing. Then she invited me back to hers. I was happy to go.'

'Uh-huh,' Fisher is saying.

Stewart's sweating and shivering at the same time. Struggling to maintain control.

'We went back to the house.'

223

'Hold up,' Fisher says. 'I want more detail than that. Tell me about the journey back. Tell me about Cope and Winter and what happened in the taxi.'

Stewart blushes. 'The old guy, Winter, he was struggling. He'd been drinking. A lot. We got him out to the taxi. We were all in the back. I was in the middle. Zara was next to me on one side. Winter was on the other. The atmosphere was pretty bad. I guess he drank a lot. I don't . . . I don't think he treated her well. I thought maybe she wasn't—you know—interested in me any more. But then she . . . she touched me.'

'She touched you?'

'Yes. She . . . well . . . She touched me. She massaged . . . me.'

Fisher isn't saying anything now. His expression is perfectly blank. He's letting Stewart swing in the breeze; suffer through every detail of the story.

'So I knew that she was still interested. The taxi reached their house. We got out. I helped Winter up the path. Zara opened the door. We got him upstairs, into the bedroom. It was . . . unpleasant. Winter was saying stuff, but I couldn't understand what it was. He was aggressive. I don't think he gave her any sort of life. He wet himself. And he took a swing at me. We dumped him on the bed, and we went downstairs.'

Don't let things get out of sequence, Fisher is thinking. Ask about the arrival. 'When you pulled up at the house in the taxi, did you notice anyone else around?'

'No, there was nobody there. At least, I didn't see anyone.'

This is no killer. This Macintosh is a horrible

224

disappointment, but he might still deliver something.

'Then what?' Fisher's asking.

'We went downstairs. Zara had a whiskey. She was stressed. I think she was under a lot of pressure with him.'

'And then?'

'She . . . uh . . . took her clothes off. She helped me take mine off. We started . . . making love . . . on the couch.'

That would relieve the stress, Fisher is thinking.

Stewart can feel that he's blushing. He'll be bright red; he'll look like a silly little boy who's been caught with his pants down.

'Go on,' Fisher says. He's sitting there, expressionless. His colleague is writing a few things down, but not much. DC Davies mostly just looks bored.

'We were . . .'

'Making love, yes, you can say it,' Fisher tells him drily. He gets a dirty look from the lawyer, but who cares about him anyway?

'I heard a big bang on the door. I didn't know what it was. Then another one. There were two men in the room with us. It was terrifying.'

He knew Cope was lying to him. That's what's going through Fisher's mind right now. If that silly little bitch had just been honest from the start, the investigation could be a lot further forward.

'They didn't say anything. They just stood there. One of them pointed a gun at us.'

'What did they look like?' Fisher interrupts him. The boy wants to tell a general story. Fisher needs details.

'They were dressed all in black. They were—I

225

don't know—average. I don't know. They were all in black. They had balaclavas on. They were pointing a gun at me. That's why I panicked.'

'What did you do?'

'I tried to run for the door. I didn't even have my clothes on.' He can feel his skin burn. 'I just ran. One of them hit me. It hurt. I fell over a chair. I was lying on the floor. I think he must have hit me with the gun. I still have the lump on my head. I . . . I stayed on the floor. I was so scared. Then I heard the bang. Then I heard the front door close. That was it.'

There's a pause in the room. Silence. It all sounds plausible. It stacks up with what Cope told him. Okay, she left out a few details. The suspect is now a witness to the killing. But there's more. Now he has to explain why he wasn't there when the police turned up.

'So the killers have left the house. Then what happens, Mr Macintosh? Because, when my officers arrived at the scene, you were nowhere to be found.'

He looks to his lawyer, who nods. Time to tell the worst of it. 'I didn't know what to do,' he's saying, almost whispering now. 'I mean, you don't, do you. I've never been in that sort of situation before.'

Stewart puts his hands flat on the table and looks at his fingernails. Just try to get the picture of Zara out of your mind when you're telling them all this.

'It was Zara. She pulled herself together. She realized what was going to happen. The police were going to come to the house. She said that I needed to get out, or I'd get caught up in the whole thing. I didn't want that. My career. Everything. I didn't . . . And she said there were things in the house that she needed to get rid of. She could go to jail if they were found. They were the old guy's—Winter's—but she would be blamed. I just wanted to help her.'

Now we're getting somewhere. Now we're getting something we can throw at her for being so bloody deceitful. This is going to be good.

'She went upstairs. I don't know where to. I stayed down. I got my clothes on. She came back with these bags. I knew they were drugs. There were two wads of banknotes as well. I put them in my pockets. She said they were her partner's. She was so beautiful. She was desperate for help. I had the chance to do something to rescue her from the life he'd thrown her into. The chance to stop her from being dragged down by him. I put them all in my pockets. We kissed. It was . . . She led me to the back door. I went through the garden and over the fence at the bottom. I came out on some other street. Got a taxi back to the flat. Hid the stuff in a shoebox.'

Oh, this is very good. Possession with intent to supply. 'So my men will find it all in your flat?'

'No. She came to the flat yesterday afternoon. She took it away. I haven't seen her since. I hope she's not in trouble.'

Fisher can hardly suppress his smile. She's in trouble all right, pal, she's in big trouble. Probably the sort of big trouble that gets a little girl thrown in jail. That's what he'll be pushing for, anyway. There's a brief explanation of Cope's visit to the flat, and that's the end of the interest. Time to print up a charge sheet for Mr Macintosh. He's been useful, in a pathetic sort of a way. Silly little boys. The trouble they get themselves into, just for a free shot at a little whore like her.

Fisher's upstairs, feeling confident about his investigation. He'll get a conviction against both Macintosh and Cope, that's for sure. The killer. Not Macintosh. Cope might be involved. She's looking more culpable. If she knows anything, then she'll be compelled to speak.

He's shouting across the room, telling anyone who's listening to get in touch with Higgins and Matheson and tell them they won't find a weapon. Tell them to keep looking for any sign of drugs and money, though. Patting a hand on the table, trying to work out the next move. The comedown. You get progress, and then you hit a brick wall. Arresting Cope will be enjoyable, but the stories suggest that she won't know who the killers are. That means more digging around. It means we're no closer to catching the ones that matter most.

41

In a small flat there are only so many places that a person's going to hide illegal belongings. They worked the bedroom first, considering it the most obvious place to check. They got word from the station to look for a shoebox. There were four of them on top of the wardrobe, all with shoes in them. They put them in bags, just in case. The bedroom yielded no results. It was even less interesting than an average bedroom. Clearly the occupant just slept in the room and spent very little time there otherwise. No TV. No magazines of an interesting nature. No condoms in the bedside cabinet. Nothing that suggested the occupant lived an interesting life.

Into the bathroom. More awkward hiding places here. Opening the cistern. Checking inside the shower head. Checking to see if there's a false back on the cabinet above the sink. Nothing. Another site of extreme boredom. Clearly these are young men who use their flat very little. A bed and a toilet, a place to eat occasionally. Into the flatmate's bedroom. Condoms in the bedside cabinet. Three unflattering photographs of a nude woman tucked away in the back of a drawer; the photos were obviously taken for Tom. A little snicker at the woman's ill-judged attempt at modelling, then carry on. Nothing.

They're doing the living room now—nothing there. Tom is still sitting in the kitchen, his head in his hands. He's called his sister, but she hasn't arrived yet.

'I don't understand any of this,' he keeps saying.

'You're not under any suspicion, sir,' Matheson tells him for the third or fourth time. 'If you could please move into the living room so that we can search the kitchen, we would appreciate that. I know this is difficult for you, but any help you can give us we would be grateful for.'

'I don't know what I can do,' Tom's saying, moving mechanically from the table to the doorway.

He's one of those people who thinks that criminals aren't like him. He can't understand that a friend might have been involved in something terrible. Sheltered lives. They're pulling everything

229

out of the cupboards, getting in under the sink. Pulling apart cereal packets and emptying biscuit tins. Messy business, but they're never the ones who have to clean it up. Serious business, though. Looking for anything that might be incriminating. Anything at all. Nothing. What a boring little flat. It's rare that you go through a place like this, owned by two young men, and don't even find a bit of weed.

'Okay, Mr Shields,' Matheson is saying to him, 'we've finished our search. We're sorry that we had to be so disruptive, but you can understand that this is a very serious crime and requires a very thorough investigation.' He pauses, waiting for a response. Tom's looking up at him from the couch with a desperate look on his face. He's not going to say anything. 'Okay then,' Matheson nods. 'We're heading back to the station. We have a few possessions of your flatmate's that we're going to take with us; nothing of yours. I expect there'll be someone round to question you more thoroughly about your flatmate in due course.' He was supposed to thank him for his cooperation, but the boy had done nothing to help and clearly just wanted them to leave.

Back at the station. Shift over. In the changing rooms, getting out of uniform.

'Fisher's still upstairs, still calling the shots on this one,' Matheson says casually.

'I dunno why he's got such a bee in his bonnet about the woman and the guy we arrested tonight. Neither of them were involved. Winter was a dealer; the killer will have been working for another dealer.'

'Aye, true. Still, Fisher's the sort of mad bastard

that's gonna catch a killer like that.'

'Mad?'

'The guy's obsessed. Obviously doesn't have a life away from the job—he's always here.'

'Well, I do,' Higgins is smiling, 'so I'm off. I'll see you tomorrow.'

Higgins is back in his own flat, but he can't sleep. There are things he feels he has to do. He owes people. Young warned him about Shug Francis. It was a warning. He told him about Shug, and then this happens with Winter. Winter's killing doesn't make a lot of sense until you throw people like Shug and John Young into the equation. Winter was small-time. He was a nobody in the grand scheme. You needed people like Shug and Young to make Winter important. But which one of them was Winter working for? Usually he would have said almost certainly Young. But now? Young had warned him about Shug Francis because of this.

Higgins is picking up his phone. An emergency number. He looks at the display for thirty seconds before he presses dial. It rings. It rings some more. He glances at a clock. It's after midnight. He doesn't want to do this, but he has to. The danger of doing nothing is that Young takes action. Ruins his career. Ruins his life. He warned Higgins about Shug Francis to force him to help. To make him more active. This is the price you pay for the favours you've received, and the ones you may request in the future. You don't have to like it, but you do have to live with it. The phone's still ringing. Maybe he won't answer. Maybe you'll have a get-out: I called and called, but I couldn't get through to you.

'Hello?' Slightly confused. Still half-asleep.

231

Definitely Young.

'John, can we meet at the flat? I have something to tell you.'

'Okay. Be there in ten minutes. I'll be there in twenty.' He sounded awake by the time he finished that sentence.

Already Higgins is regretting it, but these are the consequences. So you have to suffer a little—that's too bad. You took their help when you needed it, and you know you'll need it again. Your family needs help. Not the sort of help you can give them. You will need Young again. You have to make a good impression. He has to feel that you've earned the help you intend to ask for. So make a good impression. Get to the flat.

By the time he arrives at the flat Young has a bad feeling about it. He's parked his car two streets away. He's walking through the drizzle to get to the meeting place. A cop calls you up and tells you he wants to see you. He calls you in the dead of night. He calls you because he has something important to say. He's never called you before. Took Young an age even to find the mobile that was ringing. Young has several, all for different people. He didn't expect the one dedicated to Joseph Higgins to be ringing. Maybe the cop has decided to confess to his superiors. Maybe he's decided to set Young up. Or maybe he's decided to do it a different way. When people are in your pocket, they sometimes try to fight their way out. Even a cop can be dangerous.

In the door and up the stairs. At the door of the flat. Key in the door. A dull light inside; a lamp is on along the corridor in the living room. Follow the corridor in. Higgins sitting in a chair alone, looking nervous.

'Hello, Joseph, how are things?' Young asks him, sitting opposite. Trying to sound relaxed. Make the boy feel at ease with the situation, because he's clearly nervous. Then again, he's always nervous when he's in this flat. Quiet and a little depressed. Trying to relax him is nothing new.

'Things are okay,' Higgins is saying, but it doesn't sound like he means it.

He's clearing his throat, as if he's building up to something real important. This better be good, young man. This better be worth all the aggro.

'I thought you would want to know that we've arrested someone in connection with the Lewis Winter death.'

Shock. Holy shit! Calum. He's a good boy, he won't talk. A big loss. Shit again.

'The guy's name is Macintosh. Stewart Macintosh. They don't think he's involved in the actual killing, though. They thought he might have been, but not since they questioned him. He was there when it happened, but not to be involved. Seems like he was there to have sex with Zara Cope while Lewis Winter was asleep upstairs. They're going to arrest Cope too, for hiding drugs and money that had been in the house at the time.'

Relief. Huge relief. Calum is okay. The job went well. They're arresting people on the periphery. That's usually a good thing; means that they're distracted from the actual murder.

'What about the actual killer? Any word on that?'

Higgins is shaking his head. 'They have nothing. Seems to have been a real professional job. They have nothing to go on right now.' He pauses. He's

233

not sure if this is the right moment. If this isn't, then when is? 'I suggested to DI Fisher—he's leading the investigation—that Shug Francis might be a name worth looking at. I was careful. I told him I'd been tipped off by a contact that I didn't much trust.' He waits. He's looking to see what Young's reaction will be. A nodding head. Not angry. That's a relief.

Young's not sure how to react. Is it too soon to be throwing Shug's name at the police? No, never too soon. This is one of the reasons you brought it up. You need to put Shug on their radar. You need them to start getting awkward with the bastard. The boy has done well.

'I'm glad you brought his name up. It's important that the police are aware of what a growing threat Shug Francis is. I think the man's going to become a really big problem for this city. I do hope you and your colleagues will be able to do something about it.'

'We'll be looking at him,' Higgins is saying, 'that's something.'

'What about you, Joseph, how is life treating you?' Time to be nice and polite. Make sure he knows that you appreciate and care.

'Things are going okay for me,' Higgins is answering, nodding his head. There's something in his tone that suggests he doesn't expect that to last. 'It can be a challenge sometimes, though, looking after that family of mine.' He says it with a smile, but the implication is clear.

'You know, Joseph, any time your family needs my help, you only have to ask. Just let me know what might need doing, and I'll be on top of it. I want to help you. You've been a help to me, so it's only fair.'

Higgins nods and says that there's nothing right now. Fair enough. He needs to think about it. He needs to think about how much help he wants to ask for, and in what area. He'll ask, though. He'll throw himself even deeper into the hole. Young knows he will. Young knows he has to. He knows why too. He knows because he's been working hard to make it happen. Get the family back into debt. Get the sister running around with another bad crowd. Get them into all sorts of trouble that they can't hope to get out of without his help. He organizes the trouble. He organizes the help. It's part of his job. Keep valuable assets like Higgins dependent on you. It's one thing to get them into your pocket; it's another to keep them there.

'Why don't you head off home, Joseph,' Young is saying. 'I'll stay behind. I have a phone call to make anyway.'

Higgins nods. He gets up from the chair, shakes Young's hand. Always so polite. Christ knows where he got those manners. Not his infested, degenerate family, that's for sure. There's no call to make, but there are things to consider. There are problems still to overcome. Good news that Shug is on the police radar. Get him implicated in drug deals. Link him to Winter. It's not the meeting with Higgins that he's thinking about. It's the hushed call from Frank MacLeod. A call that suggests the next step is about to be taken. The question for Young—and, as strategist, it's he who must find the answer—is who steps first?

Tempting to go after Davidson. A nice opportunity to slap down the enemy. But who do you use? Frank is out of action. It's not safe to use

235

Calum twice in quick succession. Not safe to order two hits in such close proximity anyway, no matter who you use. Tempting to take the next step. Might be wiser to let the other side have a go. Let them make their move. Let them dig themselves in even deeper. If they hit one of our men, it gives us carte blanche. There's nothing that can't be justified after you've been attacked. Easy to win support amongst other organizations. Let people see that Shug is dangerous. Let the rest of the industry see that Shug is a threat to them too.

You might have to sacrifice someone to get that message across. That's always a sad consequence. A horrible decision to have to make, letting someone on your own side fall by the wayside. That's life. You might have to sacrifice Calum. That would be a shame, but he's worked for a few other people in the trade, so it would make a real impact. Well connected, well respected. He would be a loss, at a bad time. Without Frank, you'd have to find someone else. Third choice. Calum was the best candidate. Still, could be worth it. Wait a little. Give Davidson the opportunity to make a move on Calum. See what happens at the end of it. No need to give warnings yet. Sit back and let things happen.

42

Fisher bounds into the changing rooms. 'Where's the other one?' he demands to know of Matheson.

'Joseph? He's away home. You just missed him.'

Damn! You need these young plods to feel like

they owe you. You need them to think you're including them in everything, doing them a favour. That's how you get their loyalty. That's how you're able to mould them into decent coppers.

'Never mind. You can come with me, and find someone else to come along. We're going to pay a visit to Zara Cope. I've got an arrest warrant and a search warrant.'

Matheson finds some other plod, another youngish-looking fellow. As long as it's not Greig, Fisher doesn't really care. They're in the car, on the way to Cope's flat. Put the pressure on her there. See if she gives them the shoebox, without the need for a great search. She'll be awkward. Fisher knows it. She's the kind of cynical, smart, nasty human being who will make life difficult. She'll come up with sob stories. She'll come up with subtle little lies. She'll manipulate the information to her benefit. Finding a way to incriminate her. Making sure she goes to jail. That's the key to this. Then we find our killer.

That's the depressing thought that's settling on Fisher as they make their way into the building. None of this brings us any closer to finding out who killed Lewis Winter. How many times does this happen? You set off on one investigation and get sidetracked by something else. Happens a lot with organized crime. All of the people involved are so immersed in criminal behaviour; you can find all sorts of things to keep you busy. Fisher leads the two plods up to the flat's front door. All familiar to him. Should have got a search warrant last time he was here. Would have saved some bother. Saved some time. Didn't know that at the time, though.

237

Knocking on the door. It would make life so much easier if Cope still had the gear. Brilliant bonus if she knows all about the killing. That's the prayer. You have enough pressure to get her to talk freely. She tells you she knows who did it. She knows why. She gives you everything you need. It can happen. Probably not this time. No answer. It's late. Knock again. Knock loudly. Knock until she answers. He's thumping the door. His nerves are starting to fray a little. An investigation slipping away from him. Only a consolation prize. People will say well done, you got two people for breaking the law. There's still a good chance that you can catch the killer. Nope. The likelihood is running away. Unless something happens that you don't expect. Unless someone talks.

The door opens. A nervous face looks out. A young woman, eyes still adjusting to the light in the corridor. Clearly just got out of bed. Wearing a vest top and shorts, no make-up. Genuinely scared. She doesn't know who could be knocking on her door.

'Zara Cope, we have a warrant to search your flat. We also have a warrant for your arrest on suspicion of possessing a class-A drug with intent to supply, and withholding evidence in a police investigation. I'm sure you don't mind if we come in.' He's trying to say it to sound matter-of-fact. It comes across sarcastic and a little bitchy. Who cares? She deserves nothing better.

Zara opens the door wide and stands aside. She needs to think. They're going to charge her over the drugs and over withholding evidence. Her first thought, when she heard the mention of the drugs, was Nate. Had he grassed her? No, not Nate. He's too involved in the industry. But how bitter is he

238

towards her? Revenge—a dish best served cold, and all that. Then Fisher said withholding evidence. That was when the penny dropped. Nate knew nothing about her withholding evidence. The drugs aren't the evidence. The evidence is the second witness. Stewart. He's talked. Either they got him, or he went to them. Probably the latter. Bitter about her not wanting anything more to do with him. Pathetic. One day he'll get what's coming to him.

Fisher is pushing past her, marching into the flat, switching on lights. Make yourself at home, why don't you? He's standing in the simple flat, looking around menacingly.

'Why don't you spare us all some trouble and tell us where the shoebox is?' he's saying.

'Shoebox?' Damn you, Stewart. I should have known you were too pathetic a little prick to rely on. I should have found another way. If I had known Greig would be the first cop on the scene . . . If only I had known.

'Aye, shoebox. We know you had drugs and money in a shoebox, and we know you took it to this flat. If you just tell us where it is, then we can spare all sorts of trouble.'

Spare all sorts of trouble. That does sound tempting. But then what happens? You tell them that you've already got rid of it, so they ask you who you gave it to. You can't pretend you don't know. She would have to tell them that she gave the gear to Nate. Then he would be arrested. Oh, they would throw the book at him. They would spend an age trying to find other things to charge him with. They know he's dangerous. He's on their radar. Has been for a while. They just can't get him for anything. So he would go to jail. No, can't have that. Not much of a mother, but Rebecca is obviously close to her father, and it would destroy that. No, he's made the effort to be a parent. You owe him this.

'I have no idea what you're talking about,' she's saying, a little sleepily. 'A shoebox? What do you want with a shoebox?'

Fisher is looking at her, a bitter look on his face. 'We know you had drugs and money in a shoebox. Where is it now? Have you got rid of it already?'

'I really don't know what you're talking about. You can feel free to search this place; I have no drugs and no money. I don't own any of the furniture, so try not to break anything.'

There's a confidence in her voice. She's obviously got rid of the stuff already. If she hasn't collected any money for it yet, then it might be hard to find tangible evidence that she's ever had it. Her word against Macintosh's. Bloody hell, she moves fast. Oh no, you're not going to wriggle off this hook.

Fisher turns to the two uniformed officers. 'Right, search the place. You,' he's saying to Zara, 'can stay here with me. Take a seat. Let's me and you have a wee chat about life.'

The plods are going through the flat, pulling things apart, making the sort of mess that the owners are going to be furious about. Fisher is sitting opposite Zara at the kitchen table.

'You know that we have a witness that can put you behind bars,' Fisher is saying. He's speaking low, almost conspiratorially. 'Your only hope of staying out of jail here is to make a good impression. You tell me everything you can. Maybe

I can help keep you out of jail. You'll still get a conviction, but I'll make sure the judge knows what a good little girl you've been.'

Tell me everything you can. He's not just talking about this crime. He's talking about all the things you know. All the people you know. You could give him a little treasure trove. That's what he's praying for. You'll be some pitiful little woman, terrified of the big scary cop, and you'll tell him absolutely everything you know. Prepare to be disappointed.

'You spoke to Stewart, huh. I don't know what he told you. God knows what was going through that idiot's head. A little fantasist. All I did was try to help him out. You know what a trial would have done for his career prospects? Well, he's about to find out. He was desperate for my help. Crying all over me. So I said, go. Just go, and I'll pretend you were never here. Christ, you try and do a person a favour.'

She's a good little liar, this one. So full of shit, but the sort of liar that some dim-witted old judge could be manipulated by.

'So you admit that Stewart Macintosh was in the house at the time of the shooting.'

'Yeah,' she's saying, 'he was there. He was begging me to help him. I don't know. I'd just heard Lewis being murdered. I wasn't thinking about anything. I said, yeah, I'll help you. You go, I'll say nothing. He was so grateful. It just felt like the right thing to do. Not now, obviously. At the time it felt like the right thing to do.'

She's beginning to hit her stride. She's making her little story hang together well. She's being honest about the things she can't possibly lie about. She's avoiding the things she can.

241

Fisher pauses to let her hear the sound of two policemen ripping apart her bedroom. No reaction. She's not nervous in the least. So there's nothing to find. Shit!

'He says you went upstairs and got drugs and money. You came down and gave it to him, then told him how to escape. You went round to his flat yesterday and collected the stuff. He put it into a shoebox for you. You went off with it.'

She's shaking her head, a little smile on her lips. 'Nonsense. What garbage! You believe that? Jesus, you must be dumb if you do. Stewart wanted to see me again. We didn't exactly finish what we started, if you know what I mean. He wanted to see me again. I went round to his flat. I spoke to him. Told him it wasn't going to happen. Tried to let him down gently.'

Damn it. She's admitting going to his flat. If she denied it and they had proof, then he would be able to back her into a corner. She's covering every angle. Doing it like a pro.

'He kept telling me how much he wanted to see me. How he wanted to be with me. Said that he didn't care what trouble there might be. Didn't matter to him what had happened to Lewis. He just wanted me. I told him no. Too soon for me. Not good for him, either. He was emotional. I just left him there. I thought that was the best thing to do. His life is better without me in it. One day he'll recognize that. He's obviously sore about it just now. Lashing out. Rather childish.'

She is good. You can hate a person, but respect the skill they bring to the table.

'So you're not going to tell me what you did with Lewis Winter's drug stash?'

'I have no idea what you're talking about. I know Lewis was involved in things he shouldn't have been—I'm not totally naive. He didn't tell me about any of it, but he didn't need to. I knew. I turned a blind eye, because I loved him. I know one thing: there were never drugs in our house. Never. He knows . . . he knew what my reaction would be.'

Nope, nothing. She's locked up tight. 'Fine. It's a shame you're making this so difficult, Zara. You know what the consequences are going to be. We'll go down to the station. We'll get you a lawyer. When it goes to court, the judge will know that you made life difficult. He'll know that every piece of information had to be dragged out of you. That's not going to serve you well.'

The basic search of the flat is finished. Nothing. Almost literally nothing. She has very little of her own there. Just a few items of clothing. That's it. The rest is the furniture that comes with the flat. She has little to her name right now.

'Okay, we're taking you into the station,' Fisher is saying. He's keeping it matter-of-fact. He wants to make sure she has nothing to complain about. 'I'm arresting you on suspicion of possessing a class-A drug with intent to supply, and withholding evidence relating to a murder inquiry.' He goes through the formalities, lets her put on a pair of jeans, a hoody and a coat, and leads her out of the flat. The two uniformed officers follow on behind, silent.

She says nothing to them in the car on the way to the station. She just looks angry. Angry with the world at large. They often look that way, when they get caught. They can't believe they've been found out. They can't understand why it's them, and not one of the many other criminals they know. They curse their luck, as though that's to blame for it all. They find ways to justify the things they've done, and can't understand why the police can't follow their logic. Everyone in the criminal business does it. You find a logic that you can apply to your situation. You find a justification for any action. Once you find it, you cling to it. You just can't understand why the world doesn't agree with you. Cope's as likely to suffer from that criminal mindset as anyone else, Fisher is thinking to himself.

They're walking into the station. As Fisher leads Zara to the charge desk, so that the night-sergeant can book her in, she sees a face she knows. Walking along the corridor, in casual clothing, a sports bag over his shoulder, is Paul Greig. Must be going off duty. He was supposed to be helping her. Yeah, right. He'll help as long as there's money in it for him. He won't help if it becomes inconvenient. She might tell them a few tales about him. Then it becomes her word against a copper's. They wouldn't believe her. Or they would, and they'd do nothing about it, out of embarrassment. Besides, grassing him gets a lot of people in the criminal world angry. She can't have that. She's going to need all the friends she can get.

Greig sees her. Sees Fisher. There's a slight pause in his step. For just a fraction of a second he considers stopping to say something. Ask what she's in for. No. Don't let Fisher know you care. Don't give him anything to be suspicious about. He hates you already. If she's in trouble, then that's her problem. Law of the jungle. You have a

244

responsibility to keep yourself safe and free from trouble. Nobody else has a responsibility to look after you. You have no right to complain. She knows that. She'll keep her mouth shut. Cope glances at him as Fisher talks to the desk sergeant. He raises an eyebrow slightly. A 'too bad' look. She knows how this works. He's walking past and heading for the door. Just hope Fisher didn't notice your hesitation, or the fact that Cope looked at you. You don't want him on your tail.

They've got a lawyer for her. She's had twenty minutes sitting alone with him, spilling her guts. She's probably spun a fantastical tale for him, a web of lies that he'll be thoroughly stuck in. A weak lawyer and a strong client are a troublesome opponent. Going to have to fight our way through this one. She's had enough time to concoct her story—time to go in. Fisher leads DC Davies into the interview room. He sits opposite Zara. He looks her in the eye as he goes through the formalities.

'Before we start,' Zara says quietly, 'I want to ask you what you're doing about finding the people who killed Lewis. I thought that was what you were supposed to be doing.'

It hurts. A very accurate shot. Even she knows that your real investigation is getting away from you. Even she can see your failure. Prove her wrong.

43

Some nights you just can't sleep. It has nothing to do with a guilty conscience. That's what Calum always tells himself. He doesn't feel guilty about the things he's done. He's found his justification. It's just that, sometimes, you can't rest your head. You go to sleep, but within an hour you're awake again. Often waking with a start, fumbling at the duvet, pushing it off yourself. There's something in the room. Something on the bed. No, there isn't. It's your imagination. Too much time spent running around in the dark. Too much time living on your nerves. It's not particularly worse after a job. It's just constant. The challenge is not letting it get you down.

Calum's awake now. Sitting up in bed. Sitting in the darkness. People would say it was because he was afraid. He has thoughts of Davidson and of the phone call running through his mind. Not really. He's not dwelling on it. He's lived the life long enough to know that he's done all he can. He's alerted Jamieson through Frank. They'll know by now. Maybe they've already done something about it. Davidson could be dead already. Not that it matters. It's not Davidson that's the real threat here. Maybe that's what unnerves him most. Davidson is just an employee of someone else. It's the employer who poses the threat. That's who you have to fear. No matter what happens to Davidson, his employer can still be dangerous.

For days Jamieson and Young have been relying on Calum to get the job right. They've been sitting in their office, hoping that he would do it right. Hoping that he would do it. They've been living with the unknown. It's tough, when you don't know what's going on. Now the roles are reversed. Now you're sitting in your bed, hoping they're doing something to help you. Quid pro quo. Only, they paid you for your service. Well, they will pay, when it's safe to do so. You're an employee. You're just a piece on the chessboard. They can do as they please with you. They don't have the same obligations to you as you have to them. They might want to be seen to help you. They might want their other employees to think they're the kind of people who act to help their men. Or they might not care.

This is why he doesn't want to work permanently for someone. You do a job, freelance, and you get out. It's so much simpler. You avoid becoming a part of other people's games. You can't rely on any of them. They're all playing their little power games. That's what the industry's all about. Sure, at the lower levels people are just obsessed with money. They do all the things they do to try to get rich quick. At the top level that's not what matters. The difference between someone with a mid-sized operation and a big, national operation is not financial. The guy at the top won't be making a huge amount more than the guy with the relatively small, regional operation, because his costs will be astronomical. They always are, for the biggest movers. The difference is power. That's what they crave, and they spend good money to get it.

Sitting up in bed. Sitting in the darkness. Living in the darkness until someone tells you otherwise. This is not the way to live. Freelance—that's the way to live. Making sure everyone knows you're not tied to a big player. Making sure people never consider you important to someone else's empire. Once that happens, you become a walking target. It's a warm night. Made warmer by the agitated state Calum was in when he woke up. Can't remember why now. He reaches for the little bottle of fizzy apple juice on the bedside cabinet. Damn it! Empty. Is it worth getting up for another one? Not really. He lies back down.

He can't get back to sleep. Perhaps it's age. Perhaps, as he's got a little older, he's lost the fearlessness he used to have. He's still cold inside. He can still switch off his emotions when he's on a job. He can still overcome any emotional consequences of what he does. It's been said before, though. You get a little older, you realize that time is against you. If you want to have all the other good things in life—the things that the job gets in the way of—then you're going to have to hurry up about it. That could be what it is. You get tied down to Jamieson and the job will get in the way more than ever. You get targeted by Davidson, and all those things that have started to feel more important lately will never be yours.

Yep, he does need that drink after all. He's too awake now anyway. Calum pulls back the quilt. He wears boxer shorts and a T-shirt to bed, in case you're wondering. You're probably not. He sits on the edge of the bed for a couple of minutes. Thinking about the reality of his life. If he had a job to do, how could he hide it from a wife? How could he hide this from a wife? The worry. The fallout from a job. Even when the job's done well, you still have consequences. You're up in the middle of the night, because you can't sleep. She would notice that. You would have to try to explain it away. This job and a normal life are not compatible. It's a horrible reality, but it's true. This job is so abnormal, you have to sacrifice the things other people take for granted to do it.

He's on his feet, moving to the bedroom door. He stops and looks back at the digital clock at his bedside. Ten past two in the morning. He seems to spend a lot of his life up and about at these hours. Working in the darkness. Would you have it any other way? Admit it, you love the job. He smiles a little to himself. The freedom to live like this. The ability to do what you please. To be reasonably well paid for a job you find easy. To enjoy the rush. Okay, there are sacrifices, but there's nothing that says they have to be permanent. You do this for a few more years. You find a way out. If that's possible. Then you live a more conventional life. When you have enough money to not have to be truly conventional. To not have a nine-to-five. To be able to move about at whatever hour you choose.

He's a few feet into the kitchen when he catches a glimpse. It's dark, but his eyes are used to it, and movement can't be hidden, not unless it's pitch-black. There's a moment. It's a split second when you know the danger. You understand immediately what it is, and how much trouble you're in. It's a human instinct. It doesn't come from working in the business. Everyone has that instinct; it's just that if you're in the business, then you get to use it more often. Calum has used it before. He knows. He can tell that he's in a world of trouble, and that it's most likely too late to do anything about it. You understand the reality. But you still fight. That's another human instinct. The need to survive. The will to fight.

It's a large figure that moves towards him. The immediate thought is Davidson. He's a big figure. So Young and Jamieson did nothing about him. Charming! Now there's really no point. One advantage. One little advantage. Calum's eyes are much more accustomed to the darkness than Davidson's. The bigger man is moving towards him, raising a hand. Raising it higher than expected. Not a gun then. A knife. Going for a silent kill. Break in, kill him in his bed. Body isn't found until the following day. Davidson long gone. It's a nice attempt. One of those little quirks of fate that Calum happened to wake up when he did. Or did Davidson forcing the lock wake him? We'll never know.

Calum's raising a hand. Get your feet right. Take a good position to try to fight back. Instinct says let him have the first swing. He's bigger than you. He's got the knife. You have nothing. React to his first move. Then go for the knife. The dark figure makes a swing of the knife. It's not intended to kill. It's a slash, intended to force Calum into a more defensive position. Into a position that won't allow a counter-attack. Now it's a test of courage. How much can you take? Stand your ground. Let him slash your arms. Let him injure you. The key is staying alive. You won't come out of this unscathed—throw that dream away. This is a fight for survival. Calum holds his ground. One arm raised. On his toes, ready to strike back. The large figure swings the knife again; it slashes across Calum's forearm. It snags. It feels like it's scratched through to the bone. There's a sharp pain. Don't let that slow you down. Now is the time to react.

A fraction's delay. That's the opening. Lunge forward. Head-first. The top of his skull crashing into the large figure's lower jaw. A stifled growl of pain. A backward step. An opening. Make a grab for the knife. Doesn't matter if you cut your hand on the blade; the priority is staying alive. A grip of something. Pulling and pushing. A few seconds when all seems lost in the darkness. Are you winning the fight or aren't you? What's the other guy doing? Seconds of mystery. Seconds of nothing. The large figure twists his body, trying to pull away. Something comes loose. Light-headed. Blood running onto your hands. You want to fall to your knees. You push forward, trying to take advantage. A knife into flesh. It slides in so easily. No resistance. A twist. The fight is over.

EPILOGUE

Just getting his trousers on is difficult. His hip is stiff, but it's getting better. Not ready for a big excursion yet, according to the docs, but getting there. It's going to have an excursion, though, like it or not. This is something Frank has to do. He has the trousers on each leg and he's getting to his feet. Boy, is he out of shape. Not sure sitting on his arse in Spain is going to help that, but that's where he's going next week. The journey will be a test. Been more than a month since the surgery. Spent the first couple of weeks with his leg up on a stool. Tedious and embarrassing. An active man with a young spirit shouldn't be spending his days in that position. Fortunately the only people that matter who saw him like that were Peter Jamieson and Calum MacLean. Peter knew what to expect, didn't mind. And Calum. Well, poor Calum.

He's got his trousers up, thank God. Tucking his shirt in and closing his trousers. Belt. Where's that belt? Found it. Putting it on. Tie. Got that too. Now he just needs his coat. This isn't going to be a pleasant start to the day. These things are always sad and awkward. Frank's consumed by the knowledge that it could so easily be him. Right now, though, he's feeling pretty good. He has his car keys in his hand. First time since he had his hip replaced that he's driving. A little sooner than was advised, but so what—he feels good. The more he thinks about it, the better he feels. He's actually smiling as he goes out the front door and down the path. Into the car. Struggling just a little to get his leg to bend into position. Stiff, but not painful. That's progress. The pain has gone; now he just has to build up his strength.

Frank drives like an old man. Always has. Drives like a man who knows how not to draw attention to himself. Forty years' experience turns early lessons into long-standing habit. He couldn't drive any other way now. Eternally careful. He knows the streets, knows the city. It's always changing, but he's always learning. Nearly there, not sure what to expect. He's swearing under his breath as he pulls up at the side of the road. He has the correct address. Should've known it would be awkward. A visit like this was always going to be as unpleasant as sod's law could make it. It's a second-floor flat, and what's the bet there's no lift? Bit of a struggle to get his weight up and out of the car in one movement. Not sore, though, that's what's keeping his spirits up. Nuisance value he can deal with.

No buzzer on the front door. No sort of security at all. Frank's in through the door and glaring at the stairs. No lift, of course. With a sigh he's starting the climb. Up to the first floor. Puffing a little, but not in pain. Up to the second floor. The hip's stiff and heavy, but that might not be a bad thing. Not with the trip that's coming up. Sitting on a plane, getting through airports. Good to exercise it in advance, put a little pressure on it. It's not hard to find the flat he's looking for. It's a small corridor, gloomy, with three doors. He's looking for number eight. Knocking on the door. There's a peephole, and he's making a point of standing right in front of it. Waiting twenty seconds and the door is opening.

Calum looks a mess. His left hand is heavily

bandaged; he looks pale and thinner than before. He's nodding a wary hello to Frank.

'Good to see you, Calum,' Frank's saying. Friendly. Genuine. 'Can I come in?'

Calum's leading him along a short corridor to the living room, offering him a seat. 'Do you want a higher chair from the kitchen?' Calum's asking him. He's looking at the hip, but not mentioning it. Looking at the wrong hip, as it happens, but Frank's not going to point that out.

'That would help.' The old man's smiling.

Calum's disappeared into the kitchen and come back with a chair. Playing the good host, but only playing. They both know he's buying time. Considering this unexpected visit. Calum's thinking about the last time he saw Frank. Then it was Calum making the visit. It was business, dressed as social. This will be the same.

There's an unpleasant atmosphere already. Not threatening, but tense. As soon as Jamieson suggested this meeting, Frank knew it would be horrible. Calum's too smart for this. Plenty of morons you could visit, and they wouldn't get it. They wouldn't know that the boss had sent you to lean on them. Calum's not one of those morons. As soon as he saw Frank through the peephole, he'd have known. Now he'll be on high alert. Listening for Jamieson's voice in Frank's words. He's sitting opposite Frank. Looking at him. Trying to look friendly, and failing. He looks challenging. Like he's daring Frank to speak. Daring him to be anything other than a puppet for the boss. Frank's clearing his throat.

'Look at us, huh? Pair of wrecks. The hand. I'm hearing it was a bad one.'

Calum's nodding, raising his left hand a little. 'This one was. The other hand wasn't so bad. The cut on the arm wasn't deep, either. It'll heal, just needs a little time. Could've been a lot worse.'

Frank knows all about the diagnoses. Jamieson told him everything. Told him about Jamieson's own doctor looking after Calum. Stitching him up, getting him healed and back to work. The doctor's suggested that Calum isn't following the physio he was given. Hinting that he's not rushing back to health. The doc's a pill-popper. Unemployed, officially. Signed off sick from his practice a couple of years ago. Gets money and drugs from Jamieson for his skills now. Frank's not a fan. They couldn't take Calum to a hospital, though—that would have put him on the radar. Young man turns up with stab wounds to both hands and his right arm. Not hard to guess who the hospital get on the phone to. There would have been a cop at his bedside within the hour. Within five minutes, if the docs realized some of the blood wasn't Calum's. Frank sat and listened to Jamieson voice his fears about Calum's commitment. About him using the hand injuries to swing the lead. All Frank was thinking about was how the boy handled the job.

Admiration, in the most part. Jealousy, too. Frank picked Calum for the job. His recommendation. Eventually, his replacement. That's how it'll be. The bright young thing comes in and does well. He becomes the backup to the senior man. Time passes. Frank slows down. Calum earns the respect to become the lead man. Frank knows he's sitting opposite the person who's going to push him into the slow lane. But he knew that, when he picked the boy. No complaints.

Maybe a little fear. A gunman wants to work until he drops, or until someone drops him. The bright young thing could push him onto the sidelines. Frank's smiling, hiding his thoughts.

'I heard how you handled Davidson,' he's saying. 'You did brilliantly.'

Calum's nodding, shrugging a little. So complacent.

He's not so sure he did brilliantly. All he remembers is the blood and the fear. Trying to get to his feet. Davidson dead on the floor. The adrenalin rushing. Overwhelming everything. He knew he was in pain, but he wasn't even sure where he'd been cut. Trying to clear his head. Took two minutes of standing in silence. Then he went to the phone. The blood making it hard to press the buttons. Called George. Told him to come round. There was work to do. George came. It was difficult, but they got rid of the body. Waves of tiredness. George doing all the manual work. The fear of being caught. The fear of passing out. George was terrific. They got rid of the body. George took Calum round to his own flat, then went to clean up Calum's. Calum didn't want to contact Jamieson. Not until all the dust had settled. George decided otherwise. He wanted help cleaning up. A professional job.

That was when the organization moved into action. Someone was sent round to deep-clean Calum's flat. A safe house was found for him. A doctor was sent round to look at his wounds. All the things he couldn't organize for himself. The loving arms of the organization wrapping tightly around him. Protecting him. Holding him firmly in place. Doing it all silently. Making a show of how much they're helping him. Never actually saying what he owes them in exchange. Didn't need to be said. A nice safe house, then a tidy little flat for him to live in. The old flat emptied and cleaned. His wounds tended by the organization's doctor. George coming round regularly with shopping. Making sure he has everything he needs. Look, they're saying, look how we look after you. What would you do without us? Calum understands.

He understands why Frank is here. Here to put the pressure on. Here to make sure the Jamieson message gets across. One thing for a wrecked former doctor to deliver it, quite another for Frank. It means more coming from Frank. A man you respect. A man who matters.

'All dressed up, huh?' Calum's saying with a smile, nodding at Frank.

Frank's looking down at his formal attire. He's of a generation that dresses for things. Doesn't seem unusual to him. 'I'm on my way to lunch with Peter. Have a chat about Spain. He has stuff for me—keys to the villa, and the like. Lay out a few ground rules. No wild parties, that sort of thing.' Now they've brought Peter Jamieson into the conversation, and he's going to hover over everything that's said.

'So you were just passing by,' Calum's saying with a knowing smile.

Frank can handle this any way he wants, it doesn't matter. Calum's already sussed it, and nothing Frank says will change that. Calum knows that Frank's here to deliver a message. All Frank can do now is deliver.

'How are you feeling about it?' Frank's asking. Sounding genuine.

258

'About my injuries? Give them time, they'll be fine. That's what the doc says.'

'Uh-huh. What about the job?'

'What about it?' Not making this easy. Why should he?

'You happy with the way everything was handled? I have to say, I was impressed with how you handled it yourself. On the night. Getting rid of that shit Davidson was a service to the city. The way you handled the removal as well. Impressive. You happy with how everyone else handled it?'

This is it. If he's happy with the job everyone else did, then he has nothing to complain about. If he has nothing to complain about, then he should hurry back to work.

'Everyone seemed to handle it well enough,' Calum's saying. A bit of a shrug. 'I'm not sure it was wise to get people so high up the chain involved so early, but . . .' he's saying and trails off.

'They're looking after you, though,' Frank's saying. Not a question this time, an observation.

'Yeah.'

Frank's nodding. Sitting with his hands on his lap, looking uncomfortable. 'They will look after you too. You're a smart kid. You have talent. You've been able to keep all that talent to yourself and do well with it. Things change, though. Gets to a point where you need people looking after you. Only way to stay safe. That's the gunman's maturity,' he's saying with a smile. 'You start out independent and determined to stay that way. The thought of working for an organization is horrible. You want your freedom. You end up the opposite. You're in an organization, and you know that going freelance would kill you. Being tied to someone

259

isn't such a bad thing,' he's saying. 'If you have the right people around you, being in an organization is the smartest thing you can do.'

Frank's gone now. Looked like he was struggling with his hip as he made his way down the stairs. Calum's struggling with his hand. It's why he didn't offer a cup of tea or coffee. Even taking a piss is a struggle.

If he was freelance? He'd be a sitting duck. Easy target for anyone wanting rid of him. Wouldn't be able to hide away like this. Would struggle for cash. Frank learned to love the organization. As good as admitted that he couldn't survive without it these days. Maybe, in time, Calum will learn to love it. Maybe not.

Calum's back sitting in the living room. Staring into space. All alone in a flat that doesn't feel like home. Trying to stare into the future. Looking at the inevitable. He can't run from Jamieson—too dangerous. Staying means more of this. Common sense says you stay and you suffer it. You do the jobs. They pile up on top of you, and one day you get caught out. Then it's all over. That's the inevitable. Unless . . .

Maybe a chance comes along. A chance to defy the inevitable. Then you just need the guts to take that chance.